One Enduring Lesson

Jamal Merchant came to England from Tanzania, East Africa, in 1972 and qualified as a Chartered Accountant in 1976. He then settled in London where he is now self-employed as a property finance broker.

Jamal has travelled widely including to India, China, Egypt, USA, Canada and the Middle East. His interests include reading, current affairs, movies and cricket. *One Enduring Lesson*, a love story based in India, is his debut novel.

One Enduring Lesson

JAMAL MERCHANT

RUPA

Published by
Rupa Publications India Pvt. Ltd 2017
7/16, Ansari Road, Daryaganj
New Delhi 110002

Sales Centres:

Allahabad Bengaluru Chennai
Hyderabad Jaipur Kathmandu
Kolkata Mumbai

Copyright © Jamal Merchant 2017

This is a work of fiction. Names, characters, places and incidents are either the product of the author's imagination or are used fictitiously and any resemblance to any actual person, living or dead, events or locales is entirely coincidental.

All rights reserved.

No part of this publication may be reproduced, transmitted, or stored in a retrieval system, in any form or by any means, electronic, mechanical, photocopying, recording or otherwise, without the prior permission of the publisher.

ISBN: 978-81-291-4767-7

First impression 2017

10 9 8 7 6 5 4 3 2 1

The moral right of the author has been asserted.

Printed in India by HT Media Ltd, Noida

This book is sold subject to the condition that it shall not, by way of trade or otherwise, be lent, resold, hired out, or otherwise circulated, without the publisher's prior consent, in any form of binding or cover other than that in which it is published.

Contents

The Sound of Music	1
Welcome to Paradise	14
A Good Woman	31
The Graduate	40
Rat Race	51
An Inspector Calls	61
Pretty Women	79
Marry Go Round	87
Charade	94
Ten Commandments	101
A Chance Meeting	109
Pride and Prejudice	114
That's Life!	121
Date with an Angel	126
Life of Pi	130
Goodbye, My Lady	136
Come September	142
Alienation of Affection	164
Midnight's Children	170
Paradise Lost	172
The Guru	182
Great Expectations	194
Heaven on Earth	205

The Last Day	220
The Good Die Young	234
Guess Who's Coming to Dinner	242
Psycho	254
One Enduring Lesson	269

The Sound of Music

My father, humming an old Bollywood film song, came down to join my mother and me for breakfast with his British passport in one hand and a flag of India in the other. He had disturbed my mother mid-lecture. I had just turned twenty-seven, was single and out of work, and was in no mood to hear her make yet another attempt to reverse my ambitious plans. In the last twelve months, I had been made redundant from my job at the NR Bank and my love landscape was parched with my long-term girlfriend, Tasmin, having left me.

'There is no way I am letting you go to Mumbai, Rahul. You are fine here in London.'

Groaning theatrically, I decided to opt for the language of business, the only one she understood. 'My proposal to go to Mumbai to study filmmaking isn't new. I have put it to you and Dad many times over the past two years.'

The past year was truly an *annus horribilis* for me and I just wanted to move on to better times.

There was a brief silence during which neither parent spoke.

'A career in the film line is for school drop-outs,' added my mother meekly. 'Not for a London University Business Management graduate.'

My mother would usually give in after a few minutes of

token resistance, but this time it was proving more difficult to find that sigh of resignation in her voice, that note of final capitulation. My father, a big man, bigger than he was when he was younger, looking older than his years, his hair now greying and thinning on top to reveal the wheatish-coloured dome of his skull, touched my mother's shoulder reprovingly. She is an Englishwoman with dark-blonde hair and aquamarine eyes, a fearless figure; a woman of lustrous beauty despite her age.

'But Patricia,' he began, 'I have already said Rahul can go. I don't want to stand in his way.'

'I know that voice, Raj, and it will not work with me!'

It was a Saturday morning, the day of our big weekly breakfast. Weekday breakfasts were usually just a quick cup of tea and some buttered toast, but Saturday breakfast was a ritual. We all had two eggs, one fried and one an omelette with coriander, chopped green chillies, chopped onions, some milk and hot Indian spices, to be eaten with parathas freshly made by my mother. Tea was Indian-style and made from loose leaves. Chai. No tea bags on Saturdays. Saturday breakfasts were eaten together, as a family, not wolfed down on the run.

'The family that dines together aligns together.'

This was one of my father's many tongue-in-cheek aphorisms, most of which he had purloined from my grandmother Sona-bai, a gloriously sassy lady whom I met only once years ago, when I was two, on a visit to Dar es Salaam, Tanzania.

Another silence had descended over the table, and my father casually scanned the sports pages of *The Times*, his Indian flag tucked into his shirt.

Eventually, he said, 'I think I will go and post my British

passport renewal application.'

Then, without looking up at my mother, he half mumbled to himself, 'After that I may go to Lord's to watch the One Day International cricket match between England and India.'

'You came to England some forty years ago, as Raj Patel!' said my mother with a snort of antipathy. 'You have since changed your name, acquired a British passport and made England your home. Yet, when it comes to cricket, you support India and wave the Indian flag at cricket matches. You have failed the cricket test, as Norman Tebbit once commented.'

'What's wrong with that? All NRIs support India,' replied my father, ignoring my mother's furious glances.

'What do you mean NRIs?' my mother demanded scornfully.

'Come on, you know what I mean. Non-resident Indians.'

My father expected all NRIs to wave the saffron, white and green Indian flag at cricket matches.

'To you, those NRIs who don't are Not Really Indians.' My mother clicked her tongue, frowning.

'You will never understand,' mumbled my father, to her intense annoyance.

'I wish I had never married you,' my mother grumbled, between clenched teeth.

'Every woman says that to her husband,' rumbled my father, gesturing with all his poise and self-confidence, secure in the knowledge that my mother would never leave him despite her martinet tongue which he sometimes dreaded.

'Oh! Just forget it,' hissed my mother, standing up and deserting the table, leaving my father and me looking wordlessly at our feet.

'By the way, Dad, why did you change your name?' I

asked my father after my mother left the room.

'I found Patel too common, my son. I mean there are more Patels than Smiths in the telephone directory.'

'But why Saxena?'

'Because it's both Indian and anglicized and originates from Saxby in England,' replied my father with his usual robust smile.

That evening, my father, his face now really woebegone, stumbled as he returned to the house. It was obvious India had lost the match. If they'd triumphed, he'd have come in shouting with exuberant good humour: 'India has won! India has won! Winner, winner, chicken dinner!'

This was another ritual. Whenever India won a cricket match in any part of the world, be it a 20-20, a One Day International or a Test, my mother would cook one of my father's favourite chicken dishes, at his insistence. It might be curry or biryani, jalfrezi or tikka masala, or tandoori, but it would have to be chicken. However, there was no chicken tonight. Just dal and rice, the poor man's food, to match my father's scowling mood.

'India fumbled in the very last over, batting second,' said my father. 'Their last three wickets just tumbled. It is a clear case of match fixing. They won the toss and should have batted first.'

'Had they done that and still lost,' I suggested, 'you would have said India should have bowled first, like the cricket commentators always say on TV after every match.'

Dejected, sleep-starved, his eyes red with anger and exhaustion, he slumped into his chair, not bothered about the two missing shirt-buttons, and turned on the TV to watch the replay of the last few overs. Slapping his thigh with one hand and then scratching his head with the other, he lowered his eyes and muttered in a low voice that the match was fixed for the benefit of some crooks back home. I saw no reason to believe India threw the match, but my father was convinced. He became restless and annoyed, pacing the lounge like a caged tiger, smacking his forehead with the palm of his hand. When angry, he would wave his hand in a dismissive manner and descend into gloomy silence with his size-18 ego. If forced to speak, he would speak in single words. *Yes. No. Later. OK. Perhaps. Tomorrow. Possibly. Bullshit.* Cold sweat would stain his shirt. In this bitter mood, he would conveniently forget the three important words: *Please. Sorry. Thanks.* After he had emptied his word tank, he would soon get bored and start yawning.

At that moment, the phone rang. 'Can I speak to Saxena, please?'

It was our next-door neighbour, Pankaj Virani, also an Indian with a British passport. He usually rang my father whenever India lost a cricket match, and always called him by his last name, Saxena, which my father liked very much. I knew they would talk for many minutes, sometimes hours, and left them to it, climbing the stairs to my bedroom where I had secretly begun packing a suitcase.

∽

On Sunday mornings, I often go to the local church to pick my mother up. My father usually goes to collect her, but not on the first Sunday of each month. On that day, he telephones all his friends and relatives back in India. They never call him. No matter what happens, all the calls have to be from London. When someone dies in India, my father calls the bereaved family from London. When someone dies in London, my father also calls India to let them know.

My father is of the opinion that people from India don't like calling abroad because it costs money; even in India they give missed calls and expect the other person to call them back. So my father calls India regularly. And he no longer shouts into the phone on long-distance rambles. 'England has taught me to talk softly...and to say *please, sorry* and *thank you*,' he says.

During the languorous lethargy of Sunday afternoons, my father usually takes a nap from 3 p.m. to 5 p.m. He calls it his 'three-five'. For those two hours, he sleeps like a baby in a basket, sometimes with his mouth open, often snoring away like a buffalo. Nobody dares disturb him and he is free to dream himself back to the days of his youth, or forward to those of his dotage and eventual death. I often wonder whether I will end up like this at his age. It is clearly something England has done to him, even more reason to make my eventual escape.

That Sunday, after his 'three-five', the afternoon pouring with rain, we all sat in the lounge to talk. It felt as if the decisive moment was upon us.

My mother emerged from the kitchen, her back straight, her head held high and her hair pulled back into a stern donut bun, and stood in front of us, with arms akimbo and a vacant stare.

'Please sit down, Mum. You are making me nervous.'

'Rahul, why don't you get married and produce children instead of producing films? I don't want you to get married at thirty-something like your father and me,' interjected my mother in a cavalier blistering tone. 'A good wife will fill your days with joy and your nights with pleasure.' My mother was clearly in a mood for some adult talk and was not going to give up that easily.

'Times have changed, Patricia,' asserted my father, hoping attack was the best form of defence—for both of us. 'Career comes first. I am happy for Rahul to go to Mumbai and join Film International.'

'But have times changed for the better, Raj?'

My father ignored this question, which he often did when he didn't know the answer.

'I see nothing wrong with a career in films,' added my father in a voice of moderation and reason.

'You and Dad both left home at the age of twenty,' I said, or rather stammered. 'Why can't I?'

'Rahul, have you considered the problems of living in India—with its pollution, its chaos, its corruption? All the claustrophobic pressures of an overcrowded country? Every other day, gangs paid by political thugs turn into murderous mobs and go on a rampage, destroying property and killing people!' she said in an alarmed voice, punctuated by horrified gasps.

'I am sure Rahul will find it all very challenging,' rallied my father, half-defensive, half-defiant.

But she wasn't to be deterred. 'And what about Bollywood itself? Almost every Bollywood film is a flop, with the producers losing all the money. You will end up burning your fingers, Rahul. If not losing them altogether!'

'That's not strictly true, Mum…'

'Then there is the problem of piracy and threats from the underworld. You will lose your head too!'

'You just need passion, Mum. You can succeed against all

odds if you have passion.'

A deafening silence followed her intense interrogation. Silences were bad news with her, as everyone knew. Contrary arguments could be formulated in the minds of intransigent mothers during a long silence. I decided to break it.

'You just need a brilliant idea and a great script. A good script is no good; it has to be a great script. This is where films fail...the producers have to realize this,' I said calmly.

'This morning you told me that a film career is for school drop-outs. Film courses are now highly professionalized. Producing isn't an art, it's a business. My degree in Business Management will give me a solid start. I know I'll succeed,' I continued, with my father looking on and nodding.

My mother snapped back like a crocodile. 'I have heard that Bollywood is full of jealousy. When you are successful, there will be a lot of jealous people around you.'

'Well...that's the whole point. No success, no jealousy,' I tried to say with a weak smile. 'Once the jealousy comes, the success will already have preceded it.'

I leaned over and took her hand. The corners of her mouth quivered as she tried to suppress her anguish.

'I'll be making films from the heart, not just with cameras and computers. Then, when I'm a big enough name, I'll move to Hollywood and you can both come and live in my mansion on Sunset Boulevard.'

My father laughed.

'What's funny about that?' I demanded. 'I thought you are on my side.'

My mother sighed and stood up folding her hands across her chest, looking thoughtful.

Then my father put in, 'You can't stop him, Patricia. He

is over eighteen.'

'So am I!' she wailed. 'I am on the wrong side of fifty and I want my only son to be with me.'

A counterattack in a tearful voice, from a mother with energetic tear ducts! She'd saved her greatest weapon for the last. It was both her strength and her weakness that her despair would translate into copious tears. Often, she would stiffen her face and her resolve in order to impose her point of view. Not this time. My father held her hand, with me standing next to him shoulder to shoulder. She was surrounded.

'Rahul has passion for filmmaking. He will convert his passion into a profession and his profession into prosperity. I think you should stop your mollycoddling and let him go.'

I looked eagerly at my mother as she listened intently to my father's persuasive enticements. But she hesitated. I felt crushed, my temples throbbing, my heart pounding.

'I think you should support Rahul...' said my father. This caused my mother to sit down quietly on a chair in a corner of the lounge and purse her lips in intense deliberation. I could see that my father was winning and winked conspiratorially at him.

'Please stop turning a deaf ear to Rahul's wishes,' my father tried to reason with her.

'I don't have a deaf ear like you. Both my ears are working fine,' replied my mother angrily in a determined tone.

Another gloomy silence fell. This time it was not to be interrupted. My mother would not be rushed; we would have to let her think it over. My father and I held her hands for what seemed like an eternity. Finally, she burst into speech.

'I will speak to Father Brown tomorrow and ask him to come over and bless you before you leave for Mumbai.'

She wiped away her tears with the back of her right hand. My father smiled ruefully. My heart pounding cheerfully with boyish excitement, I hugged them both. At last there was a complete goal congruence within the three Saxenas as regards my future.

'Make sure you cook chicken tikka masala for Father Brown. It's his favourite,' said my father with one of his hopeful smiles, his eyes sparkling with appreciative radiance.

My mother nodded meditatively, mutely accepting my father's kiss on her left cheek.

'My worries will never evaporate,' said my mother in a thin voice, blowing her nose—something which she always did after a good cry. Searching desperately for words, I took both her hands in an affectionate grasp to reassure her. Her benevolent gaze, which proclaimed the generosity of a noble matriarch, overwhelmed me, making me feel as if my heart was going to jump out from my chest from under my ribs. She smiled—her first smile in many days. I was relieved. She was at last emerging from the depths of despair.

The next morning, the sun came out like it was on my side. I woke up nice and early, wide-eyed and energetic. I was ready to go. But in the traditions of a true Indian family, I wouldn't have wanted to leave without the blessings of both my parents. If my father was regarded as the head of the family, my mother was the heart, and I loved both equally. So, immediately after breakfast, I booked my flight to Mumbai by Queen Air, just in case my mother changed her mind. The next few days were filled with anxiety, excitement, and expectation. My parents were happy and sad, and I tried to keep our conversations light and optimistic.

Mumbai! I was going there at last. Back to India, where,

I felt, an essential part of me originated. I couldn't wait to go away, yet I was also reluctant to leave the only life I'd ever known—it was a rollercoaster of emotions, up one minute and down the next. The waiting was the trouble. The anticipation. The expectation. Then the day of departure came, and along with it came the tears. We said our goodbyes and I left in a taxi. I didn't want my father to drive me to the airport; my mother would insist on coming along. I left. On my own. At last.

And so, this was the life I was leaving in England to start a new one in India. An idyllic life in many ways, but also claustrophobic and restraining. I wanted more—to see more, to feel more, to experience more. But there's an old saying: 'Be careful what you wish for…you might just get it.'

∾

The plane took off on time. It was a ten-hour direct flight to Mumbai. A Gujarati couple sat next to me. They were travelling back after a holiday in London.

'Hello!' announced the husband, a large man with a thick moustache, as if I was an old friend. 'I am Dhiraj Desai. This is Shalini.'

When he shook hands with me, I noticed that half his index finger was missing.

The man wanted to talk, the woman didn't.

'Oh, hi,' I replied reluctantly. 'I'm Rahul Saxena. Nice to meet you, Mr and Mrs Desai.'

'Just call me Dhiraj. And this lovely lady is not my wife. Mrs Desai has gone to Baroda to look after her sick mother. Shalini is my secretary.'

This was information I really didn't need to know, but

Dhiraj Desai told me anyway, and with a hint of braggadocio. He must have seen the quizzical expression on my face, because he leaned over and whispered in my right ear.

'She is actually my mistress,' he said with a cheap, wicked smile. 'She is my number two, if you get my meaning.'

It was clear Shalini was putting up with him for the good time and the money. Black money, undeclared money, untaxed money. In India, they call such funds 'number two'. I got his meaning alright. I talked a little and he talked a lot; talked and talked and talked, throughout the ten-hour flight.

'I have been spending money like a sailor on shore leave.'

And he complained about everything.

'This tea is like urine. I may be a Desai, but I don't drink urine!'

This was a sarcastic reference to Morarji Desai, the prime minister of India in the 1970s, who used to drink his own urine. The Indian newspapers lampooned urine as 'Morarji Cola' when they heard about it.

'I prefer to drink wine; I am a wine merchant.'

Dhiraj Desai continued with his life story while Shalini slept beside him, oblivious to the constant drone of his voice, which was giving me an earache.

Towards the end, he nudged me and interrupted my half-asleep state. It had been a rough night with a lot of turbulence. He gave me his business card while the plane descended into the Mumbai International Airport.

'Come and see me in Mumbai if you need any help. No appointment necessary. We will talk over a glass of wine.'

'Thank you, but I don't drink.'

I saw my plane's shadow passing fast over the land below as it descended, finally touching down at Mumbai airport with a terrific thump.

Columbus never reached India. But I felt as excited and relieved as him when I saw my long journey to India was at last over, well, almost over. I was glad to be rid of the garrulous Dhiraj Desai as I was to see the yellow earth of what I considered my homeland. But it wasn't the countryside I was heading for. In reality, the glamour, glitz and the sound of music of films had brought me to Mumbai, and it was just the beginning of an even longer journey, I hoped, to my Bollywood dream. It was an airy, breezy day, with glorious sunshine splurging down on Mumbai. A kaleidoscope of cheer, elation and hope hurtled through my mind. I blazed with delight as I looked forward to an *annus mirabilis* with a voice inside me crying joyfully—*Indiaaaaah*! *Indiaaaaah*! *Indiaaaaah*!

Welcome to Paradise

By the time I left the airport it was noon. It was a hot day in Mumbai, with the Indian summer approaching its peak. The last time I was in this city had been seventeen years ago, when I was only ten years old, so everything seemed new all over again.

As I exited the airport, a large crowd of people seemed to be looking at me and smiling, and, for a moment, I got the impression they'd all come to meet me. One of them actually held up a sign with my name on it: *Rahul*. But it was for a Rahul Patel, which, ironically, I would have been if my father hadn't changed his surname. However, I wasn't disappointed; I was well aware I didn't know anyone in Mumbai. There were crowds everywhere, waiting to swallow me up. Suddenly, two men approached me, as if to check my papers. They both looked about thirty or thereabouts.

'Hello. I am Irfan Dongriwalla and this is my colleague, David Abraham.'

I gave them a puzzled look. Irfan was tall and forceful, with a drooping moustache, while David was a slighter, reserved presence. The latter was wearing a black skullcap and a loud T-shirt with the map of Mumbai on it. Irfan, who walked with a slight limp, his left shoulder lower than his right, wore a white baseball cap and a plain red shirt with its top portion unbuttoned, the bottom untucked, and brown rolled-up trousers. He smiled at me, putting me at ease.

'I am a tourist guide, and David is a private taxi driver. We work as a team…'

'Thanks, brother. But I'm not a tourist, so I won't need a guide. But I do need a cheap hotel for about a week.'

'Palace Hotel in Colaba is just the place for you. We can take you there.'

Without asking, Irfan started to push my trolley towards David's taxi.

'*We?*' I exclaimed. 'I said I don't need a tourist guide.'

'No, we are always together. You are in safe hands. Nothing to worry about.'

Exhausted from the flight, I decided to submit. After all, what did I have to lose?

David's car wasn't one of the regular black and yellow Fiat taxis of Mumbai, but a 1990s four-door black Volvo 740—a private car without any air-conditioning used as a taxi.

'It's an old car, but runs like a cheetah,' said David, as he loaded my luggage in the boot of the car.

'Your name, sir?' asked Irfan.

'Saxena. Rahul Saxena.'

I said it James Bond style, just for effect. Mumbai was already making me think and act in film mode. Also, the pair of them was making me slightly nervous.

As we drove through the city, my new companions had plenty of questions for me—questions that would have been an unthinkable intrusion in England. *Who was I? What was my family background? Where had I come from? Why had I come to Mumbai? How long would I be here? My marital status? My income?* And, in return, they told me everything about themselves. Even without me asking.

'Are you the only son of your parents?' demanded Irfan, still hungry for information.

'Yes. How did you guess?'

'I can always tell. So, you must have been thoroughly spoilt,' said Irfan.

'I was.'

'An only son of prosperous parents is apt to be spoilt,' he continued. 'Especially so in India!'

'You seem to have read the autobiography of Jawaharlal Nehru.'

'Only the opening sentence,' interrupted David with a cynical laugh, in an attempt to tease Irfan.

Within a few minutes, I had relaxed. It felt as if we'd known each other for years.

'So, you are a Gujarati?'

'Yes,' I replied, anticipating more questions. Of course, Irfan was surprised my surname wasn't Patel or Shah or Joshi.

I decided to investigate them. 'Irfan, you're Muslim and David's Jewish. That's an interesting partnership. What have you got in common?'

'We are both circumcised.' He laughed a hearty laugh.

'Without any anesthetic,' added David with an even bigger laugh.

'By a barber using a cut-throat razor,' interrupted Irfan with a soft smile followed by a huge laugh.

'There is nothing in the scriptures which says that a Muslim and a Jew cannot be friends or neighbours,' continued Irfan, after the laughing stopped.

These guys were an amusing double act, constantly laughing and cracking jokes, at which I laughed obligingly. I liked them, or I thought I did.

Outside, the traffic was crazy and chaotic. There were cars, overloaded double-decker buses, taxis, rickshaws, trucks, two-wheelers carrying families of five or six; handcarts with heavy goods being pulled from the front and pushed from the rear by labourers, with sweat dripping off their dark-brown brows, amongst which pedestrians risked their lives trying to cross. Ahead of us, four or five columns of cars were crammed into two or three lanes. Roads were dug up everywhere. Vehicles looking like they'd been abandoned rather than parked were everywhere you looked. And then there was the noise, loud and continuous, coming from every direction. On top of this, there were beggars, hawkers and hucksters as well as barefoot street kids sharing their space with animals and roadside slums. And then there was the heat! Overpowering, just as I remembered it. Mumbai seemed flung together by accident, a bedlam of sounds and smells, a city that truly never sleeps.

Up ahead, the traffic had been stopped by police to allow some minister's car to pass, possibly to go to the airport. My companions were unimpressed.

'They are always travelling,' said David

'Free, of course,' said Irfan.

'I have done a degree in Political Studies,' David announced, with some pride.

'And I have done a BABF,' said Irfan, who either constantly touched his Beatles-type moustache or rubbed the nape of his neck.

'A BABF?'

'Bachelor of Arts, But Failed.'

We all laughed at this, sweat dripping from our brows.

I was too hot and tired. Trusting them by now, I told them

I was going to take a siesta, and fell into a troubled sleep.

After a good two hours, we finally reached our destination. It was almost 3 p.m. The Palace Hotel was in one of the back streets of Colaba, a fashionable area of South Mumbai which was popular with tourists. By London standards, it was a very ordinary hotel, with twelve single rooms and six doubles. Nothing much to write home about. But it was quite reasonably priced, as Irfan had promised me.

David helped me to check in and I paid him his fare. 'We regularly bring passengers here. So, we will see you again, Rahul!'

And then they were gone.

In my room, I telephoned my parents in London from my mobile and had a long chat. They wanted a full report, minute-by-minute, from the time I entered the departure area at Heathrow till the time I reached the hotel in Mumbai. I was happy to talk. My mother sounded tearful.

'We love you and miss you...'

'And we pray for you...'

My father was more composed. I was hungry, so after the call, I ordered a biryani from room service, and after my dinner went straight to bed, heat-drained and travel weary.

Before I dropped off to sleep, I noticed there was a picture of Mumbai in my room. It bore the legend *Welcome to Paradise*.

The following morning, I was woken up by the beep of a text message at 7 a.m. India time. I knew it would be about 1:30 a.m. back home in England. It read: *bETa phone home. Love, Mum.*

My mother was using a bit of dramatic licence. *Beta* is a

word Indian parents use to express affection for their children and Mum had been watching *E.T.* a few days before I left. She obviously remembered *E.T.* wanting to 'phone home' and combined the two expressions in an effort to seem lighthearted, even though I knew her heart was very heavy. I called her straightaway.

Her voice sounded very distant: 'We miss you terribly. I couldn't wait till morning to talk to you…'

Then my father came on the phone. He was all business.

'You must go later today to Bandra and collect your cheque.' This referred to his money transfer, which comprised all my life savings, and a little extra from him.

'Of course, Dad. And I'm fine. Thanks for asking.'

He paused, shamefully: 'How are you this morning?'

I convinced him I was okay, and told them both to go back to sleep.

It's a habit of mine to drink a litre of water in the morning before brushing my teeth. After completing this daily routine, I left the hotel to sort a few things out. My first priority was to get a mobile phone with a local SIM card.

On my way to the phone shop, I passed the main roundabout of downtown Mumbai, a hub from which roads radiated in a haphazard manner. From this traffic circle an endless torrent of cars, trucks, buses and jeeps clogged the roads, moving hazardously, jumping red lights, all hooting furiously, seemingly headed in different directions. These obstructed the bikes, pedestrians and handcarts, which were piled impossibly high with goods, including one which carried a pile of cars' carcasses. Amongst this madness were **three** bony cows mooing, refusing to move. They called it rush hour, but nothing actually moved, let alone rushed, including an ambulance and a fire brigade vehicle, both on emergency calls with their sirens blaring. In the meantime, in and around the circle, people ignored the clamour of the crazy traffic as Mumbai struggled on in the midst of intolerable heat pouring down from a merciless sun.

Staring in amazement at the world racing past, walking beyond the roundabout, past a parade of small shops, I kept moving with a handkerchief clasped firmly over my mouth. I walked past a shoe factory, closed down after its north Indian workers fled Mumbai after being beaten up by local mobs; past a roadside mini-temple; past a pavement artist drawing a Hindu god, with pedestrians happily throwing money onto the picture; past a Muslim restaurant with some twenty beggars sitting outside on the pavement with out-stretched palms—some pointing to their stomachs; past a half-built block of flats abandoned some months ago after the builder was murdered by a gangster for refusing to pay protection money; past a cinema where some noisy, fist-shaking angry protestors, clogged up with hate, had gathered to stop the screening of a new Bollywood film unless the producer of the film apologized to a local politician running some kind of a parallel government; past beggars with no legs weaving themselves through traffic on trolleys; past some decaying buildings which looked like dying TB patients in a municipal hospital; past a government office guarded by two snoring policemen and, finally, to a new shopping mall near the local Metropolitan Bank.

Just before I reached the phone shop, I saw a long queue of men, women and children with buckets and large saucepans, pots and big plastic cans, all shouting and fighting and trying to jump in front of each other. I spoke to a heavy man with several chins who was waiting for a bus.

'What's all this?'

'You must be new in Mumbai. It's our "Watergate".'

I didn't understand.

'Slum dwellers, queuing for water.'

I saw at once they were engaged in a fight for survival—queuing for water to drink and to cook. Water to wash was a luxury these people couldn't afford. There was just one tap for the slum dwellers, kept at a very low pressure. I spoke to the man again.

'Is there some kind of water shortage?'

He pointed to a block of luxury flats across the road. 'Not over there. They get piped water under metered supplies. They also get additional water delivered by private tankers and pumped into their overhead storage tanks.'

At that very moment, three green and blue water tankers, each carrying thousands of gallons of water, arrived in front of the flats, while the queue of the fighting slum dwellers grew longer and longer.

I suddenly remembered that I'd drunk a full litre of water only an hour ago, and somehow felt ashamed of myself. It wasn't fair! Perhaps I should stop my morning drinking ritual while I was in this city—but then decided it would hardly solve the problem.

The man offered more information, just like Irfan and David the day before. This was something India couldn't sort on her own; she needed an international effort. Water would be like oil in years to come, I thought, and wars would be fought over it. Unless people woke up and did something about it right now this would happen in real life, not in some disaster movie. I wondered if all the people in this country spoke so openly to strangers and offered so much information in reply to a very simple question—a question that would probably have been met with a surly 'don't know' in England.

'Two-thirds of Mumbai's residents walk more than a mile to fetch water. My bus is coming, otherwise I would have told you about the notorious water mafia of Mumbai,' he concluded, offering this last piece of information as he jumped onto his crowded bus.

At the telephone shop, I was served by a young lady with a rude tone.

'It is not easy to get a mobile phone SIM card in India. You cannot just buy it across the counter!'

'Really? Whenever I've travelled abroad before, I've always been able to get one at the airport on arrival.'

'Not in India!'

I was shocked and disappointed. Submitting to the process with a sigh, I decided everything took twice as long in India as in the rest of the world.

To collect my father's cheque, I had to go to an address in north Mumbai to meet a man called Mukesh. I phoned first, but was told there was no such person. I phoned again and explained that I'd come from London and had to meet Mukesh urgently. I was told to call later. After several such phone calls, I was finally told that he would be available at 7 p.m. that evening.

I decided to travel on the suburban railway to north Mumbai from Churchgate. The trains were referred to as

Locals, and I was advised at the hotel to avoid travelling by a Local from north to south between 8 a.m. and 11 a.m. in the morning and from south to north between 5 p.m. and 10 p.m. in the evening. I wished I'd listened. It was the evening rush hour; thousands of passengers were entering and leaving Churchgate Station. Even before the trains stopped at the station, men were jumping from open doors. And thousands more were entering the same trains; men and women tired after a day's hard work, all heading northward. People who had left home as early as 6 a.m. or even before in order get to work in downtown Mumbai were all returning north to the 'home counties'—to the suburbs and slums of Mumbai, only to return the next morning in an ongoing cycle of drudgery.

Inside, the trains were jam-packed, carrying three times the passengers of their full capacity. A man crushed next to me saw my unfamiliarity with the level of overcrowding and told me it was known as 'Super-Dense Crush Load'. There were, on average, fifteen standing passengers per square metre of floor space. Fifteen humid bodies pressed tightly together and surrounded by fifteen more, and then fifteen more again and again and again.

That evening I was one of them.

The yellow and brown local train stopped at each station for just a few seconds to allow more passengers to jump in. I read the names of the stations as the red, white and blue signs on the platforms appeared every few minutes: Marine Lines, Charni Road, Grant Road, and then Mumbai Central. After that, I became part of the mass of bodies, welded together by pressure and steamy sweat. I tried to look through the crowd for the name Bandra on the platform, so I wouldn't miss my stop, but it was impossible to see. I felt like I was being slowly crushed by a snake.

'Could someone please tell me when we get to Bandra?' A voice from an unseen passenger replied: 'It's after Mahim Junction.'

At each station commuters were at war, elbowing each other, trying to board the train with some gripping on to the window grilles as they raced along the platform and some travelling dangerously standing on the train's footboard, holding on to the rods. The amazing thing was that all the passengers were travelling patiently, without complaint. They just accepted that this was the way it was and always would be; standing for hours in the searing heat, with no hope of ever getting a seat.

Somebody tapped me on the shoulder as soon as the train left Mahim Junction. 'Be ready to leave.'

At that very moment, the train jerked and a man leaning out from my intolerably crowded compartment lost his balance and fell.

But the train did not stop! Nobody seemed bothered.

'It happens every day,' a passenger told me in a very casual manner.

I later found out that the man died instantly, like many others who die every year on Mumbai's infamous railway tracks.

When we eventually got to Bandra, I'd already pushed myself forward towards the door. I was the first one out, and I waited on the platform to watch the other passengers leave the train. They were like rats exiting a tunnel. More were boarding to replace them as fast as they disembarked.

I took a rickshaw from the station to the address I had for Mukesh, in one of the back streets of East Bandra. The roads were overflowing with crowds, traffic and illegal hawkers with their makeshift shops. The rickshaw swerved in and out of traffic, pushing up a cloud of dust, changing lanes willy-nilly, tossing me from side to side as it went past a mass of tenements, some collapsing tin shacks, barefoot slum children playing cricket with a tennis ball and a column of broken red and brown bricks for stumps, then east of a pond of dirty water where women were washing clothes, past a mountain of garbage, past a barber cutting a man's hair in front of a mirror nailed on a tree, past a heap of scrap cars, until it finally reached a strangely quiet lane leading to a dark twisting alleyway where cars and rickshaws weren't allowed.

I walked the last few metres. In a moment, I arrived at a small, disordered office on the first floor of a rundown, dingy building with rickety stairs, no lifts and no door bell. I went up the airless stairwell and knocked at the door.

A thin, Gandhi-bespectacled man with a bald shiny head, his skin hanging loosely on his face, opened the door.

'Can I see Mukesh please? My name is Rahul Saxena. I'm from London.'

'Do come in.'

Finally, Mukesh, a fat, fiftyish, fuzzy-wigged, buck-toothed fellow appeared from one of the back rooms wearing a short-sleeved shirt showing off his biceps, which he constantly moved up and down.

'What do you want?' he asked bluntly.

'I'm Rahul Saxena from London. I've come to collect my cheque, please.'

'No cheque. In hawala, we deal only in cash. Here is your one million rupees. Just take the money and disappear.'

Startled by this information, I began to telephone my

father and tell him I was being given cash, not a cheque as expected. But Mukesh deterred me just by his tone: 'No calls from here! Take the money and leave!'

Nervously, I started to count the notes, which were in denominations of ten thousand and one thousand rupees.

'In hawala we don't cheat!' shouted the raucous-voiced Mukesh.

'I'm sure you don't, but I'd still like to count it...'

My father had arranged for me to receive money in India using the hawala system. It's an international informal money transfer system operated through a network of money brokers. It's used by migrant workers to make payments to their home countries. NRIs and others use it frequently. The commission charged by the hawala brokers is less than that charged by the banks, and the exchange rate is usually better. You get more for your pound, euro, dollar, dirham and dinar. To be frank, the system is illegal, and both my mother and I were against using it. But since I had to leave London in such a hurry and didn't want to argue the point with my father, I accepted his proposal to send money by hawala.

I left Mukesh's so-called office with a bag containing one million rupees, meant to cover my course fees and living expenses at Film International. Even carrying a tenth of that amount would've made me nervous on a public street.

It was dark in the alleyway, with only one street light and no pedestrians, just a couple of scrounging dogs. Suddenly, a man appeared from nowhere.

'Give me your money or I will kill you!'

I froze in my tracks. It was as if Mukesh had planned it, and was using the swiftest method of getting his hands on my money without actually touching it himself.

The man showed me a knife. His face was hidden behind a handkerchief mask, and I could only see his eyes. It was a blue handkerchief with small white circles on it. He spoke in English.

'It's not money.'

'Oh, I think it is.'

I would've laughed at his turn of phrase if he hadn't held the knife to my throat.

Removing a length of cloth, which looked like a noose, from around his waist, he tightened the material around my throat. He was behind me now, twisting the knot.

'Please...' I gasped. 'I've come from England to study!'

'Well, let this be your first lesson, English boy...'

'But...I need this money. To stay here...' I managed to add. 'I'm begging you.'

'Shut up or I'll take your life as well as your cash!'

I dropped the bag, and tried to loosen the noose with my fingers. I could feel myself starting to lose consciousness. Then he punched me hard on the back of my head and I fell to the ground. By the time I'd filled my lungs with air again and sat up straight, he was gone. And so was my money.

Getting to my feet, I ran after him in the direction I thought he must have gone, but there was no sign of him. He'd disappeared from sight into the darkness. I shouted in English and Hindi as I ran.

'Help! Help! I've been robbed! Thief! Thief!' But there was no one around to hear or help me.

Shattered and shaken, I went back to the hawala office. Mukesh and his colleague were cynically unsympathetic.

'I want to report this to the police.'

'You can't. It was hawala money. No records. No proof.

You will only open a can of worms for yourself. We will not cooperate. Please leave!'

There was a poised silence. Finally, I said, 'You set this up, didn't you?'

Quick as a cobra, Mukesh pulled a gun from his jacket and waved it in my face. 'Get out! Otherwise I will break your bones and your phones.'

In seconds, I was back out on the street, panting and out of breath.

I started my journey home in a daze of confusion and was shivering even on such a hot evening. I travelled by foot and rickshaw, and then finally by train through the never sleeping Mumbai. It was past the rush hour, and the train from north to south was crowded, but not overcrowded like the Super-Dense Crush Load and I was able to get a seat.

I had learnt my lesson. Never again in my life would I ever carry so much cash. Experience, however, is like a comb given to a man when he is bald.

Whilst on the train, sitting with my eyes closed to ease my violently thumping heart, I wished India government would make an emergency announcement demonetizing the five hundred and one thousand rupee notes from midnight that same day.

It was past midnight when I got back to the hotel, drenched in sweat. I tried to call my parents from the lobby, but the battery in my mobile was dead. I had nobody to talk to. I was completely lost and alone.

I thought of Irfan and David, but realized I didn't have their telephone numbers.

With trembling legs, I approached the front desk. 'Do you have Irfan Dongriwalla's number?' I asked the female receptionist in a desperate tone.

'Who's he?' the woman asked blankly. 'I have just joined today'.

'He's a guide. He brought me to this hotel, with a man named David.'

'There are many Irfans in Mumbai, sir,' she laughed. I was almost in tears.

Just then, as if my prayers had been answered, Irfan and David appeared. Their arrival felt like a blood transfusion. I hugged them and started to cry like a little boy.

'Hey, Rahul? What's wrong?'

'Can we go to my room, please?'

Once there, I told them the whole story. They weren't surprised, and agreed there was no point in making a police complaint.

'People hoarding black money face the same problem in India. They can't make a police complaint if there is a burglary in their house.'

They stayed with me until I calmed down. But there was nothing else they could do. They had their own business to run, they insisted. When they left, I used the hotel phone in my room to call home. After dialing a few wrong numbers with my hands shaking all the time, I got through. My father answered. I found it difficult to speak.

'What's wrong, son? Please speak. Otherwise I will get a heart attack.'

'I was mugged...near the hawala office. All the money I collected is gone.'

There was a pause, during which I expected my father to start shouting. Instead, his voice returned calmly.

'It's all my fault. I should have never used the hawala

system. It was illegal and we are now paying the price.'

In the background, I could hear my mother pleading: 'Come back to London immediately.'

But I didn't want to go back to London and admit defeat so soon after leaving home.

'We'll talk in the morning. I'll call you.'

I felt ashamed and exhausted when I finally hung up the phone. Ashamed because I'd troubled my parents, who'd been so good to me, without thinking, as if I was still in London and not over three thousand miles away, and exhausted from the trauma of the day—mentally, physically and emotionally.

I'd come to India to become a film producer. Now Mumbai had made me a pauper overnight.

A Good Woman

~

I woke up at 7 a.m., perspiring profusely from a terrible nightmare.

That bastard with the handkerchief mask had dogged me for hours, chasing me through a maze of twisting lanes and bazaars in downtown Mumbai. I quickly wiped the sweat from my forehead and tried to calm down. About to gulp down my morning litre of water, I stopped with the bottle halfway to my mouth. Instead, I sat on my bed and remembered in detail what I'd seen yesterday. I was under no illusion about the trouble I was in.

I'd already enrolled with Film International online in London. It was a two-year course, the first year of which was a foundation in filmmaking and the second year was a specialization year. I was going to specialize in Production. My admission was confirmed and my first year's tuition was due to start in two weeks' time. All I had to do now was to go in person to the institute and pay my fees. I should have been doing it today.

I knew my father would send me some more money, by bank transfer this time, if I asked him. But I couldn't do that. I'd already cost him the ten thousand pounds that had been transferred by hawala and snatched by a maniac the night before. He was a man of limited means and would find the money for me somehow. But it would place him and my mother in great hardship to sustain me and my dream. It would be unbelievably selfish of me to ask. I frantically considered and cast aside half a dozen options. My immediate options were limited. In fact, there was only one.

I telephoned my parents.

'Dad, I have decided not to join Film International this semester. Maybe I'll join next year instead.'

'I will send you more money, Rahul,' my father said in a steady voice. It was my mistake and I will make it up to you.'

'No. Please. I will find a job in Mumbai and earn my own money. I will save up for my fees.'

My mother snatched the phone. Her voice was shrill. 'But jobs are so difficult to find, Rahul! You will end up destitute!'

'Mum, Mumbai is called *Maya Nagari*, the city where miracles happen—the city of dreams; the city where young men and women, boys and girls, come from all over India to make a new beginning. If they can do it, so can I.'

'What about all your plans to study filmmaking, my son?'

'My plans haven't changed, Mum, they've just been postponed.'

My father must have reclaimed the receiver, as he came back on the line. He was apprehensive.

'You will suffer great hardship!'

'It can't be that hard, Dad. I still have the three hundred pounds you gave me just before I left for the airport. Thirty thousand rupees is enough to survive in Mumbai for a few weeks till I sort myself out.'

'Very well, stay on in Mumbai...you have our blessings and support. But move to a cheaper place and make your money last as long as you can. After that, if you still haven't found a job, come back home.'

'Roger!'

⁂

After my call to London ended, I waited in the lobby for Irfan and David, who arrived after a good one hour, along with a passenger from Toronto.

'I have decided to stay back in Mumbai and look for a job. I need to move to a cheaper place.'

Irfan became immediately animated.

'I know a very nice Parsee lady who lives nearby. She keeps paying guests. If you are lucky you might even get a separate room.'

David called a number and spoke to the lady on the phone. It was a swift conversation. He told me she had a room available, and that I could move in tomorrow morning. So, it was all settled. I went to a nearby bank and changed my three hundred pounds into rupees and prepared to check out of the Palace Hotel in Colaba early the next day.

My new home turned out to be in the Cyrus Baug Parsee colony, also in Colaba, and not very far from the Palace Hotel. So, I didn't have to travel far. My two friends took me there. Two people who didn't have to be kind to a stranger like me, but were nonetheless, and who seemed to ask nothing of me in return.

My landlady was a Mrs Perizaad Pestonji. She opened the door and greeted us all warmly. A woman in her late seventies, she had luxuriant snowy hair and an evaluating gaze.

When my friends had gone, she said:

'I have known Irfan and David for many years. I will give you this separate room.'

'Thank you, madam.'

'Not madam.' She paused, fixing me with her steady eyes. 'Call me PP Auntie, like everybody else.'

In India, you have to call your elders either 'uncle' or 'auntie'. It's not like in England, where you can call your mother-in-law by her first name. Protocol had to be observed, to show due respect, and I wasn't going to be the one to flout it.

'Thank you, auntie…I mean…PP Auntie.'

'I should establish the rules now, however,' she said, raising an admonishing finger in case I imagined she was a pushover. 'No dogs. No loud music. No pork. No beef. No alcohol. No smoking. No drugs. No eating paan. Rent is five thousand rupees a month, payable in advance, and breakfast is included. You can also use the lounge to watch TV whenever you want.'

I gladly accepted the terms and handed over the first month's rent, and said I would see her later. Unpacking quickly, I settled down in my room. Irfan had told me that Mrs Pestonji was a Parsee, and I knew Parsees were the descendants of a group of Zoroastrians of Iran who had immigrated to India in the tenth century in order to escape persecution. I knew a fair bit about the community from my father, who had had Parsee neighbours when he lived in Zanzibar. One of those neighbours was Farrokh Bulsara, who had settled in England like my father, and who later became famous as Freddie Mercury.

That afternoon, I bumped into PP Auntie in the lounge. The room was a cheerful light-filled space, painted a soothing peach colour, with a green sofa and dusty blue drapes.

'You have a lovely home,' I ventured.

'It's not for sale!' she said with a smile.

I sat in the lounge with her, trying not to show my anxiety

about money, looking at a picture of the late President John F. Kennedy that was hanging on the opposite wall. The picture showed Kennedy sitting in his favourite rocking chair. PP Auntie saw I had noticed the photograph.

'My late husband, Boman, was a great fan of JFK. The chair I am sitting on was his favourite chair, just like President Kennedy's in that picture.'

'How long have you been a widow, if I may ask?'

'BP suffered from high BP. He died ten years ago, of a massive heart attack, sitting on this very chair.'

I expressed my sincere condolences, and made a mental note not to sit on it myself, lest it be unlucky.

'Don't be sorry, he had a good life...'

Grief, she told me, was no longer something that required to be relieved. Over the years, she had accepted her loss. I couldn't tell for sure whether life's brutally inflicted wounds were still fresh or had healed.

'I am sorry,' I said again.

'No need. Tears have all been shed many years back. None left now.'

She pointed to her small eyes. 'See? Arid, like a desert.'

'After the grief, came the loneliness. Now I have conquered both,' continued PP Auntie.

A lump came to my throat. Her eyes were dry, but mine were glistening involuntarily. Maybe I had been destabilized by the mugging, but I found myself becoming emotional at the slightest thing.

'I hope I will also die sitting on this JFK rocking chair,' said PP Auntie, who, it seemed, loved using the acronym.

Our talk about death took a humorous turn when I asked her the most famous question about Kennedy's death.

'Where were you when Kennedy was shot?'

'I didn't do it. I have an alibi,' replied PP Auntie, roaring with laughter.

Smiling effusively, she got up from her rocking chair, leaving it to make an empty creaking sound. *Creak...creak... creak...*

Despite my English reserve, I found myself liking this small, septuagenarian woman with her fair Parsee skin, bun of grey hair secured with bobby pins, penetrating ice-blue eyes, aesthetic air and abrupt sense of humour. Once a school teacher, she told me how she spent her days at home, relaxing in her white-haired twilight.

She stood for a few moments, observing me with interest, as if she was trying to figure me out.

'We are Parsees.'

'I know...Irfan told me. Just like Freddie Mercury.'

'Hrmmmph. My son, Ratan, is a fan of his. He lives here, with me.'

'I see.'

'I seldom go out these days because of my aching bones.'

Aching bones or not, PP Auntie looked strong, and, it turned out, could move about with astounding speed.

I met Ratan later that evening when he walked in with a folded newspaper under his left armpit. A blue-eyed Parsee like his mother, he was around thirty-five and worked as a male nurse at the Bandstand General Hospital in Bandra. He was about my height, but dark-skinned, and was dressed in the casual clothes he'd changed into from his hospital uniform. He, too, seemed anxious to declare his 'Parsee-ness', as if I might run away if I found out unintentionally.

'We Parsees are a small community. We are declining fast

in numbers because our boys and girls are marrying outside the community. Their children are then not brought up as Parsees.'

'I know Parsees quite well,' I reassured him. 'My father had a good Parsee friend in Zanzibar...Porus Pastakia.'

Ratan smiled, as if the name was familiar.

'I am going to marry within the community,' he announced. 'My mother likes Ruby Daruwalla very much. We hope to get married within a year.'

'Ruby...what a nice name.'

'Yes, and Daruwalla means one who sells alcohol. Many Parsee surnames combine the name of a place or a product with the word walla meaning vendor, from or pertaining to.'

'How interesting! We call them portmanteau words. They combine the sounds and meanings of two, like Oxbridge.'

'The longest "walla" surname I have come across in our community is Sodawaterbottleopenerwalla. We Parsees are now being offered free fertility treatments to reverse the sharp decline in our numbers.'

'Really? Tell me about that.'

'Yes. Non-Parsees on the other hand are being offered cash incentives to be sterilized.'

His mother joined us in the lounge. It was as if she just appeared out of the ether, not entering through any door. Once she realized I knew she was in the room, she came forward and sat beside me.

'Now tell us more about yourself and your family, Rahul.'

In the end, I talked as if I was hypnotized. I told them everything about myself, including how I had been mugged and left high and dry in Mumbai. She didn't interrupt my soliloquy and neither did Ratan.

'That's terrible,' said Ratan, speaking quietly to me when I finally fell silent. 'Don't worry, you will soon find a job in Mumbai.'

'A criminal always revisits the scene of the crime,' said PP Auntie, raising her eyebrows a fraction. 'You must go back to Bandra and look for that villain.'

'There's not much I can do…'

We talked on like this for a while, and soon the other paying guest, Asif, arrived. I felt a warm glow as the evening progressed, as if I was part of a family of sorts, not a family like the one I'd left behind in London, but something that substituted for its absence. Asif Khan was around twenty-five, a lean and sharp-looking young man from Hyderabad. He was trying to become a Bollywood actor. He spoke to me in a mixture of Hindi and broken English.

'I was born Asif Ali Sardari. But some years back, I changed my name to Asif Khan.'

'Why?'

'For two reasons. The first was that everyone was calling me "Mr Ten Per Cent", after some supposedly corrupt politician from a neighbouring country.'

We all laughed, knowing well who he was referring to.

'And the other?' I asked inquisitively.

'The other reason is that Bollywood is full of Khans. So, I also decided to become a "Khan".'

Within ten minutes he'd told me all about himself and his background, and his struggle to get a role in a Bollywood film. Any role, no matter how small, it seems, would've satisfied him.

'I am good at breaking the ice, but I can't seem to break into Bollywood. There are thousands of us out here…young people from all over India, trying for a chance in films. It's a tough world out there, Rahul, full of bogus talent agents who can skin you alive.'

Proudly, he showed me his portfolio of photographs which he had shown to numerous directors and producers.

'"We will get back to you," I am always told. But no one ever does!' For a brief moment, he looked very despondent; almost suicidal. Then he said bitterly, 'I have now realized that to get into Bollywood, you need to be the son or daughter of a Bollywood actor, producer or director. Nepotism rules!' He then gave me numerous examples of Bollywood actors and actresses with absolutely no acting talent who had won film roles simply because of their family connections.

Then, to satisfy his curiosity, I told him my story all over again—in every detail. He was sad when, at last, I finished.

'I hope you will be able to join Film International next year,' he said warmly. 'Who knows, one day I might work in a film produced by you. In Bollywood, everyone survives on hope!'

At that moment, I received a text message from my father. I excused myself in order to read it:

Have you found some cheap accommodation?

While Auntie PP and her son chatted and Asif listened, I texted back.

Yes.
Who with?
PP Auntie.
How is she?
A good woman.

On that evening of warmth and confession, I couldn't have meant it more.

The Graduate

CHEWING PAAN wasn't allowed in PP Auntie's house—one of her many rules. I could understand why. A paan is made of nuts, pastes and spices wrapped in a leaf and chewed as a stimulant. One of the side effects, however, is spitting. Paan chewers tend to eject red jets from their mouths that leave indelible dark crimson stains on the roads and pavements of Mumbai. It is an ugly sight and PP Auntie didn't want stains all over her footpath and patio. Not that this had anything directly to do with my predicament, but a one-off munch of the magic leaf might've lifted my spirits and given me the energy I needed to get myself motivated.

Now that I had a permanent address in Mumbai, my first priorities were to open a bank account and get an Indian mobile phone SIM card. I was the last to leave the house that morning, apart from PP Auntie. People leave for work early in Mumbai in order to avoid the Super-Dense Crush Load. But it was no use; the trains were always full.

On my way to the bank, I passed a shopping mall where I was stopped by a young man aged around thirty. He was sitting on the ground, begging, dressed only in a kind of leotard.

'Can you give me some money, please?'

I had nothing to give him except some unsolicited advice. 'Why don't you get a job?'

'This is my job,' he said plainly. 'I work nine-to-five, and overtime on weekends.' The professional beggar smiled up at me and made the usual personal enquiry:

'What do you do for a living?'

'I've just arrived from England. I'm looking for a job myself.'

'You will not a get a job in Mumbai that easily. I came here four years ago from Agra. I am a graduate, but have no job.'

The graduate sounded like a very interesting person.

'I thought India was shining.'

'India is shining only for the rich and the super-rich.'

'But there is also a rising middle class,' I interrupted.

'But the majority of us are poor, very poor. Our children die of malnutrition. We belong to the "Bottom Billion"—the poorest of this world.' He was talking like an economist now. 'Poor, powerless people in India are invisible, and count for nothing at all.'

He admitted he had a degree. I wondered if it was in economics. Or was it in literature? I didn't ask. It didn't matter. A frown marred his forehead, but his smile broke out again.

'To make money in Mumbai, you have to be a crook... or a beggar like me.'

A pot-bellied policeman passed by, tapping his lathi-stick against the man's right leg. The beggar handed over a bundle of bank notes.

'What was that for?'

'That was my monthly instalment. Us beggars call it "hafta". We pay hafta to the police every month so they will not drive us away. In India, you have to bribe everyone, from the lowest to the highest...it is an overhead expense. My only overhead.'

Just then, a passing chauffeur-driven Porsche slowed to a stop in Mumbai's crazy traffic. But the owner ignored the beggar's tapping on the car's tinted windows. In between begging—or rather, going about his work—he did the Indian thing and told me more about himself and his family. He was married, had children and lived in Dharavi, the largest slum of Mumbai. He also gave me a little sermon about India's economic miracle doing nothing for the millions still living in grinding poverty.

'I am a slumdog, but not a millionaire! Not yet anyway. But I am earning good money as a beggar. Begging is quite lucrative in Mumbai. I am saving to buy a small flat.'

This kind of offbeat entrepreneurial optimism fascinated me.

'There are many beggars in India who are quite rich, but they still beg. Many of them die with huge sums of money in their pockets, like the one in Ajmer recently who had two hundred thousand rupees in his loincloth when he keeled over in the street.'

He showed me a newspaper cutting to prove it, and then continued:

'I would like to own my own home, no matter how small, but with an internal toilet and shower room. I am tired of using the open sewers in the slums of Dharavi.'

'I can understand your plight.'

'All I want is a basic toilet. I am not looking for, nor can I ever afford, a luxury toilet like the one being developed in England that can be flushed using a smartphone app.'

'I am impressed with your up-to-date general knowledge.'

'About six hundred million people own mobile phones in India, but many still have no access to a proper toilet.'

He was raising his voice now, with anger flaring up in him. Then he carried on, softly. 'A friend of mine likes a girl, but her parents are refusing to give their consent for marriage because his accommodation does not have an internal toilet.'

'Loo before you woo, eh!' I joked. We both laughed.

'What India needs is toilets, not temples!' shouted the beggar, again raising his voice and trying to fight back his anger.

The day was moving on, and I should have been about my own business, but the graduate-beggar kept talking to me, pulling me back every time I made an effort to get up and go. I listened politely, in case I offended him by going.

'I will be filing tax returns from next year so that I can apply for a home mortgage.'

I smiled.

'Unlike England, where you could until recently self-certify and falsify your income on a mortgage application, here in India we do not have any "liar loans".'

'Self-certification of income has now been banned,' I tried to update the beggar on the new mortgage rules of England.

'Yes, but you now have "gaming" under which mortgage applicants use buy-to-let to circumvent affordability rules to purchase a property they actually intend to live in.'

I was amazed at his general knowledge and looked at him astonished.

'I read newspapers during my lunch break.'

He told me that despite everything he found Mumbai very exciting.

'When you are tired of Mumbai, you are tired of life.'

'Didn't Samuel Johnson once say a similar thing about London?' I asked.

'You are right. I am plagiarizing,' replied the well-read

beggar with a wicked grin.

Our conversation then moved back to begging.

'I don't think I'd like to beg...' I told him.

He paused for a moment and evaluated me seriously. 'In that case, you should apply for a job as a male stripper at the Colaba Cougar Club. They always have vacancies for good-looking fellows like you. The C3 Club is just near the Gateway of India.'

'Why don't *you* apply?'

'I did. I passed the interview but failed the 'Oscar Ceremony'.'

'Oscar Ceremony?'

'They said my "Oscar" was too small!'

'But I thought size did not matter.'

'Not in bed. But on the stage the strippers need to be big. If you are, then apply to the C3 Club straightaway and you will earn some big money.'

Another passer-by threw some change, then another and another and another.

'It is my peak time now. Time to earn. Come back during my lunch break at 1 p.m. if you want to talk more.'

I walked away towards the bank, looking back at the graduate-beggar who was in full flow now that business was brisk. His suggestion was so ludicrous it started to seem like a good idea as I walked off under the searing sun.

When I reached the bank, the clerk was firm but polite.

'We will require three copies of all your documents.'

Then he noticed that the name of my referee was Mrs Perizaad Pestonji, whom he knew quite well, and his demeanour changed. My bank account was quickly opened.

However, acquiring a mobile phone and SIM card was a

different matter entirely. Long forms and long queues faced me when I dragged my sweating self to the phone shop. When my turn finally came, I was told that security was a big issue. It was a good three hours before I eventually got a new phone and a local SIM card. I was exhausted by the bureaucracy of it all and was grateful to get out of the shop.

Wearily, I fed in my parents' contact numbers and those of PP Auntie, Ratan, Irfan and David. Almost everybody had a mobile phone in India, even if they didn't have a toilet.

It was lunchtime, and, for some reason, I found myself walking back to talk to the graduate-beggar to ask him to expand on his employment advice.

∽

The next morning, I was boiling an egg in the kitchen when PP Auntie came in. I didn't hear her enter the room or come up close behind me, so she gave me a start when she spoke.

'Did you ever go back to the alley where you were mugged?'

'I am going there today.' I tried not to show my jumpiness. 'I will go after breakfast, to avoid the morning rush hour.'

'The local trains will still be full.'

I expected her to linger, but that was all she said. She made herself some tea and left. The presence she'd brought into the room left with her.

Once outside on the busy streets, I was surprised to pass the beggar I'd met the day before on the way to Churchgate.

'Sorry, I didn't ask your name yesterday.'

'Dharsi. My name is Dharsi.'

'Darcy?'

'No. I'm not Mr Darcy from *Pride and Prejudice*. It's 'Dharsi': D...H...A...R...S...I...Mr F Dharsi'

'I'm Rahul Saxena,' I said without asking him what his "F" stood for.

'You were lucky for me yesterday, Rahul. After you left, I did very good business.'

At that moment, David's Volvo pulled up at the kerb and he stuck his head out of the window. I could see Irfan was in the car with him.

'Hey! Can we drop you somewhere?'

'Churchgate Station?'

'Jump in.'

Once inside, David told me, 'We are just returning from the Palace Hotel after dropping off two NRIs. They were Patels and they owned motels in Los Angeles.'

Irfan sat quietly at the wheel, for a change, looking depressed.

'He is suffering from sexual frustration,' said David, laughing loudly.

'I never have sexual frustrations. I just wank them off,' said Irfan, moodily.

'So, what *is* your problem?' I asked.

'It's my mother, back home in Lucknow. She wants me to marry a first cousin of mine whom I have never even met.' He looked genuinely distressed now. 'Inter-cousin marriages are often encouraged and arranged within Muslim families. The girl's parents feel their daughters would be safe within the framework of supportive family members as her in-laws. The boy's parents feel a cousin wife will remain in the family and is unlikely to seek a divorce.'

Irfan drank some water to clear his throat, and then continued:

'I believe the only way to discourage this, and in the long

run prevent children being born with genetic defects, due to the closeness of their parents' blood, is through education.'

We were all silent for a while as Irfan gulped some more water. Finally, he blurted out in frustration, 'The practice conflicts with freedom of choice and romantic love!'

David and I both sympathized with him, but there was little we could do, and we were all silent for the remainder of the journey.

Churchgate Station was busy but not too crowded, as PP Auntie supposed it would be, and I wondered when she last took a train anywhere. My journey to Bandra wasn't uncomfortable, although the memory of my experience there loomed large in my mind for the whole trip. Truth be told, I had wanted to get out at every station on the way and travel back in the opposite direction. I decided to walk to the scene of the crime instead of taking a rickshaw, as I had done on that night, maybe because I was in no hurry to get there.

Just off Hill Road, I passed a young Sikh couple. They were holding hands and laughing, and they seemed to be very much in love. The man looked to be around thirty and tall, dark and handsome, as they say in Hollywood. He had a typical Sikh beard and was wearing a blue turban and a kara, an iron bracelet, which is a symbol of eternity in the Sikh community. The woman was in her mid-twenties, and I noticed at once that she was very beautiful. In fact, I found myself entranced by her for many moments.

I hadn't gone far past the couple, when two men on a motorcycle came towards me, riding fast along the road. I thought they were going to run me over, so I jumped out of their way. The next thing I heard was three loud bangs, like shots, and I looked down the road in the direction of the motorcycle's reckless trajectory. I saw immediately that the Sikh man had been shot. He was lying on the ground and blood was oozing out of his chest and stomach. I quickly ran back, and, within a few moments, the injured man was surrounded by a crowd of twenty people, then forty, then sixty, growing by the minute. The young Sikh woman—who was being restrained by about five of the throng—was hysterical.

'My husband has been shot!'

Only when she had stopped wailing did I go over and ask her what happened.

'Two men came…on a motorcycle,' she sobbed. 'The pillion passenger got off…he approached us…fired three shots at my husband…'

I remembered both motorcycle riders had worn helmets with the visors down.

I rang for the police and an ambulance, only to realize both had already arrived on the scene. The area was quickly cordoned off and the paramedics confirmed that the man was still alive, if barely. They prepared to rush him away to the nearby Bandstand General Hospital, while the police made a token gesture of questioning the crowd.

After five minutes, identification of the shooters was proving impossible, so the cops gave up and moved everybody along. I remembered that Ratan was working as a male nurse in Bandstand, so I offered to telephone him on his personal mobile phone and tell him what happened. Knowing this would speed things up, the medics agreed. They also asked if I'd accompany the young Sikh woman in the ambulance, to try to keep her calm. Ratan was available when I called, and he took down all the details. He told me, 'I will be waiting for your ambulance at the Accident and Emergency gate with

Dr Mittal and some nurses.'

On the way, the young woman held my hand in the back of the ambulance and spoke in a barely audible voice, through her streaming tears.

'Thank you,' she kept saying, over and over. '*Thank you...*'

Before I knew it, we were at our destination. Built on a sprawling twelve acres, Bandstand General Hospital was a multi-speciality tertiary care hospital with state-of-the-art facilities.

Ratan was as good as his word—he was the first person I saw when the ambulance doors swung wide. 'We have ten most advanced operating theatres, one of the largest Intensive Care Units and some three hundred consultants.'

The woman's husband had been rushed to one of the operating theatres. She was totally shattered and in shock, crying continuously, unable to talk under the fluorescent lights of Accident and Emergency.

I stayed with her and tried my best to comfort her. She told me her name was Julie Singh and her husband's name was Robin. I tried to take her mind off the situation by doing the Indian thing and telling her a little bit about myself and how I was robbed in the close vicinity of the place where her husband had been shot. But nothing I said could console her for very long. At the same time, I tried to disguise how attracted I was to her.

Every passing minute seemed like hours. Then a couple of policemen arrived and asked us both some questions. They were going through the motions, of course.

'What else do you remember about the assailant?'

Julie shook her head. 'Everything happened so suddenly...'

For my part, I tried to be as helpful as I could.

'I remember one of them was wearing a red helmet with black spots.'

The two cops looked at each other, as if to say 'that's a great help', while Julie kept up her sobbing.

'I just can't understand it...my husband had no enemies or debts...'

'I hope you catch the bastards!' I offered lamely.

I was angry, as much for my own predicament as for the man who'd been shot. I held out little hope of either of the culprits being apprehended.

Eventually, the police left. Robin was still in the operating theatre a good two hours after being taken in, and no one was holding out much hope. I couldn't stay any longer, much as I wanted to. I spoke to Ratan, and he arranged for a counsellor to come sit with Julie. She held onto my hand and didn't want to let it go. This gave me a warm feeling inside—I was being protective and felt strangely needed by her. It was already 6 p.m.

'I'll pray for your husband,' I told Julie, as I left her in Ratan's company.

On the way out, I realized I'd come to Bandra to visit the scene of one crime and ended up being a witness to another. Two serious crimes in two days. At least mine was only a roadside robbery. This one was an attempted murder! And I was the only real witness...I was scared to death.

Rat Race

Two days later, I went back to the Bandstand General Hospital to see how Robin Singh was doing. Ratan wasn't around, but I met Dr Mittal, a confident, well-spoken young man in his mid-thirties.

'His wife had him discharged just two hours ago,' explained the doctor. 'She is flying him to Amritsar. We tried to stop her, but she insisted.'

Disappointed, I left the hospital. I had missed seeing Julie by just two hours. I badly wanted to see her and talk to her again.

Over the following days her image gradually faded from my mind as my job hunt took over. The search took many forms, starting online using Ratan's computer, which he kept in the lounge. He set up a username and a password for me. I composed a CV, and started sending job applications. I also made phone calls responding to job advertisements and applied to companies which hadn't even advertised. I tried cold-calling, visiting offices, stores, hotels and factories asking for a job, any job.

I got nowhere.

I was beginning to experience first-hand the harsh realities of surviving in Mumbai. I quickly realized that the job market wasn't nearly as buoyant as it was made out to be. Corruption was rampant in the recruitment process. Nepotism and bribery favoured the less competent and undeserving over the talented and worthy, and even education wasn't enough to swing the balance in your favour if you didn't have the contacts or the money.

Two months had passed since I was mugged and I still had no job. I soon lost count of the days. My money was running out fast. I took local trains, travelling on all three lines—the Western Line, the Central Line and the Harbour Line. I travelled by bus, I travelled by rickshaw. There were days when I was forced to count the change in my pocket to determine just how far I could progress by public transport. If I didn't have enough money, I would walk, trying not to swallow too much dust as I trudged wearily through the teeming streets, and the dark nameless alleys and by-lanes of Mumbai. My shoes started to wear out from my daily pounding of the streets of the city. I walked as far as my legs would carry me, but I eventually grew too tired to continue, with both my feet hurting and my hips complaining.

My job hunt took me everywhere and I ended up exploring the entire city, from south to north, east to west. What I discovered was a callous world that had narrowed into a neighbourhood but not broadened into a brotherhood. Sure, India was shining. Mumbai was shining—in the shopping malls and in the new multiplex cinemas and in the nightclubs and in the five-star hotels, and in the glitz and glamour of the high-income class, all living in modern luxury. There were London-priced properties and jam-packed bars, and call centres where your credit card details could be stored or stolen. That was the money-is-everything side of Mumbai.

But I also saw the other side.

I saw the blemished Mumbai, the blemished India. I saw the pathetic slums and the less fortunate homeless people sleeping rough. I saw dirty ragged little kids playing in the gutters and men, women and children defecating on the roads and on the railway tracks. I saw the open drains and the manholes and the mountains of garbage. I smelled the stink, tasted the foulness, heard the weeping, tripped over the rats and was bitten blood-raw by the mosquitoes. From time to time, a cocktail of odours filled my nostrils—human and animal faeces, rotten food and fish, compost, sewer gas, stagnant water, perspiration, exhaust fumes. At one point when I was walking around I almost collapsed when I inhaled an overpowering stench of raw sewage.

Mumbai was a city of monumental contradictions. A schizophrenic city where the richest people live cheek by jowl with some of the poorest. It was truly 'a tale of two cities', and I would have to learn how to become immune to one of them—how to walk around with my eyes closed and pretend it wasn't there.

The city was becoming more and more noisy every day, or perhaps it was my increased capacity to respond to that noise which was making me burst with exasperation.

On my way to my first job interview, I passed Mumbai's wretched red light district with its dark crowded streets where young women stood waiting for customers, or leaned out of upstairs windows. Wearing heavy make-up, and dressed in excessively bright and garish colours, these prostitutes with tight clothes and loose morals smiled constantly, trying to lure their next customer into their small filthy rooms, with small single beds and old, tattered mattresses covered with soiled multi-coloured bed sheets. Some passers-by just walked these streets window shopping, watching thrusting bosoms and navels, laughing, wolf-whistling, making kissing noises and gestures, and exchanging lusty comments. There were also some serious customers who went in and out quickly, adjusting their trousers on their exit. The noise, the loud music, the hustle, the chaotic traffic in the neighbourhood made the sadness of the place even more distressing. I swiftly left and vowed never to go back again to that HIV death trap.

My first proper job interview turned out to be a set-up. The man wanted me to invest in an illegal investment scheme offering ridiculously high returns. What I wanted was a job—a real job that would earn me enough to live on and allow me to save for my two-year course in filmmaking. I'd started to eat less in an effort to save money. I wasn't starving, at least not yet, but I couldn't afford tandoori chicken or mutton biryani any longer, and I had to make do with dal and rice.

One day, I was sitting in a café on Mira Road. The Hope Café, with its mismatched table and chairs, was a typical working-class restaurant crowded with customers and waiters running around; a noisy place with Bollywood songs blaring out from a huge music player, while flies buzzed around and orders were screamed to the kitchen. There were no printed menus. The waiters would list all the food available in the restaurant. 'Mutton masala, chicken masala, mutton biryani, chicken biryani, samosas, kebabs, pilau rice, dal, parathas…' Some food items were listed on wall-mounted boards which also proclaimed a few injunctions: *No Alcohol. No Kissing. Putting Make-up Not Allowed. Betting On Cricket Not Allowed.*

I was sitting there drinking tea and looking at job advertisements in *The Times of India*, when a classified jumped out at me from page 40: *Night Rat Killers Required.*

At that moment, a man sitting at the next table moved across, uninvited. He spoke to me in a whisper as he mopped a streamlet of perspiration and black hair-dye running down his forehead and neck.

'Looking for a job?'

I nodded nervously.

'I can help you migrate to England.'

I pretended to show interest.

'I can send you to England under a special scheme.'

'A special scheme?'

'It is designed to allow highly skilled people to immigrate into the United Kingdom to look for work or self-employment opportunities.' He smiled in a knowing sort of way before continuing. 'The beauty of it is you don't even have to be highly skilled. I know someone who will arrange all your bogus certificates and upgrade you from unskilled to highly skilled on paper. He can even help if you don't speak or write proper English.'

The man leaned in closer to me.

'Myself Rajagopalcharianandswamy Srimadaddankithiraha.'

Incredible! It was one of those very long multi-syllable south Indian names. I could never have remembered it but for his business card which he pushed in my hand at the time.

'You can call me Raj,' he said, to my relief. 'It will cost you two hundred thousand rupees. I am here every afternoon if you need my services.'

'I will meet you tomorrow,' I lied to get rid of him, and sat for a further hour in despair.

When I reached home, I saw PP Auntie showing a thin bony man around the house. He was wearing narrow silver-rimmed spectacles, and had just finished chewing off a paan.

'This is Mahendra Jiwa,' announced PP Auntie. 'Our new lodger from Baroda.'

'Hi, I'm Rahul, I am from London.'

He went cold and made a face. Sweat suddenly started to pour down his neck.

'I know many NRIs in England, Canada and America,' said Jiwa, whose paan-reddened tongue spouted out when he talked. 'They are all a pain in the arse.'

It soon became obvious that Jiwa made no secret of his dislike of NRIs. PP Auntie left the room to go back to the lounge.

'Stop impressing us with your English Cheddar cheese, Lurpak butter and Ribena...'

I tried to tell him I wasn't one of those people and, in fact, I was quite humble about my status here in Mumbai. But he didn't want to listen.

'And why do you all speak with such bizarre accents? Why can't you speak with a proper accent, instead of pretending to be what you are not? I hate Indians who take up a foreign name like James or Michael and pretend to speak in British and American accents which do not even suit them. That's why I never took up a job at a call centre!'

'I hate NRIs. My sister was married to one from Canada. She has now come back to India because the bastard was already married.'

More anti-NRI abuse followed. 'I was conned by this same Canadian NRI into investing in a bogus website, where I lost money. It was a dot.con rather than a dot.com website!'

He went on and on, his arms gesticulating wildly as he strived to hone home his argument. I wondered if this resentment of NRIs was a general thing in India or if it was confined to people like Jiwa who'd had a bad experience or in his case several bad experiences.

'Why don't you NRIs just pack up your bags and go back to where you came from?'

I was too tired to start a big argument, but I did try and defend the NRIs.

'There are millions of Indians scattered all over the world. We do contribute to the Indian economy by remitting billions of dollars every year.'

He started to cool down.

'I have come to Mumbai to learn filmmaking.'

At the mention of this, he was suddenly a different man. 'I love films…both Hollywood and Bollywood,' he said with a pleasant smile.

I told him about what I had been through since arriving in Mumbai.

'Keep trying, my friend. One day you will succeed.'

That was the extent of his advice. The subject of conversation then became himself, in the Indian fashion. 'I was married as a child, but I refused to recognize that marriage. Instead, I am now married to a Gujarati girl and live with my rich in-laws as a "ghar jamai", a live-in son-in-law.'

Just then, PP Auntie walked in with some tea and grilled cheese sandwiches. She joined our conversation: 'The system of ghar jamai works well sometimes, but the poor ghar jamai has to be ready to bear insults and jokes and be dominated by two women—his wife and his mother-in-law.'

'My case is worse,' laughed Jiwa. 'I am a ghar jamai of another ghar jamai. My life is a hell with three women on my nerves—my wife, my mother-in-law and my grandmother-in-law!'

All this talk of other people's situations wasn't doing me any good. I was still without a job and my money was running out fast. I was ready to do anything. I politely excused myself and left PP Auntie and Jiwa to talk about the chains of marriage.

Night Rat Killers Required.

The following day, the advertisement appeared again in the newspaper. I decided to apply, and was called in for an interview.

I was horrified by the state of the building when I finally arrived at the interview. Must be rat-infested, I thought, as I approached it past the garbage and many illegal constructions that encroached upon the footpath. With the lift not working, I was breathless by the time I reached the shabby fourth-floor office which was situated next to a smelly toilet—with the flush not working, I am sure.

The interviewing officer, a fortyish, tall, thin man, his hair flattened down with hair oil, decided to give me a lecture, as if I was applying to be his personal assistant.

'With the rat population on the rise in Mumbai, the municipal corporation has decided to recruit more night rat killers.' In between drinking tea from a saucer with a slurping noise, he explained to me how the job should be done. 'Armed with a long stick in one hand and a torch in the other, you would be required to go out six nights a week.'

'At what time do I start?'

'At 1 a.m., when Mumbai is asleep, but the rats aren't.'

'I understand.'

'You first blind the rat with the torch and then hit it with the long stick and kill it and put it in a bag.'

'How many shall I kill?'

'A minimum of thirty per night. More the merrier. Next morning at 7 a.m., you will be required to count the dead rats in front of a council supervisor.'

'What if I kill less than thirty?'

'Your pay will be deducted.'

There were four other candidates at the interview. We all had to pass a written test followed by a physical, testing us for speed and stamina. We had to carry a fifty-kg sack on our shoulders to prove our fitness. I was accepted for the job along with three others. One applicant who fell down whilst carrying the fifty-kg bag was rejected. The salary would be three hundred rupees per night.

I immediately told Irfan and David about my first job in Mumbai. They were disappointed that I hadn't been able to find something more in keeping with my education and qualifications, but were nevertheless supportive.

So, the following night, in lashing rain, I started my job as an NRK—a night rat killer.

The rat-infested areas of Mumbai were a world apart from the shopping malls and multiplexes and luxury apartments of the more affluent areas. It was a parallel city without parallel.

Rat killing in Mumbai reminded me of the rat problem back home in England where it was becoming increasingly more menacing. I had heard that there was even a rat at 10

Downing Street that was finally caught by Larry the cat, a four-year-old tabby.

I had come to India as an NRI. Now Mumbai's rat race had made me an NRK.

An Inspector Calls

Most cities in India use traps, cats, poison, fumigation or glue strips to get rid of rat infestation, but in Mumbai, with a population of twenty million, the municipal corporation preferred to use stick men or NRKs—a rare breed in India. The method, though brutal, was simple and effective. I was assigned to 'C Ward' in the old city, just a few blocks from the exclusive Queen's Necklace shoreline. The buildings were decomposing, and populated by poor people. Dozens of rats scurried along the walls and heaps of garbage or lurked behind carts and parked bicycles or crouched under discarded newspapers. The rodents could be anything up to eight inches long, and I had to be quick and blind them with my flashlight before they leapt into the air and escaped. The technique of killing them with a single blow to the head with my metal-tipped pole took me a while to master, but the fear of one of the monsters biting my face soon made me proficient in the art. If the first blow didn't kill the rat, then I'd have to catch it by the tail in mid-air and smash its head against the nearest wall.

One night, an NRK colleague of mine horrified me.

'In Mumbai, we kill rats, but the Musahars of Bihar in northern India eat them to survive.'

I was shocked into an amazed silence to learn this.

'Caste-based repression of more than one thousand

years has deprived them of their basic dignity. India with its nuclear weapons and a space programme has failed them in an unpardonable manner,' added my colleague.

When it rained, the rats would migrate with the street-dwellers into the dark alleyways and dimly-lit underpasses for shelter. There were plenty of rats. The figure of a half-million killed by NRKs every year in Mumbai seemed like it was only scratching the surface of the problem, but at least I'd never be out of work again. Six days a week I fanned out with the rest of the city's NRKs, from midnight till dawn, making my quota of thirty rats per night. In the morning, the tally would be entered into the oversized ledgers maintained by the pest-control bureaucrats from the comfort of their desks. Mumbai, as Asia's largest slum, was an ideal breeding ground for the rats.

Some of my NRK colleagues liked to hunt the rats barefoot so the rodents wouldn't hear them coming, but I always wore sandals. Samples from our kill were combed for fleas, which were then tested for bubonic plague. This is what made me finally give up the job, this fear of being bitten and infected.

And a better offer, as well.

One day, after two months of earning seven thousand and two hundred rupees per month, which was below the taxable limit, and gave me a take-home pay of the same amount, I was having breakfast with two of my NRK colleagues in a restaurant after a night's work. The tea at the restaurant was horrible. The awareness of this suddenly reminded me of Dhiraj Desai whom I'd met on the flight from London, and his 'urine' monologue came to my mind as I sipped the lukewarm liquid in the restaurant that morning. I still had his business card and although I believed his big words on the plane were just a form of bragging, I nonetheless decided to go and see him at his office the next day.

'Mr Desai is not yet in,' said the young receptionist in a polite London-style tone.

'You are welcome to wait in the reception.'

It was a highly sophisticated and ultra-spacious office in downtown Mumbai on the fortieth floor of Regent Chambers. His staff of ten was an encouragement and relief. Maybe he really was somebody after all?

I waited and waited, but he didn't arrive. After about two hours, I fell asleep in the reception area and was woken by somebody shaking my shoulder. It was Dhiraj Desai and, to my utter surprise, he recognized me. He'd put on a bit of weight—about the same amount as I'd lost since seeing him on the plane. His smile was welcoming.

'Hello, Rahul.'

He shook my hand and took me to his office, a luxuriously furnished room with elegant fittings and floor-to-ceiling glass windows that provided a panoramic view of Nariman Point and Marine Drive. His secretary brought us tea. This was a different secretary, not Shalini, and I decided not to ask about her. I assumed she must have left him and he now had another mistress.

'Our tea does not taste like urine.' We both laughed at this reference to our previous meeting, and I told him what I'd been through, and my current job as an NRK, in case he smelled the slums and the rats off me. He was horrified.

'Why don't you join us?'

I accepted immediately, without even discussing the terms.

'Your salary would be ₹36,000 per month, to be reviewed after three months.'

This was only three hundred and sixty pounds in UK currency, but it was a lot more than the hundred and thirty pounds a month I earned as an NRK.

'You can start tomorrow if you like. You will be in charge of the inter-company wine trading that I started with my brother Paresh's company about a year ago.' I smiled. Sometimes it pays to talk to strangers on planes.

So, the next day, a Thursday, I reported for my new job, excited and nervous and eager to make a good impression. Things went well for the first six weeks. I was qualified enough to do the work and it was clean and safe, away from the rat-infested alleys. Both brothers were polite and courteous to me, and I thought I'd landed on my feet at last. Then I noticed that no payments were actually being made between the companies with respect to the inter-company trading; also, that Dhiraj was paying very little VAT to Customs, and Paresh was not paying any at all for wine sales to his brother.

One Monday morning, I decided to ask Dhiraj about the potential mounting VAT liability. When I got to the office, both the Desai brothers were there along with three other people—a police inspector and two others in dark suits.

'I am Police Inspector Jagdish Raj. These two are VAT officers. You are under arrest, Mr Rahul Saxena, for VAT fraud.'

I was dumbstruck and unable to answer the inspector who addressed me in this accusing way. I looked at Dhiraj and Paresh.

'The Desai brothers are also under arrest,' said the inspector.

We were all taken to a customs detention centre in Charni Road and questioned further. Computers, accounting records, VAT documents, invoice copies and many more papers from both companies were seized and taken away by the VAT officers to help with their investigations.

From the questions I was asked, and from the comments made by the VAT officers, I was able to build up a picture of what had been going on. It was apparently agreed between the Desai brothers that Dhiraj would buy wine from Paresh who would then not file any VAT returns and deny all knowledge of the inter-company trading. The invoices created showing Dhiraj Desai buying wine stock from his brother were, therefore, bogus invoices, or 'fresh-air invoices', as the VAT men called them. Dhiraj would insist that there was a bona fide inter-company trading agreement and that the VAT was the responsibility of Paresh's company.

In the midst of all this, Dhiraj would retain the VAT money collected from the genuine external sales of wine and siphon off the funds. It was a clever fraud, but even in India, it couldn't be sustained for long.

Of course, they blamed me, the new man.

'You invented and perpetrated this VAT fraud jointly with the Desai brothers. You knew, or should have known, that VAT fraud was being committed and just turned a blind eye to it!'

I protested my innocence.

'I joined the company only six weeks ago! The inter-company trading has been going on for more than a year.'

The VAT officers were not convinced.

'I am only an employee of Dhiraj's company and have nothing to gain from the alleged VAT fraud!'

I was very polite and careful throughout the investigation as I didn't want to be beaten up. But it didn't help. I remained under arrest.

The next day, I was handed over to an overweight, silver-haired, baton-waving custody officer with a toothless smile, who laughed in a macabre manner and spat copiously. He led me down poorly-lit hallways to a stairwell smelling of urine, finally to a basement cell, also poorly lit, where I was thrown barefoot into solitary confinement. I crossed to one corner of the cell, trying, unsuccessfully, to avoid puddles of urine.

To my surprise, it was not a solitary confinement after all. As I sat down on the floor, I was immediately swamped by mosquitoes and cockroaches. I screamed, loud and fierce. It scared off the little bastards, but only for a few seconds. I sat on the floor of the cell in a state of shock, shaking and sweating as if I had malaria at an advanced stage. After two hours, I was given some dal and rice for my dinner, which I did not touch at first. Later, oppressed by the tyranny of hunger, I ate in the company of the mosquitoes and cockroaches, and surrounded by the unbearable smell of urine. I did not sleep the whole night, as the little rascals had decided to keep me company. I kept pushing them off with my hands and legs, which, by the morning, were almost paralysed due to exhaustion.

Finally, dawn came.

'Come on. Out!' Screamed the toothless officer. 'My duty is coming to an end.'

I was shoved up the same maze of hallways and stairwells, and on reaching the ground floor my face was covered in a black cloth as if I was about to be hanged. I was then pushed into a police vehicle.

'Where are we going?' I asked anxiously.

'You will soon find out.'

I recognized the voice. It was one of the VAT officers

from the day before. Was I being driven to the gallows to be hanged without a trial?

In a panic, I imagined hanging by the neck, with my eyes bulging, my face turning blue, my tongue sticking out...

For the rest of the journey, I felt as if I was sinking into quicksand, the swamp of anguish and gloom. I had no idea where we were heading. The van's pace was erratic. Crazy speeds, sudden stops, lunatic hooting. I had no idea what the hell was going on, as I was repeatedly thrown left and right, and then left again as the van criss-crossed through Mumbai's insane traffic.

Then a loud bang! A sudden halt! A loud, sharp, shrill cry! What had happened? An accident? Had we been hit? Was there a multiple car crash? Had anyone been killed? No one was prepared to tell me...

'Just shut up!' hollered the VAT officer, as our van finally started to move.

At last, after a hellish two-hour journey we reached the VAT Head Office at Nariman Point where the black cloth from my face was removed. I felt like a human wreck.

I was taken in a lift to an interview room on the fifth floor. Again, I was pushed. I was interviewed for the second time—the same officers, the same haughty tones, the same questions, the same answers.

'Wait here. We will come back to you,' said one of the VAT officers at the end of my interrogation.

After the longest night came the longest day, as I sat starving, all alone in the interview room behind closed doors, not knowing what was going to happen or where I'd be sent next. Gloom engulfed me. I had nothing to do except sit and worry and look at the picture of Gandhi on the wall.

Ironically, the British treated him well in the jail. Today's India was different when it came to dealing with detainees. Then, at about six in the evening, the VAT officers returned.

'You are being released without charge.'

'What about the Desai brothers?' I asked in a weak voice.

'They have been charged with VAT offences. They will be tried in a court of law. For the moment, they have been released on bail.'

The past thirty-six hours had been hell. I felt defiled and degraded—solitary confinement, denial of food and water, brutality, lassitude, disheartenment—I didn't deserve any of that.

Once outside on the street, I ran without looking back and went straight home.

PP Auntie was sitting on her JFK rocking chair, saying her prayers. Ratan was also at home, it was his day off. Neither of them seemed to have noticed my overnight absence and were too preoccupied to see the state I was in. I didn't feel like talking, so I took a quick shower and went straight to bed. It was my second night in succession without eating. All in all, I felt lucky to be alive.

The following day was a Saturday, a working day in India. It was also the day for our big breakfast back in London, and I really missed my home and my parents and my friends and my life back in London. I wanted to go back.

Even though I was hungry, I couldn't face breakfast. My stomach was tied up in knots with worry. I decided to go straight to work. Both Dhiraj and Paresh were already at the office when I reached. They looked calm and relaxed. Dhiraj, looking like a powerful mobster, removed his sunglasses and gave me a roguish smile.

'Nothing will happen to us. This is India. We have clever lawyers who will drag the case out for many years. With a backlog of millions of cases pending in various courts in India, our case will not be heard for at least ten years,' said Dhiraj, laughing like an idiot.

His brother was even more outrageous and said, 'Even then, we will be found "Not Guilty". In India, you can kill someone and often get away with murder on appeal.' Dhiraj, the co-conspirator, agreed, gesturing like a nodding donkey in a Texan oil field.

'But...what about me?' I stammered as I looked nervously at Dhiraj.

'You will be all right, Rahul. We will protect you. Silence speaks louder than words, Rahul. But, in India, money speaks even louder. We can dodge jail even if they find us guilty.'

'My father is unwell in England. I have to go back.'

I hated lying, especially about my father's health. But I was thinking on my feet and it was the only way I could get away from them without any repercussions. Dhiraj put his hand on my shoulder. Ironically, I felt like a fraudster myself.

'When must you leave?'

'Immediately.'

'We will be sorry to lose you, Rahul. You will be hard to replace.'

They accepted my story, and gave me my final salary cheque. I was glad to get out of his office and into the street.

But what the hell was I going to do now? My NRK job was gone to someone else in the queue and I hardly had the appetite to return. And I didn't feel up to going through the job-hunting process again. Once more, I felt lost and confused in an alien world. My ambition to become a film producer seemed like an impossible dream, and I needed a shoulder to cry on.

On my way back from work, I noticed that Mr Dharsi, the beggar, who had disappeared for a few days, was now back on duty.

'I had been on a holiday to Agra with my wife and children, Rahul.'

'Holiday?' I exclaimed.

'Yes, even the dregs of the earth need a break! Did you apply to the C3 Club?'

'No. I don't think I'm interested.'

Though, by now, I was interested in just about anything.

⁘

In Mumbai, it was often evening before I even realized it. Days were flying fast. Days became weeks, and the weeks became a full month in no time. I still had no job and it was my father's birthday. I phoned him.

'Happy birthday, Dad.'

'Thank you, son. But it's not a happy day. The firm where I was working has just gone bust. We all have been made redundant this morning.'

'I'll come back to London immediately.'

'No, no, don't! We will manage. You stay focused on your career aspirations.' I didn't want to tell him just how badly things were going. Instead, I said, 'Look after yourselves, then.'

'We will…you too, son.'

After sitting reflectively for a moment, I sent a text message to Irfan, asking if he and David could meet me next time they were in Colaba. A reply came quickly: *See you at Imperial near Colaba Post Office within an hour.*

The Imperial, where I had been a couple of times before, was a typical Irani restaurant with its high ceiling, wooden tables with marble tops and huge mirrors on the walls, not to mention the scent of chicken pies, meat pastries, cakes and freshly-baked rolls which tempt one as they walk in. It was one of the last few Irani restaurants in Mumbai. Most of them had been sold or had stopped trading.

The owner, a tall, broad-shouldered, soft-spoken man in his late sixties, scratched his high forehead as he spoke to me while I drank my soda, waiting for my friends.

'Our children are just not interested in taking over our restaurants…they all want to go to America or to Canada. Moreover, nowadays fast food and pizzas are becoming more popular with young customers.'

'It's sad. Mumbai will soon lose a part of its heritage and cultural legacy. Not to mention your excellent food and hassle-free service.'

Then I became aware I had company. David looked concerned when he saw me. I was beginning to look thin and haggard. He and Irfan sat down and ordered tea and mutton samosas, for which Mumbai's Irani restaurants are popular.

'We haven't heard from you for such a long time,' said Irfan, his voice full of concern.

'I gave up killing rats at night and ended up working for Dhiraj Desai.'

'You mean that "urine guy" who you met on the plane from London? What happened?'

'The bastard and his brother turned out to be VAT fraudsters. I ended up being arrested for no fault of my own, and have just been released from detention.'

'Goodness me! Have you been cleared?'

'Yes, thank God.'

'What about the Desai brothers?'

'The crooks have been charged with VAT offences.'

'Serves them right,' said David, looking relieved.

I apologized to my friends for burdening them with my multitude of troubles, but I had to talk to someone.

'Hey, what are friends for?'

One of the advantages of the Irani restaurants of Mumbai is that you can sit there for hours without being challenged by the owners. So, we sat looking at each other. Eventually, I asked: 'Have you heard of the C3 Club?'

My two friends looked at each other and grinned. 'More like "C-through" club!'

'A beggar I met said I should become a male stripper.'

'What? You mean Mr Dharsi?' asked Irfan.

'Do you know him?'

'Who doesn't in this part of Mumbai?'

'All doors are closed,' I lamented, 'except the doors of the C3 Club, it seems.'

Both Irfan and David remained silent for what seemed a long time. I took this to be a sign of their disapproval.

'I need a job, guys. I need money to survive…to save for my film course and pay for my board and lodging while I'm studying. I need money to help my parents in England. I have no choice!'

Almost simultaneously, Irfan placed his hand on one of my shoulders while David placed his hand on the other. The gesture took me off-guard.

'We understand your position.'

I just had no more than two hours sleep that night. I spent the night tossing and turning in the bed and going to the washroom at least five times to look at myself in the mirror—wondering at what I'd become and, worse still, what I intended to become.

The C3 Club opened at 2 p.m. in the afternoon, so I went there at 5 p.m. to keep the appointment I'd made over the phone with the manager, Miss Rekha Jones, a tough-looking woman of forty who carried herself with the authority and the power of a headmistress from the 1960s.

She welcomed me with a brief smile to her 'classy' club, then took me to the club's lounge, a sensuously decorated and seductive den with mood-lighting and a relaxed atmosphere.

'So...you are from England?'

'Yes.'

'And one of your parents is white?'

'How did you know?'

'I can tell by your fairness...It's a look that's popular here. Our women like fair-skinned men. It makes them feel special.'

'Your women?'

'We are not a gay club for men! We are an exclusive club for the modern Indian woman. The only one of its kind in Mumbai.'

Rekha went on to explain how conservative the society was in India:

'In the land of the Kama Sutra, you couldn't, until a few years back, show kissing on screen. Things are changing, but there is still a long way to go. We still have vandals in India who go about separating couples, even if they are just holding hands! We believe that women should not feel guilty if they have desires.'

I noticed the club had seating for about two hundred.

'You will have to strip as part of an audition. Even though you have fair skin, we will have to see what else you've got...'

With this startling suggestion ringing in my ears, the audition was arranged for the following day.

But when I went back there, the doors were locked and there was a notice saying the club had been closed down. The watchman told me that there were several surprise raids the night before in various parts of the city in order to extort money from 'Dance Bars'. Even though the C3 Club wasn't a 'Dance Bar'—rather, an exclusive women's club—it was still a victim of corruption. I went home disappointed. I'd psyched myself up to do the audition, all for nothing.

A few days later, I had a phone call from Rekha Jones, asking me to come and see her. The C3 Club had reopened, but without the male striptease show. I wondered what she wanted.

'I have another job for you,' she began. 'It requires certain skills, which I believe you possess. You are young, handsome, educated, fair-skinned...some of our ladies would like you to entertain them privately.'

'You mean a private striptease?' I asked anxiously.

'No, not quite. They would like you to visit them. Meet them, maybe go out with them...*Escort* them. Think of yourself as a male escort, rather than a male stripper. Would that suit you?'

I listened while she laid it on the line.

'You mean a male prostitute?'

'I much prefer the word escort, Rahul.'

As I ran this outrageous idea over in my mind, she kept on talking, explaining more and more about the world of opportunities in front of me. All the while, the thought of my parlous financial state never escaped me. It was either this or killing rats, I told myself.

'...Mumbai is a city which never fails to shock and surprise. Here, women buy sex from men willing to sell their bodies.'

The headmistress was now softening up, and talking in a friendly and persuasive way.

'We have rich, bored women, single women, middle-class housewives, company executives, wives of industrialists, page-three personalities, all looking for sex and excitement. And willing to pay for it.'

She saw my apprehension, and tried to reassure me.

'It's all very discreet, of course. Our ladies will be impressed by you. You are polished and sophisticated. They will feel they can trust you.'

She looked straight into my eyes, as if she was trying to hypnotize me into agreeing.

'They are beautiful women, Rahul. It's a beautiful life… travel…money…everything will be at your disposal.'

Without thinking, I blurted out, 'I'm not interested. I'm not for sale.' Despite my predicament, I just couldn't contemplate selling my body for money. It was against everything I believed in.

'Consider it carefully,' she called after me, as I left her office without drinking the coffee she'd served.

Two days later, Rekha called again and asked me to meet her. And when I returned to her office, she once again served coffee.

'I haven't changed my mind,' I told her, ignoring the cup of coffee in front of me.

'I'm not asking you to.'

She was clearly not going to give up.

'In Japan, they have a "Rent-a-Friend" scheme, where men and women socialize with others for a fee. Only a small proportion of the trade involves sex, most hosts and hostesses aren't prostitutes, and customers are only looking for a good companion to talk to.'

Rekha made powerful eye contact with me.

'So why don't you just start off as a "friend"? I will only send you to clients who are looking to talk…for now, at least.'

'Only talking?' I asked, the idea becoming more appealing. Talking, I could do.

'Of course. See how you go. You will make more money than you've ever made before.'

After a moment's hesitation, I said, 'Alright.'

'Good boy! You'll need a *nom de guerre*, of course. How about…' And here she pondered, as if searching for a name not currently in use, '…*Radium*?', asked Rekha, her plump matronly face now glowing radiantly or rather, shall I say, "radiumly".

'Why not?' I replied. Radium was as good a name as any. Radium, an almost pure-white chemical element with the atomic number of 88 (as I discovered when I later looked it up on the internet), a number symbolizing fortune and good luck, a powerful number made up of the energies of the number 8, doubled and amplified. Radium—just the kind of name for a 'friend', a conversationalist, an escort; how astute she was, how professional. I looked her straight in the eye, just as she'd done to me.

'What's in it for you? Apart from money, of course?'

'My customers' happiness.'

'I'm sure…And what is your actual percentage?'

'Ten per cent of your fees. But don't worry, my dear Radium, our customers are rich. You will make so much money that even after my cut you will be left with plenty.'

I was still reluctant. I could never touch a woman I didn't love. But what about Radium?

'Look, you can start off as an escort and work your way up. You call the shots...take it as far as you want and no further. But, the further you go, the more money you make.'

I wanted to leave the coffee untouched and walk out of the room and never come back. But I didn't, because I wasn't in control of the situation any more. Radium was making the decisions now.

'Radium is ready,' I whispered to Rekha.

'Good boy! You'll be my best escort, I know you will. Do you have a suit?'

'I brought one from England.'

'You will be working in a recession-proof industry. There will be no boom and bust. Rather there will always be bust-boom.'

I smiled whilst secretly admiring Rekha's charming cleavage, which she was flaunting in a lovely cobalt blue dress with a plunging sweetheart neckline that only just protected her modesty. I felt I had somehow become Radium in the past five minutes.

'One who curdles the milk with lime juice owns the cheese. From today, you are mine.'

I didn't mind this kind of possessive talk by Rekha, so long as it brought in money for me and got me out of the mess I'd made in Mumbai.

'Work hard and the sky's the limit. You snooze, you lose.'

I drank the coffee before I left, with the promise of an

assignment the following day. I had come to India as Rahul. Now Mumbai had turned me into Radium. My fortunes, at last, were beginning to change.

Pretty Women

Rekha was checking out my Marks and Spencer beige-coloured suit which I had bought from the Marble Arch store two weeks before my departure from London. 'Make sure you make Roxy Ambani really happy.'

'It's not Armani, but I hope it will do…for now,' I said nervously.

'Yes. Remember she is not looking for sex. Not even a kiss,' said Rekha as she brushed some loose hair from the shoulders of my jacket.

When I rang the bell of the fourteenth-floor apartment of Ganesh Towers on Worli seafront, it was opened by a tall, barefoot woman in a red and green salwar kameez. Roxy was beautiful—a rich woman living all alone in this luxury flat with a caged African grey parrot.

She let me in and was quick to break the ice.

'I brought this parrot from Congo two years back. His name is McEnroe.'

I listened politely, but was more interested in Roxy. I was taken aback by the ease with which I had slipped into the persona of Radium.

'You're very pretty.'

'Tell me something I don't already know. Shall I tell you a story…what's your name?'

'Radium. I'd love to hear your story.'

I leaned forward and looked directly into her eyes. 'Listen, Radium...what a name! I've known a few men like you, so there's no need to overdo the attention thing.'

'I understand.'

'And you're not a robot either!'

I didn't quite know how to respond to that. She was a bold, confident woman. All I could say was,

'What about your story?'

'Well, you say the first sentence and I will continue.

I was impressed. Roxy wasn't anything like I thought she'd be. On the way to her apartment I imagined an overweight, middle-aged matron with an inferiority complex. The reality was quite the opposite. And I wondered why she had to hire men like me. But that was none of my business. Wondering how I should start the story off, I saw a portrait of a woman hanging on the wall.

'Once upon a time, there was a *pretty woman*...' I started.

'I know all about her! Her name was *Mary Reilly*,' said Roxy.

After a pause, she continued.

'She had a *Mona Lisa smile*. She lived on *Ocean's Eleven* Boulevard in a small town in Georgia, USA. She would *eat, pray, love* and though she looked as delicate as a flower, she could be as tough as steel. Her friends called her *Steel Magnolias*.'

Roxy then asked me to continue.

'It was *Valentine's Day*. She told her *stepmom* that she was going out to be with her friends, with whom she had *something to talk about*,' I said in continuation of the story.

I wondered where this was leading. Surely, I wasn't being

paid to take part in some clever word play based on some film titles of a famous film star. But I wasn't complaining. Roxy continued.

She said, 'After that I will attend *my best friend's wedding*; she is marrying *Michael Collins* in the old church in the neighbourhood of the *Mystic Pizza* restaurant, owned by *the Mexican* widow *Mrs Erin Brokovich*.'

I wondered if I was expected to join in again. Why not?

"'Be careful. There's a big *law and order* problem in that area," said her stepmom, who always pretended to be *closer* to her than she really was.'

Roxy smiled, showing a set of perfect teeth. She was enjoying this.

"'*I love trouble* and I am not afraid of *dying young*," Mary replied as she left.'

"'*Everyone says I love you* but I have yet to *hook* someone," said the *pretty woman* to herself as she was driving on *Ocean's Twelve* Avenue.'

'But a truck crashed into her and there was *full frontal* damage to her car.'

It was a dialogue now, a game, and no longer a one-sided story, with each of us trying to outdo the other.

'There was a *conspiracy theory* that her stepmom, known to some as *The Ant Bully* had been planning her murder for some months. She was getting all her ideas by watching *Miami Vice*.'

The onus then shifted to me.

'Mary wasn't injured. She was the great survivor. A *grand champion*.'

'Some years later, her stepmom wrote a letter to *Baja Oklahoma*, the local police inspector, who described it as the *confessions of a dangerous mind*.'

'My hands are *blood-red* she wrote.'

'The wicked stepmom killed herself in a *firehouse* before she could be arrested, and this was one *crime story* the police had the *satisfaction* of solving, without even trying. Mary, once a *runaway bride*, is now married to *Larry Crowne*. And now she lives happily with her husband in *Notting Hill*, London, in a lovely house called *Charlotte's Web*.'

I clapped my hands and admitted defeat. Over coffee, Roxy talked about films.

'I love movies, in particular, the films of Julia Roberts,' she said as she looked at the portrait on the wall.

'Why don't you write novels? You have a fantastic talent for telling stories.'

'You think so?'

'Certainly. You know how to tell a tale...and a good story well told will transport your readers into a never-encountered world and give them an experience they'll never forget. You could do it!'

Roxy nodded and gave a huge laugh.

The parrot imitated her laugh. 'Ha-ha-ha-ha.' And then screamed, 'Pretty woman! Pretty woman!'

'Stop it, McEnroe!' said Roxy in an angry tone.

'You cannot be serious!' screamed back the parrot.

Roxy and I ended up laughing with McEnroe joining in a few seconds later.

I felt like flattering her. After all, I was being paid handsomely. 'You have the capacity and the talent to be an author with authority and authenticity.'

'I like you, Radium. You know how to lie to a girl.'

'I'm not lying, Roxy.'

'Of course, you're not.'

Then, without warning, she started to cry. I glimpsed the cracks in the tough facade of this woman who could buy a man's time to lie to her. I handed her a handkerchief and waited; I didn't try to put my arms around her or to console her in any other way. I was waiting for my cue.

'I'm sorry. I had a dog but he…died last week,' said Roxy, who was clearly living in the grip of profound solitude in this golden cage.

It was approaching lunchtime, and I could tell she was distracted.

'My lunch comes from my mother's place every day,' said Roxy.

At 1 p.m., the bell rang and a tiffinwalla arrived with food in shining chromium containers.

I examined the tiffinwalla's expression to see if the man knew what was going on in the apartment; if he had an employer who he might report back to or if there was any danger. The tiffinwalla must have assumed I was curious and took this opportunity to advertise his services.

'We are Mumbai's tiffinwallas. We bring home-made meals for our customers!'

After the tiffinwalla left, Roxy put the food on a dining table and I helped her to set it up for lunch. The food was vegetarian—curry, dal, chapattis, with some papads and jeera rice. Roxy went to the kitchen and brought out pickles, chutney and yogurt.

'My maid is not in today to set the table. She had to suddenly go back to her village in Uttar Pradesh. Her mother died yesterday in a stampede at an event where free saris were being distributed to poor women by a local politician.'

'There must have been chaos…'

'Yes.'

Roxy was clearly distraught about this.

'In India, stampedes occur frequently and people die...at free sari distributions, at railway stations, at crowded temples, at VIP funerals, at free meal hand-outs and sometimes even at long ATM queues.'

'It seems nobody cares.'

'Every time an inquiry is set up and the matter is then just forgotten.'

She saw my bemused expression.

'Sorry. I love to talk. Sometimes my husband and I used to eat an entire meal together and not say a single word.'

'Your husband?'

'Akshay was always jealous and suspicious.'

'It seems he was suffering from the "Othello syndrome".'

'Othello syndrome?'

'A delusional jealousy leading people to suspect a partner of infidelity. It's named after Shakespeare's tragic hero.'

'You seem to be well-read,' she said with a laugh.

She was laughing with her mouth, but there were tears behind the laughter. I waited patiently. I really didn't want her to suggest any intimacy, and considered telling her this was my first time.

'Some people are good from far and far from good. Akshay was like that. I married him after I became pregnant. We never took precautions. It's a myth that a woman will not get pregnant if the guy pulls out before coming. I know that now.'

Oh God, I thought. She's turned the conversation around to sex. I had wondered how long it would take. Tears finally appeared in the corners of her eyes.

'I'm sorry to hear that,' I muttered.

'There is no point in crying over spilt milk…or spilt semen!' said Roxy, bitterness now showing in her voice.

She quickly got to her feet and wiped her tears before they could roll down her face.

'Sometimes, he would not withdraw, even though I would tell him to do so.'

'That's technically rape, even between husband and wife.'

'You talk like a lawyer, Radium. I like you.'

There was again an abrupt silence; then she burst out: 'We are soon to be divorced. I have a son, Pritam, who is studying at a boarding school in Panchgani. He is coming tonight to stay with me for the weekend.'

'You must be looking forward to seeing him again.'

'We still have time before…shall we go for a drive? I have a new car.'

'I'd love to.'

In a few moments, we had walked through to the garage, and were sitting in her new vehicle. She had a silver S-Class Mercedes saloon, which she'd bought only ten days back.

'This car is an ultimate luxury limo and a fantastic example of cutting-edge technology.'

'You love driving, it seems.'

'Yes, I drive myself.'

'Who said this…"Fasten your seatbelts; it's going to be a bumpy night"?'

'Bette Davis said it in *All about Eve*.'

She obviously had a great interest in movies and had a good memory for names and trivia.

'After Julia Roberts, Bette Davis is my second favourite movie heroine.'

Roxy explained she was worried about getting a visit from

the Income Tax Department enquiring about the purchase of her new car or, even worse, a phone call from the underworld.

'Hey, I enjoy your company,' she suddenly offered, wind blowing her hair from the car's open window.

Once we returned from the drive, Roxy gave me an envelope bulging with cash. To my great relief, she'd talked the whole way and I'd just listened.

Roxy Ambani was a *pretty woman* indeed.

Marry Go Round

~~~

Two weeks later, Rekha called to inform me that Roxy's husband had died after scoffing a big meal and drinking a lot of alcohol, before having sex with a woman half his age. Way to go, big man, I thought. But Rekha wasn't surprised.

'This pattern of death is common with men who are having extramarital affairs.'

Then, professional that she was, she went back to her business.

One Sunday evening, I went to see a woman named Aasma. She lived in a bungalow on Madh Island, off the coast of Juhu, north-west of Mumbai. The Sunday traffic in the city was normally tolerable but that night it was horrendous. It was Janmashtami, the birthday of Lord Krishna and one of the most loved festivals in Mumbai. When my taxi finally reached Madh Island, I was already an hour late.

'I'm sorry to have kept you waiting,' I said as I gave her a small gift I had brought for her.

The woman was in her late thirties and quite good looking, though not as pretty as Roxy Ambani. She had a decent figure, and I guessed that she didn't have any children—although I could have been wrong. Her clothes were expensive and her perfume was discreet and sophisticated. The bungalow itself was quite fabulous and exquisitely decorated inside. Aasma had two maids and a driver, who slept in the basement. The maids brought tea and samosas.

Aasma sat on her emerald green brocaded sofa in the main lounge glittering in chandeliered brilliance. She was silent for a few minutes, so I decided to break the ice.

'You have a lovely name.'

'Aasma means "high status"…but my status is low right now.'

She wanted to tell me her story. And I listened intently. After all, it was what I was being paid to do. For the first time since landing in India, I felt I had found my vocation.

'I was born Aasma Malik, in a small village near the Dhuandhar waterfall, close to Jabalpur, in Madhya Pradesh. After my parents died, I moved to Mumbai where I met my husband, Dharam Khanna.'

'Khanna?' I asked.

'Yes, Khanna. He was a Hindu. It was a love marriage and both our relatives were against it. I met Dharam a few years back when I was waiting for a bus. He offered me a lift in his van.'

'Sounds like a scene from a Bollywood film,' I suggested.

'Yes, Radium, it was love at first sight. He was young and handsome. I djdn't mind the scar on his left cheek.'

'A birth mark?'

'No. The legacy of a knife attack in his younger days.'

'What happened next?'

'A love marriage, of course.'

'How romantic,' I said sincerely.

'Yes. Dharam worked as a driver for a gang who smuggled gold into India from Dubai. We had such a happy marriage, until he started coming home late at night.'

'Pressure of work?'

'That is what I thought, until one day he told me he was seeing another woman and he wanted to get married to her.'

I saw there were tears in Aasma's eyes.

'Go on...'

'After five faithful years, I was devastated. I cried day and night like a little orphan girl. I stopped wearing mascara. Sleep was hard to come by. Dharam assured me that he still loved me. But he also loved Benazir, who was from Ajmer, and he'd already bought a wedding ring for her. I almost had a nervous breakdown. But, after many weeks of argument and inner torment, I came to accept that Dharam wasn't going to change his mind.'

'The law in India does not allow two wives. Am I right?'

'Yes, but that little obstacle was no problem for Dharam.'

Boldly, I continued, 'So, did he ask for a divorce?'

'No. Dharam just became a Muslim and changed his name—Dharam to Karam and Khanna to Khan. Karam Khan then legally married Benazir. No one could stop him. He used Islam for his convenience, to legally practice polygamy. From two Khannas, we now became three Khans. Karam Khan, Aasma Khan and Benazir Khan.'

And here she stopped her story, suggesting we have dinner. The aroma of the sumptuous meal cooked Moghlai style made my taste buds go crazy. Mutton masala, chicken korma, saffron-flavoured lamb biryani, along with three vegetable curries and butter drenched parathas—it was a lavish banquet for two! I hadn't realized how hungry I actually was until I looked at the food laid out in front of me. I was delighted to oblige and immediately sat down to eat.

Wiping her mouth on a napkin, Aasma took up her tale

again. 'The practice of Hindus converting to Islam just to marry a second time is not uncommon in India. It was a legal loophole which Dharam and many others have exploited. But the Indian Supreme Court plugged this legal loophole in May 2000. If it's now found that a man has embraced Islam only to have a second wife, he could be prosecuted.'

'So, bigamy for Hindus has been finally outlawed?' I asked innocently.

'Yes, but in India we have clever lawyers and it is difficult to prove intentions. The practice still continues. Over the years, Karam learned all the tricks of the smuggling trade and became a smuggler himself. He went from strength to strength, becoming richer and more powerful. We changed houses a few times, moving up the social and housing ladder. There were parties, music, dancing, cars, servants and chauffeurs.'

'So, life was not bad after all,' I suggested, scouring my plate with a piece of roti bread.

'Yes, but a couple of years later, Karam started coming home late at night again.'

'Pressure of work?'

'No. He declared his intention to marry yet again. Dharam's conversion to Islam became a source of pain for both me *and* Benazir.'

I paused, and stopped stuffing myself. I leaned over and took Aasma's hand. I sensed she was glad I had done this; her face brightened as she continued her story.

'The law no longer applied to him. As a Muslim, he could lawfully take a third wife. Her name was Chandni. She was a Muslim from Hyderabad.'

'Didn't you try and plead with him?'

'We did. Both Benazir and I argued and pleaded with

Karam not to marry again. But he was in no mood to listen.'

'We all moved to a bigger house. Karam had the money and could afford three wives.'

'Was life not chaotic?'

'It was,' she said, frowning. 'A marriage involving one husband and one wife can lead to all kinds of difficulties. Ours was a case of one husband and three wives. It was a nightmare.'

'So, did he then go on to marry a fourth time?'

'You guessed right. A year or so later, Karam declared that he wanted to get married yet again. As a Muslim, he could have four wives. The laws of India allowed it. We, his other three wives, were devastated. Was it never going to end?'

'What was her name?'

'Dilshad—a Muslim from Aligarh and a graduate from the Aligarh Muslim University. Although highly educated, she didn't mind marrying a less-educated person with three wives.'

I squeezed her hand. 'Because of Karam's money?'

Aasma gave a brief nod, a tilt of just a few degrees. 'We moved into a still bigger house.'

'So, how did he cope with four begums?'

'Oh! He was proud of his four-wife status.'

'Did he treat you all well?'

'No! He soon started calling us A, B, C and D, for Aasma, Benazir, Chandni and Dilshad. He even started calling us his Vitamin A, Vitamin B, Vitamin C and Vitamin D. He'd say a man had to take his daily vitamins for good health.'

I waited to be told about Karam's weekend vitamins.

'Karam boasted about taking multi-vitamins in Dubai on Fridays, Saturdays and Sundays.'

I continued to listen, showing genuine interest in what

my client was telling me.

She told me how Karam often threatened his wives with divorce. '"All I have to do is to say *Talaq! Talaq! Talaq*! I can then easily have four new wives," he would tell us boastfully.'

I knew well what the three five-letter words meant—'I divorce thee.'

Always having had a passion for making anagrams by rearranging letters of words, I quickly formed the word 'Qatal' in my mind meaning 'murder' in Hindi. At the end of the day 'talaq' was no different to 'qatal', I thought. Both acts slaughtered the innocent woman.

Aasma paused to sip cranberry juice, while reclining on her sofa looking totally exhausted.

'We all developed the fear of TATT,' she continued in an embittered voice.

'You mean "Tired All the Time"?' I asked. I knew about this syndrome as my father had once suffered from TATT for a few months some ten years ago.

'No. Talaq All the Time,' replied Aasma.

After a further pause, a longer one this time, she continued, 'Life for all four wives became more and more intolerable. The fighting, the shame and the sheer insensitivity of it all got on our nerves.'

'Was he ever violent?'

'He developed an erratic temper over the years. Our marriage started to corrode. Once or twice he slapped us. From better halves, we became bitter halves, and then battered halves.'

'You should have left him.'

'I finally did. I decided I had enough and left. I moved to this bungalow, which Karam had put in my name for some tax-dodging reason. I also had some money which I've invested well. I am financially independent. But money isn't everything.'

By now, tears were streaming down her cheeks.

'So where is Karam now?'

'Karam had made huge investments in Dubai, but when the crash came, he lost everything. Benazir, Chandni and Dilshad have also left him now. I haven't seen them or Karam or heard from any of them for more than two years. But we are all still technically married to him. He still has four wives.'

It was getting late, and I suddenly felt exhausted. This listening-for-money wasn't as easy as I'd first thought, especially when I began to feel for my clients. It was alright as long as I could just listen, pretend interest, pretend to be Radium. But the part of me that was still Rahul got in the way, and I started feeling sorry for these women, and that's when it got tedious. The telephone rang, but Aasma ignored it. It was past midnight.

'You will not get a cab now. My driver will drop you home.'

Aasma put a folded envelope into my shirt pocket. It bulged with more notes than Roxy's.

On the drive home, I thought about Aasma's life. I liked this woman and believed the marriage laws allowing up to four wives at a time for Muslims should be changed. I also felt that the system of triple talaq or, shall I say, triple qatal was wrong and should be outlawed. Both systems brought misery to innocent Muslim women and violated their rights. I yawned and began counting the cash. Then I stopped. It was easy to become callous in this business, I thought, and put the envelope back in my pocket, catching the driver's steady gaze in the rearview mirror.

Charade

~

AFTER DOING so well on my first two assignments, Rekha sent me to other clients all over Mumbai—rich single women, busy career ladies looking for a quick date at short notice. There were the haves and the have nots. Some did not want or have the time for relationships. There were women with husbands, with boyfriends. Some with both—all hiring me for excitement and to spice up their love lives with existing partners. Some notified their desires in advance, whilst others yearned for the 'boyfriend experience'. As time went by, I became more confident and more relaxed in my duties.

I learnt to be charming. Always sugar-sweet. Always punctual. Always showing interest in my clients—an interest that appeared genuine. I was generous with my compliments. I was attentive and switched on, and my mobile was always switched off so that I could give my clients my undivided attention. I forced an enchanting smile and loved it when women smiled back. A woman's smile was a turn-on, not her cleavage or her legs; a woman's smile was the first thing I saw when she opened her door to me. I also learnt to make my eyes mesmeric. During conversations, I would lean forward and look into a lady's eyes appreciatively and attentively, with appropriate nods of my head at whatever my clients were saying. My eyebrows became articulate. When in repose, they made me look cool. When raised, they were wicked. I was always well-groomed; my touch gentle and my voice soothing, reassuring, hypnotic. I could afford well-made clothes after a while and I dressed fashionably but not ostentatiously. The women loved my old-school displays of chivalry and classic gentlemanly gestures such as opening doors, helping them on with their coats, pulling out a chair for them and generally doing things their husbands and boyfriends had long ceased doing. My hand gestures were lavish and theatrical. I would always let the woman be in the driving seat when it came to talking. I would ask questions in an interested way and let her go on about herself, her past, her likes and dislikes, allowing her to open up and feel comfortable in my cheery presence.

I was quite knowledgeable, and my clients often asked for my advice. They loved my English accent and my light skin, and I kept my body in good shape. I became skilled in the art of pleasing women both in and out of bed. I turned myself into the fantasy my ladies desired me to be and they loved me for it. I grew up left-handed, but was ambidextrous when it came to pleasuring women who loved the magic in both my hands with their visible blue veins. The business e-mail ID of yours truly was radium@hotmail.com. Some of my clients, however, suggested I change it to radium@hotmale.com. Yes, ladies and gents, Radium, the Mumbai escort was now in full swing—ready, willing and available to kill, thrill and chill Mumbai's rich women and begums.

I decided to stay on at PP Auntie's house, even though I could now easily afford to rent a flat of my own. PP Auntie and Ratan were always good to me, and they needed my rent money to clear some debts which Ratan's father, BP, had left behind. They didn't ask where the money and clothes came from, and I didn't feel like telling them. I tried to save as much as I could, always keeping in mind my goal of studying filmmaking. I was looking forward to that day—the day when I could say goodbye to Radium.

I called my parents regularly, but never mentioned anything to them about Radium. They wouldn't have understood, to say the least. To them I was Rahul, their good son.

Mr Dharsi, the beggar, was still there on the same corner, trying to build up a deposit for his mortgage on a one-room flat. He knew I was now Radium with the C3 Club, and he gave me a knowing grin whenever I passed him in the street. Irfan and David also kept in touch. They were my best friends in Mumbai, and they never criticized anything or stood in judgment. David even mentioned to me a couple of times that he had a client for me, but always seemed uneasy when it came to telling me more about her. I decided not to pursue the matter.

One day, almost three months after I began at the C3 Club, my mobile bleeped. It was a text message from Rekha, asking me to go and see a new client, Gayatri, at Malabar Hill.

To my surprise, a man opened the door when I rang the bell. I could see from the doorway that it was a high-ceilinged, two-floor duplex flat. I recognized him after a moment or two. It was none other than Dr Mittal, the doctor at the Bandstand General Hospital, where I took the injured Robin Singh with his wife, Julie.

'I'm sorry. I think I've come to the wrong flat,' I stammered, and began to walk away.

Dr Mittal called me back.

'No…Gayatri is here.'

'Is she unwell? You must be her doctor.'

'No. I am her husband.'

Dr Mittal led me into the flat and Gayatri joined us.

We sat in the lounge, the three of us, looking at each other. The silence was awkward. Somebody had to say something.

'It's a hot day, but your flat's nicely air-conditioned.'

It was small-talk. I said the first thing that came to my head. Gayatri took the cue, as tea and bhajiyas were brought in by the maid.

'We married three years ago.'

Dr Mittal joined the conversation. 'We should not have...I am...gay.'

'Sorry,' I said, with alarm, 'but I don't do gay clients.'

'No, Gayatri is your client. I will be leaving shortly to go to the hospital...night shift.'

After a few tense seconds, Dr Mittal continued.

'I was a victim of Section 377 of the Indian Penal Code that criminalizes gay sex between consenting adults.'

'In India, parents compel children to get married. Otherwise the rumour industry within friends and family starts working overtime,' said Gayatri.

Having 'come out' and off-loaded his chest, Dr Mitttal suddenly looked less tense.

'My parents were very old-fashioned and arranged my marriage with Gayatri. I was not willing to get married, but they would not listen. I could not tell them of my secret boyfriend. It would have created havoc in all our lives and most probably resulted in police harassment.'

I listened intently, and felt the eyes of his wife on me.

Gayatri spoke up, 'My parents persuaded me to marry Dr Mittal as he was good-looking, well-educated and from a rich family.'

The doctor cut in. 'I never told her that her husband-to-be was gay.'

'Surely,' I asked, 'you two can divorce now and lead your separate lives?'

'It is not that easy. This is India,' replied Dr Mittal.

'Divorce would be a disaster. To flourish in the community, you have to be married,' said Gayatri.

'As a divorcee, she would be shunned by her family.'

'As the ex-wife of a gay man, I would be an outcast.'

'Life would become intolerable,' added Dr Mittal.

Dr Mittal put on his jacket and began to head towards the door. His parting words were tinged with sadness. 'Divorce is stigmatized in India…and homosexuality more so. Social ostracism is our biggest worry.'

Gayatri asked the maid to bring some more tea. 'Luckily, my maid doesn't speak English, only Marathi and Hindi. Our secrets are safe.'

'I have a life, but my wife hasn't,' said Dr Mittal, feeling genuinely sorry for his wife. 'I am gay. But in India I am scared of saying this in public for fear of FIRs and troll abuse on the social media.'

'We can't divorce and we can't commit suicide,' said Gayatri, tears rolling down her cheeks.

'I am sorry I spoilt your life,' said Dr Mittal.

'We have no option but to remain together…' said Gayatri.

'Till death us do part,' added Dr Mittal as he shut the door on his way out.

After he had gone, the maid finished her day's work and left too.

Gayatri then took out an album of photographs and we sat on the sofa looking through it. There wasn't much else to be said, so we flicked through the pages which showed how Gayatri grew from a lovely child to the elegant woman now sitting next to me. She commented every now and then about when the photos had been taken, adding little bits to the story of her life. I listened as usual—all the time moving closer. Until our heads were touching, and then our knees.

'I am not a nymphomaniac, but I do like being made love to,' said Gayatri as she led me to her bedroom with an unhurried grace.

'Treat me like a bride,' said Gayatri, who had dyed her hands with henna like an Indian bride. I touched her chin, and turned her head towards me. Then I kissed her, lightly, carefully, letting her know I was in no hurry. She responded by closing her eyes. I slowly undressed her. Her lovely looks, her skin with its scent of sandalwood, her radiant eyes, gleaming hair, thick erotic lips and her deep navel were all a delight to my senses. Soon we were exploring each other, kissing, cuddling and squeezing. My right hand worked on her breasts, which I sucked like juicy golden Alphonso mangoes. First the left breast, then the right and then left again. I saw her nipples rise up majestically in gallant attention. My left hand, in the meantime, was busy stroking between her legs. Soon enough her body language with her parted legs and arching back was telling me she was ready. 'Come in please, and don't come out.' she whispered with a moan. I got her meaning or rather her double meaning!

Later, when we were showering together in her marble-tiled bathroom, she put a 24ct gold chain around my neck.

'Today, Radium, I feel like a bride, like a complete woman.' Her words were almost whispered, as if to herself.

As I prepared to leave, she hugged me tightly, kissed my

left cheek and put cash into my right hand.

On my way home, I wondered about Dr Mittal, and the many sad men like him in India who were married in public and gay in private—a charade forced upon them by society.

Ten Commandments

~~

My ancestors were cobblers from Visnagar, where my grandfather had been born, and from Mansa, where my grandmother was born. Taking a break from my work as Radium, I decided to travel north to the state of Gujarat to visit these two villages. They were no longer villages but had grown into fair-sized towns. The old-fashioned cobblers, or mochis, as my ancestors were called, were gone. Instead, I found smart shops selling shoes manufactured by local factories. Shoemaking was my heritage, my ancestry, and I wanted to travel back in time to see it for myself. But time had moved on.

It was good to get away from the madness of Mumbai, and I longed to see more of rural India. I yearned to find myself in the hills and on the road, to stay forever in the bosom of my motherland. I wanted to be Rahul, a true Indian. But my visit in-country was just that, a visit. I was a tourist, not a true Indian living in the interior of my country.

Radium made sure my vacation didn't last long. Rekha was eager that I get back to business. I had noticed that I hadn't been getting any new Muslim clients, nor had any of my existing Muslim clients asked for a revisit for a while now, which other satisfied women had been doing. I spoke to Rekha when I returned from Gujarat.

'Have I done anything wrong?'

'No, it's the holy month of Ramadan, when many Muslims abstain from pleasure.'

I was relieved. I was getting quite used to my role as Radium, and I had become addicted to the appreciation.

At that moment, my mobile phone flashed. It was a text message from Irfan, asking me to meet him and David for dinner at Memon Mohalla at 9 p.m.

By the early evening, I was on my way to the prime Muslim heartland of Mumbai. The traffic was crazy around Crawford Market, and my taxi driver Sulaiman, a Muslim in his early fifties, was continuously screaming at a rival motorist, also a Muslim.

'You bastard. Are you blind?'

'Fuck off! I will crush your balls.'

'You motherfucker! How dare you say bad words during Ramadan!'

'I never say any bad words in the month of Ramadan. You sisterfucker.'

I just sat back and listened in amusement to the vituperative vocabulary of the two Muslim drivers screaming at each other in Urdu, in typical Mumbai-style, each claiming the moral high-ground in the name of the holy month of Ramadan. In the end, Sulaiman advised me to walk the last mile to avoid being late for my appointment.

Finally, I met my friends. I noticed that Irfan was now wearing a taweez around his neck.

'It is for good luck and protection.'

David was wearing his usual Jewish skullcap, even though he was in a predominantly Muslim area. He saw my quizzical expression.

'The people of India believe in religious tolerance and communal harmony. Hindus, Muslims, Sikhs, Christians, Jews, Parsees all want to live peacefully side by side here. It is the politicians who are responsible for most of the riots in our country. They either instigate them or turn a blind eye to the killings.'

Irfan joined in the debate as we looked around the stalls. 'The same politicians then visit these areas to build up their minority vote banks.'

Irfan then took David and me for a tour along the by-lanes of Mohamed Ali Road and Memon Mohalla, a vibrant and dynamic area buzzing with heat and humanity.

'This is where we are going to have our dinner today.'

He pointed to the many food stalls on the way. It was a lively, chaotic and crowded area, intensely lit, with food outlets on all sides selling chicken tandoori, tava mutton, bhuna ghosht with chillies, onions and tomatoes and baida roti, khichda, mutton rolls, kebabs and fried fish. Yellow malpuas were being made on the spot and fried till they were crisp. And phirnis, the milk-based sweets, yellow or plain white, were being served in flat little earthen pots. There were open fires roaring with tavas sizzling on top. My mouth was watering by the time we had walked fifty yards. There was loud music and earnest sermons and calls to prayer blaring out from all directions. Handcarts trundling everywhere, piled high with clothes, caps, shoes, fancy goods, household items and toys competed for business with each other, all obstructing stalls piled high with sweets and sticky dates, the traditional food with which one broke the fast at the end of every devout day.

The relentless noise of screeching traffic, the vibrant scenes of busy streets, a push or two in the ribs from passers-by, along with the mouthwatering fragrance of food urged us to stop for a bite.

We had a sumptuous roadside buffet. It was a meal I wouldn't forget for a very long time.

'This goes on almost all night. Ramadan is here in all its glory. ... A wonderful carnival that lasts an entire month,' said David, talking like an excited Muslim who had just broken the fast.

Afterwards, Irfan told us he lived in the nearby area of Dongri, and invited us to his place for sherbet. That's when it dawned on me why he was called Dongriwalla. But it was late and I was tired.

'I'll come next time,' I assured him.

Irfan understood. Waving goodbye, he walked away towards Dongri. David offered me a lift home which I gratefully accepted.

Once we were in the car, David said he had a client for Radium.

'It is very confidential.'

'I promise nobody else will know.'

'Her name is Josephine and she is Jewish. I have known her for many years.'

'Is she single?'

'Married. Josephine and her husband don't have any children despite being married for five years.'

'Why don't they try fertility treatments?'

'They have tried everything,' he said matter-of-factly.

I wondered what he expected Radium to do about that. Being an escort was one thing, fathering children was something else entirely.

'Josephine's husband is prepared to go along with the idea

of another man fertilizing his wife for him.'

I was skeptical at first. Then worried.

'Radium's job is only to please a woman, and he always uses a condom.'

'She is clean. Not using condom will not put you at risk. Please think about it...'

He dropped me off at PP Auntie's house, where I tried not to think about it as hard as I could.

⁂

A week later, David called.

'So, what have you decided?'

I paused. 'I will go along...and play it by ear.'

'Josephine and her husband live in a one-bedroom flat in Dadar.'

He gave me a few more details about Josephine. We agreed it might be better for me to go see her on her own initially, when her husband wouldn't be at home.

When the woman eventually opened the door, I saw sadness in her face, as if she had been crying the whole night. She was modestly dressed, wore no make-up and her hair was tied up instead of flowing around her shoulders. It was as if she'd gone out of her way to make herself look plain and unattractive.

I sat on the small sofa while she brought me tea. There were no pictures of the woman's husband anywhere in their lounge. Josephine's teacup rattled on its saucer and her teeth were chattering with fear. Suddenly she burst into a flood of copious tears. I tried to comfort her as I usually did with most of my clients who were sad. She pulled away from me.

'No, it is not right!'

'What's not right? You've hired me.'

'This whole idea of me going to bed with you.'

'Who said anything about going to bed?'

This calmed her a little and she looked at me in surprise. I gave her a minute or two to compose herself.

'I am sorry, I am not prepared to go through with the idea of becoming a mother using another man's seed. Not even by artificial insemination, let alone by sexual intercourse.'

'Hey, don't worry. I'm not going to touch you.'

I poured her some more tea and asked if she'd like me to leave. She wanted to talk, just like the others, and listening to women had become my speciality. So we talked, or rather she talked, about how she and her husband had tried unsuccessfully for five years to have a child.

'We were so desperate we considered taking help from a temporary partner. But now I am not prepared to go through with it.'

'I can understand perfectly. Can I give you some advice?'

She nodded, smiling wistfully. I smiled back. 'Or rather... your husband...?'

'Please, tell me...'

'OK, let's see...to begin with, tell him to eat plenty of fruit and vegetables and whole grains.'

'Next?'

'Also, he should exercise regularly...and meditate, it's important to meditate.'

I looked at the ceiling thoughtfully. Josephine found a pen and paper and started writing down my words of wisdom.

'He must also stop wearing tight underwear...that is, if he does wear tight underwear.'

We both laughed at the mental picture of her husband

modelling underwear, tight or otherwise.

'And stop bathing in hot water...a man's testicles have to be at the right temperature for efficient sperm production.'

She laughed again, louder this time. I laughed with her. She sat with her pen, poised, waiting for my next set of fertility instructions.

'Reduce caffeine intake...'

'Next?'

'And make love early in the morning.'

She smiled.

'Does he ever tell you "Not tonight, Josephine"?'

'Often.'

'Well, he mustn't. Make love regularly and have fun. And you must orgasm as well as him.'

She blushed.

'The female orgasm helps to push the sperm up into the cervix.'

She continued to write everything down, bowing her head so I wouldn't see her embarrassment at my more explicit suggestions. Then she raised her head, still smiling.

'Oh yes,' I added. 'Brush and floss your teeth regularly.'

This wasn't my joke. This was one of grandmother Sonabai's aphorisms, one of her tongue-in-cheek truisms.

'And if you want a boy, eat a full breakfast and a high-fat diet...a low-fat diet favours girls due to selective loss of male foetuses.'

I paused. Surely this was enough. 'How many pieces of advice is that?'

'Ten.'

After the dictation was over, she read back what she had written down.

We sat and looked at each other, saying nothing. It was clear she wanted me to leave now. I'd done my job. There was nothing left for me to do.

'I will convey this to my husband,' said a bubbly and giggly Josephine. 'I will call you when my baby is born.'

'Please do so. I will be delighted to hear from you.'

'I will treat them as the "Ten Commandments".'

A Chance Meeting

It was the day of Eid al-Fitr, better known as Ramadan Eid, the Muslim holiday marking the end of the month of fasting. It was a public holiday in India. The holy month of Ramadan had ended the day before with the sighting of the new moon. Eid was being celebrated with traditional gaiety, joy and enthusiasm across Mumbai. Muslim men and children, wearing white kurtas and caps, packed the mosques across the city to offer prayers. On that day, David and I met Irfan at his Dongri home to wish him the best.

The main road led into narrow streets, and the streets led into narrower lanes, and then even narrower by-lanes. The place was well-known for its bazaars, mosques and restaurants, and they had unique sound, smell and sensation. Being Eid, the place was buzzing with excitement.

Irfan lived alone in a one-room accommodation on the fourth floor of a four-storey building without a lift, a fact I didn't mind, as I have a lift-phobia. As with many other buildings in Dongri, Meheboob Mansions was an ancient and dilapidated tenement. It was located in the middle of a narrow lane, where buildings faced each other like armies on an ancient Moghul battlefield. The walls inside were in a state of disrepair and looked like they hadn't been repaired or painted for forty years. On every floor I could see a maze of electrical wiring lying exposed. There were no fire exits or extinguishers anywhere and, if a fire did break out, the lane was too narrow to allow access to the fire brigade. The building was one big death-trap. Irfan told us that most buildings in Dongri, Bhindi Bazaar and other nearby areas were like this—old, dilapidated and dangerous. People lived in one or two small rooms with common toilets in the corridors. There was a water shortage in the building.

'But people are happy,' he said. 'Life goes on.'

Irfan was philosophical about it as he served us sherbet. He asked us to stay on for a traditional Eid lunch of mutton biryani and chicken samosas which he'd ordered from a Muslim restaurant nearby. We sat on a mat on the floor and ate what was probably the most delicious biryani I'd ever tasted.

After lunch, David stayed behind, but I took a taxi to Bandra. I still hadn't given up on my movie aspirations, and I needed to buy a book on the early history of Bollywood. It was a rare book called *Bollywood Before 1970*. It wasn't available in any of the shops I'd visited so far, and PP Auntie suggested I try Bollywood Unlimited on Hill Road in Bandra. I'd already phoned them earlier that morning and had been told by the shop assistant that they had one copy, but it had been reserved by another customer.

'But, I must have it…please!'

'You will have to come and talk personally to the owner. It's Eid and we will be closing at 3 p.m.'

Bollywood Unlimited was an upmarket music and film bookstore which sold all kinds of films, DVDs, CDs, books, magazines and film merchandise. I noted with a shiver that it was close to where Robin Singh had been murdered. For some reason, I found myself thinking of him and his beautiful wife, Julie. I wondered if his wounds had healed and if they were still in Amritsar. I wanted to meet them again. Well, I wanted to meet Julie Singh again, to be perfectly honest. It wasn't the first time she'd come to my mind.

The owner wasn't there when I arrived, but the assistant told me she'd be along shortly. For me, with my interest in filmmaking, the store was paradise and I was quite happy to browse while I waited.

Time passed. It was already 2:30 p.m. and there was still no sign of the owner. It would soon be 3 p.m. and closing time. Then the store assistant shouted at me from the checkout counter.

'Here she comes!'

In came a slender woman of twenty-something, looking ravishing in a white salwar kameez, wearing large sunglasses and holding a white matching clutch-bag. The woman was Julie Singh. I couldn't believe it. She was just as beautiful as I'd remembered her. I'd just been thinking about her a few moments earlier, realizing how close I was to the scene of that bygone tragedy. She recognized me straightaway and we stood there looking at each other in disbelief. Then she ran across and hugged me.

'How is your husband?' I managed to ask.

Tears welled up in her eyes.

'Robin is no more,' she said, weeping copiously.

I was shocked, and we stood for a moment in silence.

After a while, she took me to her office at the rear of the store. There she explained what had happened.

'Dr Mittal and his team tried their very best to save Robin. On the third day, I decided to take him to Amritsar because he knew he was dying and wanted to be near the

Golden Temple.'

'Were you able to take him there?'

'Yes, in a wheelchair. And he died there.'

'Oh...I am really sorry.'

'I had a miscarriage a month later. Not only did I lose Robin, but I also lost my baby.'

I tried to comfort her and wished Radium was there. He was better at this and would've known what to say.

'I returned to Mumbai from Amritsar after Robin's death and bought this shop from the inheritance he left me.'

I wondered why she chose a place like Hill Road, so close to the scene of Robin's murder. Was it because it made her feel close to him in some weird way? But I didn't want to ask.

'Thank you for everything you did for me on that day. The police have still not found the man who murdered my husband.'

'This is a fantastic and unique shop. I really love it.' I still couldn't believe it was her. Fate had brought us together again after all this time. I had come here to buy a book and found Julie Singh.

'So...what do you do, Rahul?'

'I came to Mumbai from England to study filmmaking so I can become a film producer. Eventually.'

'How are you getting along?'

At this question, I felt immediate shame. 'My plans are on hold for the time being due to some personal circumstances.'

Of course, I didn't mention Radium.

'Listen,' she said quickly, 'I have only one copy of *Bollywood Before 1970*, but it has been reserved by another customer.'

'Could I have it...please?'

She telephoned the customer and it was agreed that I

could have the book. She pulled it out from her drawer but would not accept any payment.

'It's yours. For what you did…'

'Thank you,' I said. 'We must meet again.'

She smiled shyly at me. Chance had brought us together again, and I wasn't going to let her get away again.

Pride and Prejudice

~~~~

Within a few months, I'd improved my Hindi and Gujarati, both of which I could now also read, and picked up a little bit of Marathi as well. Back home in England, my father often spoke to me in Gujarati, but when he was angry he would always speak in English. It's a thing with Indians—being angry in English! And English was also part of Radium's charm. My clients loved the compliments I showered on them in that enigmatic language. My reputation was spreading. By now, I was a well-heeled and confident companion to some of Mumbai's richest ladies.

My health was consistently good. I neither smoked nor drank.

The month of Ramadan was over. Rekha sent me to Shabnam, a client in Goregaon West in North Mumbai. She was a pharmacist, living in a large house with four dogs. The house had an unusual smell, which gave me one of the most terrible headaches I'd ever experienced. It could have had something to do with the dogs. The headache lasted a good three days. I took two Panadol Extra tablets every six hours and kept an ice pack on my head, before I finally started to feel better on the fourth day. I was totally housebound and felt like a disabled person, and it made me think about what it must be like to be in that condition all the time. I realized that there were many people in this world who were serving a sentence of virtual house arrest without ever having committed any crime.

And then it happened, as it was bound to eventually. Rekha called me into her office.

'Would you mind going to a disabled client?'

Without thinking, I said, 'No way!'

'I am discouraged by your reply. All our clients have found you charming, generous and compassionate.'

I said nothing as she continued. 'Maybe you are conditioned by the fact that "the disabled" didn't exist in India at one time. Then somebody decided to recognize that there were, in fact, "disabled people" in the country and, in a world of political correctness, they were now referred to as "physically challenged" or persons with "special needs". And they have no one to love them.'

I listened quietly to Rekha, all the time staring at the floor and into nothingness. When I looked up, my eyes were brimming with tears. Maybe I had been under a lot of pressure recently, but I felt overly emotional all the time.

'I am sorry. I should not have objected.'

'Her name is Anjali Khan.'

Rekha was pleased to hear that I was now willing to visit Anjali, who wasn't a member of the C3 Club, but actually someone she knew from her college days.

It was the day of Ganesh Visarjan, the eleventh day of Ganesh Chaturthi, and I was in the mood to walk the streets. Statues of all sizes of Lord Ganesha were being carried through the streets of Mumbai in a procession—the small ones on shoulders, or in people's arms, while the monumental ones were pulled along on huge wooden carts by hundreds of devotees. And all were to be immersed in the sea at Chowpatty, near Marine Drive. I joined the final stage of the procession and found myself shouting *Ganpati bappa morya* with the others, accompanied by drummers, trumpeters and singers, some clearly high on drugs. There was much excitement and some chaos created by a band of noisy ruffians shouting political slogans.

Anjali lived alone in a lovely sea-facing flat in Marine View, on Marine Drive. She was an attractive thirty-something, with a welcoming smile and long black hair that covered her shoulders. I tried not to make it obvious, when she opened the door to me, that I recognized she was in a wheelchair, and that I saw, through her thin dress, that her legs were somewhat wasted.

She was friendly and talkative, and I made myself at home. She had inherited her husband's flat after his death in a horrific car accident on the Mumbai-Pune Highway some eight years ago. She had been badly injured in the same accident and had been in hospital for two months.

'I came home in a wheelchair and have remained in it for the past seven years.' Her light-hearted mood changed abruptly. 'Maybe it would have been better if I had died as well.'

She tried to smile, but it was forced. Then continued: 'Despite my wealth, I have no real friends. Nobody invites me out. Nor is anyone prepared to visit me, including my own widowed mother or my brothers or sisters.'

'Relatives, eh!' I said, trying to lift her mood. 'The nearer in blood, the bloodier they get!'

'My in-laws are the worst. Clogged up with hate, they

refer to me as "langdi", "the lame one". It seems I have just disappeared from society.'

As usual, I gave her my undivided attention. I listened and was deeply interested in what she was telling me. 'In a country like India, it is a real nightmare to be disabled. Here, social attitudes are so unsympathetic. There is so much prejudice, and disability is considered a social stigma.'

My expression echoed her hurt. I held her hand in both of mine as she continued to talk.

'Despite legislation, disabled access to public buildings, shopping centres, railway stations and airports in India is practically non-existent.'

'With roads and bazaars being so crowded, you must be finding it impossible to move around with a wheelchair.'

'Yes, Radium. It is terrible.'

Anjali wiped her tears before continuing.

'And, bad as it is for the men, disabled women face a double disability.'

'You mean gender discrimination?' I asked.

'Yes. Not only do I have to face challenges posed by my disability but I also face discrimination for being born a woman.'

'I think the government should act urgently.'

'The government treats disability as a charity and welfare issue.'

I suddenly felt like a politician. 'What is required is awareness, a change of attitude…help and support.'

'You are right, Radium. We need to be treated with honour and dignity, not sympathy.'

Her voice broke. She stopped talking in order to drink some juice. She finished what was in her glass, and then I poured her some more.

'I feel so deprived...'

I knew what was coming. Her deprivation wasn't just access to airports, railway stations, shopping malls and bazaars. It was much more. I waited for her to broach the subject. It was always better that way—let them make the move, let them think they are in control. Anjali wasn't as reticent as Josephine when it came to talking about sex.

'A sex life, relationships and pleasure are not supposed to exist in the dictionary of a disabled woman.'

I responded cautiously. 'I think people are wrong. Such dictionaries are out of date.'

Her face lit up at my words. *He understood*! This man actually understood! It gave her the encouragement she needed.

'Sometimes I feel absolutely suicidal. The chances of me finding a boyfriend or another husband are next to nil. When my husband was alive, we had a great sex life. Today my sexual needs are still unchanged. I am still the same woman. So what if I have become disabled?'

Working with a disabled client was a completely new experience for me, and I didn't know what to say.

'Society is so silent about the sexual desires of a disabled person.'

I listened as I prepared myself mentally and emotionally for the challenge.

'People feel ashamed and embarrassed to even have a dialogue,' she said. 'There is silence, even at a professional level amongst medical and care workers.'

I realized then that a disabled woman had the same desires as other women, the same sex drive, the same libido. Sex wasn't something that only 'perfect' women enjoyed. Sex was sex, whether you were able-bodied or disabled. There were no 'special needs'. Every woman was special in her own way.

'Society has denied people like me any kind of sexual fulfilment resulting in an annulment of our femininity. Sexual desire is considered inappropriate for us, which, in fact, destroys our self-esteem.'

Despite my reservations, I started to look at Anjali like she was any other woman.

'I was so relieved that Rekha did not brand me as "sex mad" when I discussed my desires with her. She said you, Radium, were her best escort…the most subtle…the most sensitive. It wasn't an easy decision…but I finally agreed to see you.'

Flattered, I said, 'I am so happy I came to see you.'

'I would have liked to have become a mother…'

Then the talking stopped. Anjali had nothing more to say. I stood up and pushed the wheelchair to her bedroom.

Anjali's body was quite beautiful despite the wasted legs. As we kissed, I could feel her breath on my face and neck. There was a scent of jasmine in the room that filled my head. I could touch the fragrance of her—the woman—smell her woman's smell and taste her woman's taste. I kissed her lips passionately and then her breasts and then her stomach, opening her dress as I went. She undid the buttons of my shirt and licked at my ear with her tongue. Suddenly, Anjali stopped, maybe realizing what was happening, and her body began to convulse in short spasms. I held her shoulders until it stopped. Then it passed and we relaxed again, and made our own kind of music until the critical moment arrived. Our bodies were conjoined with our hearts thumping and our breathing in unison.

'You have got a fantastic fanny.' This was one of my several compliments to her that evening.

After it was over, she lay still and breathed heavily, making cooing noises for a long time, basking in the greenhouse effect of our recent congress. She continued to hold me. The sweat from our bodies made a damp stain on the bed sheet.

'I loved your lip service,' said Anjali, suppressing the giggles.

'Lip service?' I was puzzled. I was sure all my compliments were quite genuine.

'Kissing, Radium! I mean your kissing,' she explained to my great relief.

I was flattered, but only hoped that she wouldn't now go on to call me Mr Kissinger!

Her giggling continued, now no longer suppressed as she put her left arm around my shoulders and an envelope into my shirt's pocket. Ruffling my hair flirtatiously, she whispered, 'Thank you, Radium. You were really great.'

As I stepped out into the jasmine-scented night, I felt virtuous, almost euphoric, as if I had been given a difficult challenge and had emerged victorious.

That's Life!

Rita Kapoor lived in a sea-facing bungalow in Versova in a crescent of identical bungalows, part of a brand-new retirement facility with lofty terraces, open courtyards and canopied balconies built for the super-rich of Mumbai. She was delighted when I gave her the book on Indian film.

'Wow! *Bollywood Before 1970*! This is the one book I have been searching for, for a very long time.'

'I bought it especially for you.' I gave her my seductive smile.

We sat together, looking through the three-hundred-page volume which was full of pictures and stories of the history of Bollywood since it first began. There was a full-page poster of her film *Murder at Churchgate* on page sixty-two.

'I was twenty when I acted in that murder mystery, back in the sixties. Now I am myself in my sixties! Ha! Ha! Ha!'

'You look great. Not a day older than fifty,' I offered.

'Thank you. Unlike Hollywood, our actresses in India do not get lead roles in Bollywood films after the age of forty. I was big, but the pictures got bigger and the actors younger. Now, I am mostly at home, ageing gracefully.'

A lady of voluptuous beauty in her younger days, she still liked being in full make-up.

'I will die with my make-up on,' she said.

For a woman her age, she looked as good as it got, in her pink chiffon sari and her eye-dazzling diamonds.

'I never get a chance to dress up anymore.'

'What about film functions?'

'I don't get invited. It's a cruel world, Radium. So many of my Bollywood colleagues from the sixties are living all alone and, some, even in poverty.'

Like all my clients, Rita wanted to talk before getting down to business.

'I was once married to a Sikh businessman and lived in Delhi for a while. I have one son who is married and has children of his own.'

'Don't you all live together? This house is quite big.'

'The concept of everyone living together under one roof is disappearing amongst the new urban middle class and the rich in India. Children are moving out of their parental homes.'

I pondered on this, before saying: 'Unlike England where more and more children are staying on with parents because of high property prices and difficulties in getting home mortgages.'

Then she suddenly became serious. 'My husband was killed in the anti-Sikh riots in 1984, whilst out on the road to buy some groceries in New Delhi. After my husband died, I married again. Kaushik, my second husband, was a lovely person. He owned a furniture shop on Grant Road in Mumbai called Bombay Furniture Mart. One day, a group of thugs barged into his shop and ordered him to change the name of his shop to Mumbai Furniture Mart. When he refused, they beat him up.'

'How sad,' I said, genuinely moved.

'Mumbai may be the new official name of this city. But

I don't see why people should be prevented from also using Bombay, do you?'

I agreed with her. Then she continued.

'Many cities all over the world are known by different names in different languages. London is known as "Londres" in French, and "Rondon" in Japanese. Paris is called "Baris" in Arabic and "Parigi" in Italian. Why should Mumbai not be called "Bombay" in English?'

'I think a high court judge should be asked to decide the controversy via a Public Interest Litigation case,' I replied.

Rita offered me some coffee, which I declined. Time was getting on and I wanted to get down to business. But Rita was intent on getting her money's worth out of me. She had been a big star in her time, used to people waiting on her, and still had an undeniable air of command.

'My second husband developed a heart condition after the beating, but he delayed heart surgery to avoid Pitru Paksha, a sixteen-lunar day period of Hindu worship that included death rites and rituals in homage to their ancestors.'

'He tried to time his treatment astrologically?'

'Yes, and died.'

It was another Indian thing, I thought, this excessive belief in astrology, with middle-class parents asking doctors to ensure that their children were delivered when their astrologers judged the stars and planets to be favourably aligned and cosmically timing Caesarean sections for the births.

'I have money and I live quite comfortably in this house in Bombay,' she said. 'But it's not enough. I miss love and companionship and sex. So what if I am past sixty? Should I not still be sexually active? Do I not have the right to still enjoy a satisfying sex life?'

I agreed, in principle—but it was now time to get on with that sex life and stop talking about it.

'I feel like a young woman trapped in an old woman's body.'

'People can have great sex well into their eighties,' I suggested hopefully.

'Passion is possible at any age.' She said with a smile.

'I agree. A woman of eighty is as much entitled to a good orgasm as a woman of eighteen.'

'After my second husband died, I took a lover and we had great sex together. Then my son and daughter-in-law found out and they were so embarrassed, they stopped talking to me.'

'To be sexually fulfilled is a fundamental human need at any age,' I offered.

'Not in India! Here, we seniors sometimes cannot even hold hands in public or hug. We are expected to act our age. We can't stop living, can we?'

'Of course not.'

'We are expected to grow old gracefully, or rather gracelessly, and accept a sexless life as our fate and practise, celestial celibacy till we die,' said Rita, looking straight into my eyes, her hands now tightened into fists.

'There is segregation between generations, with rampant age apartheid being practised in the society. Worse still, many would like demographic cleansing of the country with us seniors all dead,' she continued, her eyes now looking glutinous.

'That's life,' she exclaimed tearfully after a pause.

'Cheer up!' I whispered as I manoeuvred Rita towards the bedroom, agreeing with her that desire doesn't die with the ageing process. At sixty-something, she'd kept herself well, I told myself. She was still slim and splendid and her hair was still dark. Probably dyed. A few silver strands were visible, but they only added grandeur to her grace.

The lovemaking was not as wild as with some of my younger women, but for Rita it was great. She basked in the tender heat of passion. In the immediate aftermath, Rita seemed intoxicated and, when she got up, she walked like a drunken doll. She sat on a swing in her lounge, a traditional Indian swing made in teakwood, beautifully carved with solid antique brass chains. She held a cigarette in a long red holder in her right hand and a peacock-feather fan in her left hand. It was a commanding show of authority, wealth, and a touch of old-fashioned glamour. She began to sing the memorable song from *The Sound of Music* in a low, flirtatious voice, in tandem with the rhythm of the gently swaying swing:

I am sixteen going on seventeen...

I sensed she was at peace with herself, ready to share her innermost thoughts with me. However, I reminded myself I was there to work, and slowly brought the conversation around to money.

'Of course, Radium,' she said, and soon returned with her gold-embossed purse.

Date with an Angel

For some reason, I wasn't able to meet Julie Singh again after our chance encounter at Bollywood Unlimited on the day of Eid. I telephoned her a few times for a chat, but she was always too busy to meet up. I wondered if she was avoiding me and, if so, why? I even thought about going to Bandra unannounced to surprise her, but always decided against it. What if she didn't want to see me? Julie told me on the phone that she'd done a degree in history, followed by a diploma in teaching, with the aim of becoming a history teacher. But that was all in the past. Now, since Robin's death, she was investing all her energy and money in Bollywood Unlimited.

Then I caught a break—I invited her out for dinner, and though she said she was too busy at first, she eventually agreed after a little bit of persuasion. She was travelling to Amritsar and we agreed to meet when she returned.

It was the day of Raksha Bandhan. I began speculating why Julie had agreed to meet me on Raksha Bandhan. Did she consider me her brother? Was she going to come along with a rakhi, the traditional gift that symbolizes a chaste, protective relationship between a brother and a sister? I hoped not! We'd agreed to meet at 8 p.m. at the New Horizon Restaurant on Carter Road in Bandra, not far from her store. I arrived there a little early and as 8 p.m. approached, I worried in case she'd changed her mind. But, right on time, Julie walked in with an orange-coloured envelope in her right hand. She was looking heart-stoppingly beautiful with her hair cut fashionably short and threaded with a ribbon.

After we were seated, and had ordered drinks and starters, I asked her what was in the envelope.

'It's a rakhi.'

My face fell. She placed the envelope on the table. 'This rakhi is for...'

Before she could complete her sentence, we were interrupted by the waiter bringing our drinks. She resumed speaking after he left the table. I was sure she must have seen the expression of dismay on my face, but she seemed to pretend not to.

'This rakhi is for someone really special. I first met him on the day my husband was shot and I look on him as a brother.'

'Can you guess who he is?'

'No...I can't.'

'You know him very well.'

'Is it me?'

The surprise on her face must have matched the heartache on mine.

'Of course not...this rakhi is for Dr Mittal.'

I was so relieved I almost burst out laughing.

'Dr Mittal tried his very best to save Robin's life at the Bandstand General Hospital.'

Her face turned sad. 'He's a good man.'

'Is he expecting you?'

'I have not met him ever since Robin was shot. I will give him a surprise.'

It was time to decide on the main course. Julie ordered

chicken with capers and some bread rolls and butter; I had the same. I didn't care. I could have eaten anything and wouldn't have even tasted it. All that mattered were her words 'of course not'.

The restaurant was quiet, with just a few tables occupied. It wasn't the most intimate of places, but probably just right for a low-profile first dinner date with a young widow still grieving for her dead husband. It was casual, like the white shirt and navy blue trousers I was wearing—clothes I'd bought from the Debenhams store in Oxford Street. I was Rahul, not Radium, and I wanted it to stay that way. Julie wore a simple button-down denim dress in soft chambray, with a mandarin collar, on-seam pockets and short sleeves. She wore hardly any make-up, just a touch of eye shadow, and it was clear she wasn't trying to seduce me—even if she had said 'of course not'. It was almost a year since Robin Singh died, but I knew she still missed him very much.

The waiter brought the food and we talked through mouthfuls of lemon-flavoured chicken and green beans and capers and small boiled potatoes. We talked mostly about Robin, and I didn't mind that as much as I thought I might. I encouraged her to tell me more about him and their life together. Only a good listener can become a good friend, and a good friend was what she needed most in her life at that point.

After dinner, she drove off in her car in order to tie the rakhi on Dr Mittal's wrist, and I watched the wheels kick up dust in the enchanted evening. But before she went, I had asked if we could meet again. Her words still echoed in the air.

'My place...next week?'

'I'll wait for your call...'

Julie was not my sister. My date had been with an angel. My only dilemma was how to break the truth about the nature of my real profession when the time came.

Life of Pi

~~

I HAD TWO missed calls from Rekha and a text message asking me to ring her. Something was urgent, and she wasn't to be deterred.

Her voice came on the line: 'Would you be prepared to see an HIV-positive client?'

Again, the first thought that came into my head was 'no way'.

Then I remembered I'd initially said 'no way' to disabled Anjali Khan, but that had worked out fine in the end. Anyway, she might not even want sex.

'She is not a member of our C3 Club, but I would appreciate it if you would go and see her. Her name is Pisces and she lives in Virar. I have told her you are from England.'

So, with a heavy heart, my mind fixated on Julie and our night out, I did Rekha's bidding.

Pisces, a simple-looking thirty-something woman, lived on the first floor of an old block of flats near Virar Railway Station. She'd just returned from the local bazaar when I arrived, and she looked in good spirits. For someone who was HIV positive, that is.

'I go every morning to the local bazaar to buy fresh fruit and vegetables.'

'Despite your HIV, you look fine.'

'Thank you,' she said, rather uncomfortably.

To make up for my clumsy opening line, I said, 'Pisces. Now that's an interesting name.'

'Yes. I was born on 1st of March. My grandmother gave me that name. In school and at home everyone called me Pi.'

'Now that sounds sensual and playful.'

'I was, but now life is different because of my illness.'

'I can understand.'

'I have my good days and my bad days. I have been HIV-positive for the past four years, after I came to Mumbai from Bihar.'

'I think HIV should not be a taboo subject…'

Once indoors, Pisces poured some tea for me.

'So, what brought you to Mumbai?' I asked.

'It was after my marriage…'

'An arranged marriage?'

'No. A forced marriage. It involved a kidnap.' I was shocked by this.

'Were *you* kidnapped?'

'No. It was the groom who was kidnapped.'

'Why?'

'It's called "Pakaruah shaadi".'

'Meaning?'

'A forced marriage—a custom which is prevalent in the interiors of some parts of northern and eastern India.'

'What exactly happened?'

With difficulty, she began to tell me her story. 'Lalu was a newly qualified railway engineer, with a well-paid job in Bihar. One day, when he was walking to work, five men armed with knives and guns stopped him and kidnapped him in broad daylight…'

I listened attentively.

'...Lalu was locked up in a dark room for two weeks and beaten by his kidnappers. He had no idea why he was being held, or what the demands of his kidnappers were.'

'Then what happened?' I asked.

'He was then drugged and taken to another house, where he was again locked up and beaten. After he recovered from the effects of the drugs, he was forced to shave and shower, and made to wear wedding clothes and a decorated turban.'

'How barbaric!'

'Indeed, Radium. Later that evening, Lalu was brought to a wedding venue fully decorated with flowers and multi-coloured lights and made to sit next to a woman dressed up as a bride.'

'And who was that woman?'

'That woman was me.'

Pisces saw the disbelief and astonishment on my face.

'It is true. The whole thing was set up by my widowed father who wanted Lalu, with his bright financial prospects, as his son-in-law and my husband. I was completely against the marriage but was threatened by my father and his hired thugs.'

I was rather skeptical of this, but she went on.

'Groom abducting in India is the result of the dowry system, of social and economic imbalance and male dominance and feudalism in the interiors.'

'But isn't dowry now illegal in India?'

'Not in the real world. Here the ever-increasing dowry demands of grooms' parents and the inability of girls' families to fulfil them has resulted in poor families hiring criminal gangs to kidnap prospective grooms and pressurizing them into forced marriages which are socially acceptable and religiously bona fide.'

'I am shocked.'

'Families take the law into their own hands. The police are corrupt and the legal system, weak. The gangsters, who are well-organized and powerful, take full advantage of the situation and make big money by abducting prospective grooms.'

Pisces's earlier good spirits evaporated as she remembered her ordeal. I gently rebuked myself as I recalled that this was the rural India I still longed for—the hills and rivers and bosom of my motherland where I wanted to stay forever, the true India of my dreams.

'Be wed or dead, the gangsters told us…they said they wanted to see blood on the bed sheets in the morning… otherwise there would be blood on the floor.'

'So, what happened next?'

'Lalu and I were then locked up in a room and forced to consummate our marriage. A few days later, we ran away separately. Lalu went to Jaipur and I fled to Mumbai.'

'So how did you become HIV positive?'

'I had been infected by Lalu. I believe Lalu did not know he was HIV positive, but on that fateful night he had told me he wasn't a virgin and that he'd slept with quite a few girls while at the engineering college.' Tears rolled down her eyes. 'I will be dying young.'

I put my arm around her shoulders and pulled her close to me. I could feel her sobs against my chest and I felt sorry for this poor girl.

'I wrote to my father and told him not only had he ruined my life, but that he had sentenced me to death.'

'What did he say?'

'Nothing. He didn't write back.'

More tears dripped from Pisces's chin.

'I was once a living doll. I have now been condemned to an early death and till then the hell of remaining single. I will miss knitting booties for my children and the joy of bringing them up.'

Pisces dried her tears but they kept returning, her shoulders shaking.

'I will miss growing old,' she said mournfully with a sigh, but then added with a laugh, 'but not my progression from slimness to old-aged obesity.'

She smiled at my attempt to revive her good spirits. 'So… here I am now in Mumbai, working for an NGO, trying to help HIV-infected patients.'

'I know that HIV-positive people face violence and discrimination in India.'

'We are a second clan of "untouchables". There is a lot of fear and misinformation and mistrust surrounding us. I think people's fears need to be dispelled.'

'You are right,' I interrupted.

'Our NGO is trying to improve the social acceptability of people living with HIV.'

She showed me some publicity material from her NGO and I looked at it with real interest.

'We are trying to explain to the public that sex using proper protection is safe, even with HIV-positive partners.'

'I know that.'

'I am glad you do. I even hope to start a marriage bureau for HIV-positive persons.'

She laughed at this, even though it wasn't funny, just in case I thought she meant the marriage bureau might be for me some day. I laughed with her, not at her. And as we began to relate to each other as a man and a woman, the spectre of the HIV faded away. She'd never had sex with anyone other than Lalu and very much desired the attention of a man.

'Please make love to me, Radium,' said Pisces as she held my right hand and led me to her bedroom.

Despite my fears, I had a desire to heal this woman. I was quite happy to provide a pleasant and emotional offering to Pisces.

Of course, I believed in safe sex in this trade. I always used a condom.

'It's not on, if it's not on!' I would tell my clients.

After the lovemaking session, Pisces was flushed and beaming.

'The colours around me look brighter and the world seems a friendlier place,' she said.

I was happy that my valiant attempt to bring a moment of happiness in the life of Pi was rewarded. But staring at the ceiling, I immediately saw Julie's face. I didn't know how much longer I would be able to lead a double life.

Goodbye, My Lady

~

When I got home, I received a shock. I came to know that PP Auntie had been admitted to Bandstand General Hospital with a very high fever. I went there immediately and met Dr Mittal and Ratan by her bed.

'The situation is grim,' Ratan admitted. 'Dr Mittal says my mother will have to be put on a life support system.'

'I am so sorry to hear that.'

I went to her bedside and held her hand, and she looked up at me with those all-knowing eyes of hers. And I wondered who she saw—Rahul or Radium?

We waited and prayed, and after a few days in intensive care, PP Auntie made a slight recovery, insisting that she be discharged from the hospital so that she could be at home on her birthday. Dr Mittal was against the idea, but she ended up discharging herself.

'If I am dying, I would rather be at home when it happens.'

That's what she said to me when I came into the lounge one evening and found her there. I sat next to her and tried to tell her she had many years left. But I wasn't as competent a liar as Radium.

'I am suffering from vascular dementia.' She knew all about her illness. Dr Mittal and Ratan had explained it to her.

'Vascular dementia is caused by chronic reduced blood

flow to the brain, as a result of a stroke or a series of strokes,' she explained.

'Are you in pain?'

'The strokes were so small I hardly noticed. They are known as silent strokes.'

Again, I sat with her and held her hand, telling her all would be well.

⁓

The next day was PP Auntie's birthday.

But which one? Her cake with only one candle, which Ratan had organized, offered no clue.

Ratan had taken the day off to be with her, and I was also at home. She had received more than thirty birthday cards, which she looked through while sitting on her JFK rocking chair.

Ruby Daruwalla, Ratan's girlfriend—an incredible cook—had arrived early in the morning to cook a special birthday lunch in honour of PP Auntie. The main course was *dhansak*, a popular Parsee dish consisting of mutton, lentils, vegetables, spices, cumin, ginger and garlic.

At two o'clock, we all sat down to a fantastic lunch.

'Happy birthday, PP Auntie!' I smiled, raising a toast.

I gave her a leather-bound copy of *William Shakespeare: The Complete Works*, because I remembered how much she loved the Bard. She was delighted! I just hoped she would get time to read some of the plays.

'Thank you, Rahul.'

I held her hand, in homage to this glorious old lady who'd taken me in off the streets of Mumbai when I had nothing and nobody and was all alone in a strange city.

She blew out the candle on her birthday cake, and we all stood and watched while she cut it with the silver knife which BP had bought on her first birthday after their marriage.

I sang, with Ratan and Ruby joining in:

Happy birthday to you! Happy birthday to you!
Happy birthday dear PP Auntie! Happy birthday to you!

And then Ruby:

For she is a jolly good fellow. For she is a jolly good fellow. For she is a jolly good fellow.

And finally, Ratan: 'Three cheers to my mum—Hip hip hooray! Hip hip hooray! Hip hip hooray!'

We all clapped, and I was lost in admiration of this most wonderful and noble lady. As we sat together, eating cake, talking, and being a family, I remembered my other family back in London, and promised that I would call them soon.

'Did you know Shakespeare died on his birthday?' asked Auntie PP, with a twinkle in her eyes.

I ignored this, as I didn't want to talk about death on this happy occasion.

'I am eighty today,' she announced grandly.

I had to admit I was rather shocked. In her seventies, certainly, but I didn't think she was much more than seventy-five.

'How does it feel to be eighty, PP Auntie?'

'Twice as good as when I was forty!'

The years had wrinkled and debilitated her body, but her spirits were high; more like a woman of eighteen, not eighty.

At that moment, my mobile bleeped. It was a text message from my mum.

Please wish PP Auntie a happy birthday from your dad and myself. Love Mum.

PP Auntie was ecstatic on being shown the text message. She was glowing with a radiance that was not of this world.

Later that afternoon, she took her pills from her plastic medicine kit, which had seven compartments, one for each day of the week. Then she fell asleep on her rocking chair while reading *A Midsummer Night's Dream*.

She never woke up. Her face in death looked serene, satisfied, smiling.

Earlier, PP Auntie had talked about Shakespeare dying on his birthday. Now she left us on her birthday, while reading one of his greatest plays. It seemed like an apt way to go.

When we had all recovered from the shock, Ratan, Ruby and I hugged each other in our common grief. I telephoned Irfan and David who came over within an hour. The five of us sat and planned PP Auntie's funeral arrangements.

'She died without seeing our marriage,' said Ratan, sadly.

Both Ratan and Ruby were upset about this. But PP Auntie had known her time was up, and had not been sad about it herself. We cheered ourselves with that thought, and we knew she would now be with BP in the heaven that she deserved.

~

PP Auntie's funeral was attended by about a hundred people, including a few Parsee grandees and some non-Parsees such as Irfan, David, Dr Mittal and me. The funeral was held at the Tower of Silence, on top of Mumbai's Malabar Hill. This was a three-hundred-year-old, forty-five-acre funeral park; with its green surroundings, it had an atmosphere of calm, peace and eternal rest.

It was a grief-charged day. The non-Parsees sat in a

special seating area, while the Parsees themselves gathered at the Bangli, a prayer room where PP Auntie was laid out for mourners to pay their last respects. Irfan and David sat on either side of me. I was tempted to take a selfie using my mobile phone of us three sitting at PP Auntie's funeral, but decided against it, as I felt Ratan may find my action insensitive. PP Auntie, I am sure, would not have minded. She would have laughed her unforgettable laugh.

The Parsee priest recited the prayers in a pure, soothing voice. Then the body was taken in a procession to the Tower of Silence, winding its way on a long path through the trees, watched by birds from the tree-tops. The procession went up the hill, accompanied by the sound of the mourners' footsteps.

When they arrived at the Tower, PP Auntie's face was uncovered for the last farewell. She was then carried into the towers by four khandiyas, the traditional bier bearers—the only men who are allowed entry into the wells. We could see no more now.

Ratan felt he had to explain to me: 'My mum's body will be placed on a stand, the white cloth covering her body will be removed, and she will then be left exposed inside in the Dokhmas.'

'Dokhmas?' I asked.

'Large cylindrical stone towers. In the towers, my mum's body will be devoured by the vultures.'

I was startled by this fact. As he spoke, we could see vultures flying overhead, descending in circles, finally lining on the wall of the Tower; some flapping their wings waiting to go down to the dokhmas, others just sitting peacefully.

Ratan pointed to some more vultures appearing in the blinding blue sky.

'Look, they know she has arrived,' said Ratan.

'After the prayers are said and the rituals performed, the vultures will do the rest. Soon, no evidence will remain that my mother ever lived in this world.'

'Except her memory,' I said in a low, emotionally charged voice.

It was a very sad moment. A feeling of deep loss and emptiness engulfed me.

That evening was gloomy, with the shadows melting into darkness earlier than usual. After the funeral, I sent a text message to my mum and dad in London: *PP Auntie is no more*.

I then looked up into the sky, which seemed mournful itself, ready to burst into tears, and whispered: 'Goodbye, my lady...'

Come September

~~

She had invited me for dinner, but, so far, all she had done was talk about Robin and cry. At the back of my mind, too, was the fact that I had been the only witness to her husband's murder. For some reason, I couldn't bring the subject up. By seven o' clock, Julie was showing me her honeymoon photographs.

'I knew Robin since we were seven...'

Tears welled up in her eyes again and rolled down her cheeks. She talked about how they'd met as children and fallen in love and got married. But now she was all alone and lost. She cried and cried; she cried for Robin, she cried for herself, she cried for her lost baby.

'I want him back. We fought every day, but loved each other every minute...every second.'

I felt like an intruder. How could I possibly match this love? How could I expect her to feel for me the way she felt for him? He would always be there in the background, haunting us like a ghost.

'I miss his five Ts.'

'Five Ts?'

'His touch, his trust, his talk, his time and his tenderness.'

But now those five Ts were no more, replaced by another T. Tears! Robin was no more. An unknown assailant on a motorcycle had put an end to Robin on that fateful day a year ago, just off Hill Road in Bandra. It was that simple, that easy. One day you're walking along arm in arm, very much in love, and the sky is blue and the birds are singing; the next day you're alone and everything is grey and sad and silent. No more love. Except there was more love—I loved her but I didn't know how to tell her. She hadn't even deleted the last voicemail message Robin had left on her mobile that morning: *Hi sweetheart. Am on my way. Will be slightly delayed. See you soon. I love you.*

She played it every day, over and over again. Now she played it for me.

There was a long silence between us after she played the message. I knew she wanted to play it again. To hear it again. But she didn't. Maybe she sensed my chagrin. But Robin just wouldn't stay away.

'Would you like to hear a song?'

She asked this question as I helped her set the dining table.

'Are you going to sing?'

'Of course not...it's a recording.'

Those words again. She didn't wait for me to say yes or no. I guessed it would be Robin singing. And it was. With my poor Punjabi, I had problems understanding the lyrics, so Julie translated the song for me, as his voice filled the room. It was as if he was there with us, and it unnerved me, but it delighted her.

This is Robin, your thorn bird, singing for you, my lovebird.

An hour later, we were sitting together over dinner. The subject had finally changed from Robin to me.

'So, do you still aspire to become a film producer?'

'Very much. I will join Film International next year.'

She smiled. 'Do you miss England?'

'Absolutely. More than that, I miss my parents.'

Sadly, she announced: 'Both my parents died when I was ten. First my mother, and then my father died a few weeks later.'

'I'm so sorry.'

She went to her dressing table to fetch something.

'My father left a letter for me with his brother, Kapil, to be given to me when I was eighteen.'

She gave it to me to read. This is what he had written:

My dearest daughter Julie,

I was unfaithful to your mother. She was a truly noble lady who never suspected that I was seeing another woman. When your mother died, I told you she had died by accident, whilst we were out boating on Jhelum River. This is both true and untrue.

We went out in a small boat, just the two of us. Whilst I was rowing, your mother stood up and started walking towards me. She lost her balance and fell overboard. I could have saved your mother. But in those few seconds I had, I was thinking of this other woman and my life with her, rather than of your mother. Your mother drowned. I didn't have time to save her.

The police have accepted that your mother died by accident. However, in the Kingdom of God, I am guilty of her murder. I have now left this other woman and will never see her again. I was a coward. I killed your mother. Now I am leaving this world, I hope I will be able to join your mother and seek her forgiveness. I have stopped taking the medication for my heart condition and will not survive another heart attack, which I pray should come soon.

I know you like Robin. I hope one day you two will get married. Please forgive me, Julie. For being unfaithful to your mother. For killing your mother. For killing myself. For leaving you an orphan.

I am leaving this letter with your Uncle Kapil, who will give it to you when you are eighteen. He will look after you. Please forgive me. I am full of remorse, regret and repentance.

Your loving dad,
Kirpal Singh

There was a spell of silence after I finished reading the letter.

'I was devastated when I read it,' she said.

So was I, I told her. There was another lengthy pause. Eventually she spoke. 'I keep busy at the shop. I get up in the morning and soon it is evening. Morning. Evening. Morning. Evening. The routine continues. Life continues,' and she smiled weakly in my direction.

Julie put her father's letter back in the bottom drawer of her dressing table. We continued our talk over dinner of rice and chicken curry.

'My economic status is secure, but my everyday life is meaningless,' she admitted. 'I have very few friends.'

'I am your friend.'

She smiled again. 'I know that. Thank you.'

I didn't want to leave her. I wanted to put my arms around her and embrace her. But I couldn't do that. Not yet. I wasn't a brother, but I was a friend. It was a start. Something to build on.

It was nearly midnight when I left.
'Goodbye, Julie.'
'Never say goodbye.'

⌢

It was two weeks since I'd been to Julie's house, and she had been on my mind constantly. Since then, I'd called her almost every day and asked her a few times to go out with me, though I didn't want to reveal my feelings too soon. She turned down every suggestion.

'I would only spoil the evening, crying and talking about Robin.'

'I'm your friend. I want you to be happy. I'm concerned about you.'

Finally, she sent me a text message, asking to meet on Sunday. We met at the Hanging Gardens at the top of Malabar Hill at 5 p.m.

When she arrived, Julie looked happier than I'd ever seen her. She showed signs that she was slowly moving away from the sadness that followed Robin's death. Of course, she still missed Robin and still talked about him, so I didn't try to stop her or to change the subject. I genuinely wanted to help her work her way through the trauma.

As we sat on a bench eating peanuts, she asked me to tell her more about myself. I told her the story of my life in London, my Indian father, my English mother.

'My friends at school used to tease me by calling me a Red Indian.'

I told her again about coming to Mumbai to study filmmaking, and how I was mugged, about PP Auntie and her death, my friends, Irfan and David—everything except about Radium.

'How interesting! What are you doing now?'

'Erm, I work as an entertainment consultant.'

I didn't elaborate, and thankfully she didn't ask me to.

'Any girlfriend?'

'We broke up about three months before I came to India. But time heals all wounds…doesn't it?'

She paused at this statement, and I immediately regretted reminding her of Robin.

'So, like most men in India, will you be looking for a virgin when you get married?'

'No…not me.'

'You are handsome and charming and from England. Any girl will like you.'

I laughed. 'And any man would fall in love with you.' She remained silent. There was sadness in her eyes.

'Robin loved me. He is still with me.' She showed me her wedding ring.

'I still feel married to him. My heart, soul and mind all belong to Robin.'

We looked at each other in silence.

'I told you I would only spoil the evening.'

'No! You have scars…deep ones…'

She smiled, but I wasn't sure if it was real or just a polite reaction.

'Can I recite a poem for you?'

'Rhyme on.'

I cleared my throat, took a deep breath and quoted:

You can shed tears that he is gone
Or you can smile because he has lived.

Julie listened attentively as I continued. I finally ended

the poem.

Smile, open your eyes, love and go on.

'It's a lovely poem. Did you compose it?'

'Oh no!'

'So, who did?'

'No one knows. I first heard it whilst watching the funeral of the Queen Mother in London in 2002. It was chosen by the Queen herself for her mother's funeral.'

'How touching!'

She smiled one of her lovely smiles, and, this time, I knew it was genuine.

'You should remember your cherished moments with Robin. But also, live for today and for the future.'

I spoke in my own clumsy way, but not with Radium's polished words. However, her smile encouraged me and I placed my hand on hers.

'A life that's not lived passionately isn't lived fully.'

It was the first time I'd actually touched her. She gently pulled her hand away from mine and there was a long silence between us. We'd finished the peanuts and I asked her if she'd like some ice cream.

'I would love some.'

We walked together across the garden, between hedges shaped like animals, towards an ice-cream vendor. It was like we were in some strange land of our own, neither India nor England, with nobody else around. Our Garden of Eden.

Later, we enjoyed the gentle evening breeze and the lovely view of the sunset across the horizon of the Arabian Sea. The sun eventually dipped below the horizon, and the street lights came on, breaking the spell. From the top of the Hanging Gardens, we could see Marine Drive transform into Queen's

Necklace with its dazzling lights. The feeling of just the two of us alone in the universe was suddenly gone. Humanity intruded upon us again, and it was time for dinner.

'Let's go to Chowpatty. It is nearby.'

'Shall we go in this?' I asked Julie as we approached a horse-drawn carriage waiting for passengers.

'Fantastic. We will travel like royalty!'

Chowpatty is the most popular beach in downtown Mumbai. I'd been there a few weeks earlier for the Lord Ganesh immersion ceremony. The atmosphere at Chowpatty on a Sunday evening was a different experience altogether. A huge crowd thronged the beach. There were hundreds of people enjoying an evening out, trying to escape from the hustle and bustle of Mumbai. The mood was party-like as we walked along the busy stretch of sand, taking in the carnival atmosphere of merry-go-rounds, camel rides, horse rides, and monkey shows. There were wayside astrologers making a quick buck telling gorgeous lies as well as balloon-sellers, masseurs, magicians, jugglers and snake charmers.

Next to the magicians' corner, we passed Kamal's Movie House, a peep show machine on a small cart, with Kamal, the owner, playing a dafli. The man was in his early fifties, with a luxuriant moustache and a swollen left cheek. He was wearing a tarboosh, a red felt cap shaped like a flat-topped cone, with a silk tassel. He was constantly smiling, showing off his paan-stained teeth, three of them golden, while merrily drumming away, turning his head from side to side, moving his surma-lined eyes in all directions, inviting children to see clips of old Bollywood movies. While the children whose parents could afford it had mobile phones to watch the same film clips on YouTube, Kamal was making a comfortable living with his peep-show machine by charging one rupee for a two-minute view, which children from deprived families were happily queuing up to pay.

Then there were the food kiosks strewn across the vast expanse of the sandy beach of Chowpatty.

'This is where we will have our dinner tonight,' I said, hoping she would agree.

Julie's mood had changed. She was like an excited kid now, dodging back and forth between the food stalls selling bhelpuri, paani puri and pav bhaji, and hot and spicy food.

'You must try the kulfi…it's what Chowpatty's famous for.'

Julie held my hand as she pulled me across towards the kulfi counters.

At the coconut counter, where we drank water from freshly beheaded coconuts, a man came and probed my ears with a fine wire rod. I was startled and tried to make him go away.

Julie just laughed.

'He is a professional ear cleaner. Let him do your ears! You don't have them in England?'

'No!' I cried.

The man showed me the wax he removed from my ears and I wasn't sure if it was really mine or somebody else's that he had hidden in his hand. I paid him anyway, because I was so happy.

'This time it was the ear cleaner who removed wax from your ear. Next time, it might be a pick-pocket who will remove your wallet, so be careful,' said Julie, reminding me of Mumbai's many perils.

It was an exciting evening, which had to end, as all things do. When it was time to say goodbye, Julie thanked me before she left.

'This evening has been most delightful.'

'I'm so glad. As you know, my name is Rahul…which means "conqueror of all miseries".'

'I will try and not be miserable from now on.'

I didn't want to leave her; I wanted to go back with her and make love to her and be with her forever. But I had to be patient. Patient. Patient.

'Let tomorrow be a new beginning. I'm sure Robin would want that for you.'

I took her home at the end of a truly memorable evening, and I hoped it was the beginning of a truly memorable relationship. I whispered to her before I turned away.

'Smile, open your eyes, love, and go on…' To my delight, she smiled.

I was already falling in love with Julie. I hoped she would also soon love me.

Over the next two weeks, I called Julie every day. Once, I was busy, and didn't get to call her till about midnight. Luckily, she was still awake.

'I was waiting for your call all day.'

This was a good sign; my calls meant something to her!

'Please send me the poem you recited the other day at Hanging Gardens.'

I typed it up on blue paper with a decorative border in silver. Blue was her favourite colour, she admitted, while silver was mine; blue and silver together symbolizing our growing friendship. I sent her a short note with the poem, telling her I missed her and would like to meet her again.

We met at Juhu beach on a Sunday morning, three weeks

later. It was an airy, breezy day with some sunshine. Rain was expected later in the morning. It wasn't very crowded at that time of the morning, and we were away from the rush and crush of Mumbai.

As we started to walk, the wind tore at her hair, tugging it loose from the velvet ribbon, tossing it wildly about, making her look ravishing.

'You look really beautiful.'

She blushed slightly and turned her head away as we walked along the water's edge.

'Do you miss love?' She didn't reply.

'Well…I miss love. I dream about falling in love. I dream about you too.'

We continued to walk along the beach, and I thought she was never going to speak again.

'I think about you…'

She said this after a long silence. There were a few other couples sitting on the sand or walking hand in hand.

'May I hold your hand?'

'You may,' she whispered.

She closed her eyes the moment I touched her.

'You're so beautiful. You're the most beautiful girl I've ever seen.'

We took off our shoes and walked into the waves. It seemed to me that I was in a dream and would wake up any moment in PP Auntie's house. The breeze became more intense and so did the sensation of our touch. At the far end of the beach, there was a bench which another couple had just vacated. I held Julie's hand and gently pulled her towards it. We sat in silence, looking at the sky and the waves and, finally, into each other's eyes. Yes! Our eyes were already proclaiming our love for each other!

'I love you,' I told Julie. My voice was hoarse and my mouth was dry. 'I've felt like this ever since we met at the New Horizon Restaurant,' I stammered blushingly. 'I'm not asking you to forget Robin...'

She looked down at the ground and remained silent. I moved closer to her. Her eyes were closed.

'May I kiss you?' I asked.

My voice was barely above a whisper. Again, she didn't reply. But she gently tilted her head towards me. She opened her eyes as I moved my face towards hers. She didn't move away. Soon our lips were touching. It was a kiss, not a passionate kiss, but it was our first kiss. It was beautiful!

I drew her towards me and kissed her again, holding her with both hands. I looked into her eyes and kissed her again. She kissed me back. I kissed her again, this time more passionately. She parted her lips and wrapped her arms around me.

'I love you!'

This time, I didn't stammer. 'I love you too.'

We stayed holding each other on the bench for a long time. For years, it seemed. For an eternity. Then we started walking again, sometimes hand in hand, sometimes with her arm looped through mine, sometimes with me walking backwards and looking at her, sometimes with my arm around her waist. We didn't say much, there was nothing much to be said.

We were in love. The feeling was wonderful. I had seen many beautiful women, mainly under the guise of Radium, but, for Rahul, Julie was the only woman in the entire world.

'You are truly beautiful,' I said again.

'Your love has made me so.'

The ground smelt of spring. The air smelt of winter. Then there was rain. First it came as a very light shower, but gradually it became more intense. I didn't care. We didn't care. Lightning, then silence, then thunder. More thunder, a few kilometres away. Soon there was a stunning display of clouds and lightning filling the moody sky. A splinter of lightning came crashing down from the heavens.

'Bring it on!' I shouted. But we did not run for cover. Love makes you do ridiculous things, like walking in a thunderstorm with wet clothes and hair, standing in the middle of a beach, while the other couples ran for shelter, and not caring about anything, as if we were in a world of our own.

In a while, the lashing rain slowed to a drizzle and then stopped followed by a lazy calm. A double rainbow pierced the majestic clouds. The sun appeared and so did a school of dolphins, porpoising in the distance in the blue sea. Then we saw three ships appear from the other side of the horizon.

'Fish and ships!' I joked lamely, as I gently dragged her towards me.

'You must be missing the fish and chips of England.'

'I do.'

'I love you,' said Julie, running her hand through my wet hair.

'Remember who said it first.'

We wrapped our arms around each other.

'Rain makes me forget my pain.'

'No more pain…from now on.'

Julie hugged me tight as we both welcomed the advent of our love and its confusing joy. My breathing intensified as she whispered, 'Love happens.'

A week after our Juhu beach meeting, Julie invited me home for dinner.

Rain had started at dawn. There was a huge downpour of water carpet-bombing the streets of Mumbai. The weather was causing chaos, and I was late when I finally reached her sea-facing flat. I had brought her a small gift—a robin-blue solid marble egg, measuring three inches in height, mounted on a wooden stand. I'd already bought it when I realized the colour might cause her distress. But it was too late to do anything about it now.

'Blue...my favourite colour.' She smiled as she opened my gift box. 'And not just blue...robin blue!'

She hugged me and tears welled up in her eyes.

'I chose blue because it's a natural colour...from the blue of the sky. It's supposed to have a calming effect and brings peace.'

Julie placed the egg on the side unit in her lounge. While it rained outside, I hoped her tears wouldn't start falling as well.

I have always loved the rain. When I first came to Mumbai, I looked forward to experiencing India's monsoon first hand, the pleasure and excitement of walking in the rain and getting soaked; the magic of the monsoons as in Bollywood films, with a rain scene showing the heroine singing and dancing, displaying her breasts under her rain-soaked clothes—something even the orthodox censors in India didn't seem to mind. But the reality was different. There were never gentle showers like we have in England, where rain might stop cricket for an hour or two. Here the rains were roaring and deafening, forceful and ferocious, exploding with thunder and lightning. Such a rainy season wasn't the pleasant experience I'd dreamt about. This rain wasn't romantic—it was a necessity, something to be tolerated for survival.

So the monsoon season wasn't something magical like I had imagined, but a phenomenon dreaded by the people of Mumbai—because of the flooded roads and the chaos, the traffic jams and the overflowing gutters, death from drowning or disease.

'The slum dwellers and homeless people are the worst affected,' Julie told me.

'And yet the mighty monsoon rains are necessary, so that India can survive and life can go on.'

'Yes, life has to go on.' I said and paused.

'Your shirt is wet. Why don't you take it off? I will dry and iron it for you.'

I hesitated for a moment. My hands were shaking as I started to undo the buttons of my wet shirt. I went on, button by button. Julie touched me, feeling the warmth of my body. I wrapped my arms around her. She closed her eyes. I pulled her towards me and kissed her on the lips and neck. This was what I'd come for. She knew it! I carried her into the bedroom. She was beautiful. Her skin was soft, and her hair was sleek and had now grown to shoulder-length, and her eyes were shining.

The room was dimly lit with little shimmering nightlights. There was complete silence in the room, except for the sound of a grandfather clock.

Tick, tock! Tick, tock! Tick, tock!

Julie was watching me as we both undressed. We were nervous, unsure of ourselves. She had a girlishness about her, something endearing, something splendid and surreal, sensuous and sublime, all at the same time. It seemed so perfectly right to be here with her. It was as if time was standing still and my soul had ceased to exist—my individual soul—and had been replaced by a cloud of sensations that could easily be mistaken for a soul. There had been so much on my mind before I came into this sea-facing flat. So much I had to do. But all that seemed to evaporate inside the bedroom. Now it didn't matter. Time ceased to exist.

I could hear music, distant, somewhere at the back of my mind. My head felt light, floating on the scent of the woman beside me, the texture of her hair, the seductive sound of her voice, the sparkle of the nightlight on her teeth, the stimulating eroticism of the situation. For a brief moment, I forgot my other life as Radium.

Once she was naked, I discovered her skin was smooth and felt like silk—warm and slightly moist in the low light glow. Her tongue found its way around my body and her hands were electric when they touched me. I moved to the rhythm of Julie, in tune with her body and its changing positions on the bed. Her voice purred like a leopard, though her words made no sense to me, nor were they meant to. They were meant only for her, and I made my own sounds. I can't remember how long we were in bed. I didn't know what day it was or what month or year.

Later, we drank pineapple juice together and hugged each other like two lost friends meeting after a long separation. We laughed as we talked about our kisses and love-bites, which were soft and painful, and about our scratches which had left marks.

Finally, time began to move again.

Over the next few days, we kept in regular contact by phone, e-mail and text, telling each other how much we loved and missed each other. I sent her a dozen blue roses, specially ordered from Valentine Florists in Andheri, which specialized in creating blue roses by dyeing white ones. They were a symbol of our love.

Julie was fast becoming the love of my life—my future—my soulmate. We spent time walking on the beach and in the streets of Mumbai, laughing and dreaming of the future. We visited Haji Ali Dargah and the Gateway of India and Marine Drive and Madh Island. At Haji Ali Dargah, I saw a Muslim fakir who said to me, 'Hello, my son.' On his forehead was a small contusion confirming his passion in his five daily prayers. He blessed us and gave me a piece of paper with something written on it. It was a one-line prayer in Hindi with a translation in English. He called it 'bandagi'.

'Sitting cross-legged, recite this bandagi in your mind for one hour every day at four in the morning, with the lights off and your eyes closed.'

'I'm not a Muslim,' I told him politely.

'You can pray to any god or goddess using this recitation. The Lord will listen. Your prayers will be answered and your problems solved.'

I accepted the prayer paper and as I was walking away he whispered to me, 'This prayer is strictly confidential and for you only.'

At Madh Island, we walked together on the beach at low tide, and then swam together in the Arabian Sea at high tide. Julie took me to see the large open-air laundry at

Dhobi Ghat, next to Mahalaxmi Station, where clothes were washed by the dhobis. I was fascinated by the concrete wash pens with their flogging stones, and the dhobis washing and drying. Julie knew this man called Ramu, who was her dhobi, and he took us round, explaining how the dirty linen was collected and washed, dried and ironed, and piled into neat bundles for the customers.

'Julie madam...your dress.'

Ramu pulled out Julie's blue dress from amongst dozens of clothes in his pile.

The scene was like something out of a bygone era, and I made a mental note to include Dhobi Ghat in my first film.

⁓

Though I was busy with my other secret life, I made time to be with Julie and, when we were together, we were totally lost in each other. Nothing else mattered. Everything was wonderful when we were together and we were sad when we were apart. There was a tidal wave of passion when we made love, and every time it was like a new experience. There was magic all over again. Julie was always surprising, always different, always more than I could ever have hoped for, always enigmatic. We loved the same things—music, food, films. We had so much in common that it was as if we were born to be with each other. I'm not saying we didn't have differences and arguments every now and then. We had our ups and downs, like most lovers. And, of course, I was worried about her finding out about Radium. I began thinking about killing him off, about smothering him, about cutting off his lifeline. But the big question was how I would survive financially. It was a dilemma I had no solution for.

I even tried to pre-empt this by warning her.

'There might be some tough times ahead.'

'I told you before, Rahul…love brings pain. Sweet pain.'

∫

Sometimes we went walking near Jubilee Lake, not far from Mumbai. We sat on the shore, looking out over the vast expanse of water, throwing pebbles to make ripples and losing ourselves in the ambience. It reminded me of a bedtime story my father had told me when I was very young, about some small boys throwing pebbles at frogs in a pond. Fun for the boys, but fatal for the frogs. I told her lots of these little stories, all of which my father had told me over the years.

'You have a lot of respect for your father,' she observed.

'When I was ten, I had to write an essay in school about "The Person I Respect the Most". Some boys wrote about football players and others about film stars, but I wrote about my dad. It was the best essay and my teacher read it out to the whole class.'

I told Julie how much I loved my mother as well. My father used to tease me in my pre-teen years, by asking me, 'Do you love your dad more or your mum? '

'Daddy more and Mummy more,' I used to reply as a child, each time my father asked me the question.

Julie was impressed.

She told me about how painting was one of her passions before Robin died. When we went back to her place, she showed me a couple of canvases. One was of a man and woman standing under an umbrella in the rain, looking adoringly into each other's eyes. The other was of a poor Indian peasant woman pulling a wooden plough in a farm, helped by her two small children, who were both crying.

'This painting is a depiction of the plight of poor farmers in India.'

'I have heard that so many of them were now committing suicide due to poverty, drought and crippling debts.'

It was a depressing subject and I didn't want to think about it. I just wanted us to stay in the state of bliss we'd been in for weeks now, and I didn't want anything to encroach on that happiness. I changed the subject.

'You must start painting again!'

'I will. You inspire me.'

∽

One evening, I went unannounced to her flat. I was carrying a small box.

'A gift for you.'

'What is the occasion?'

'You are the occasion. Can you sing?'

'No. But I can dance. I love dancing, especially at Navratri. There will be a big Navratri celebration at Bhuleshwar next week. Shall we go?'

The following week, we spent an afternoon together in Chor Bazaar, one of India's biggest flea markets. It was a maze of narrow lanes and by-lanes full of people from all over Mumbai, India and abroad—Arabs, Africans, Europeans, Chinese. The shops sold almost everything: junk, cutlery, clocks, sockets, hammers, tools, screwdrivers, pictures, old Bollywood film posters, gramophones, sports goods, stamp collections, fake jewellery and fake paintings.

'If you lose something, you can get it back from Chor

Bazaar.'

'I've lost my heart.'

'The thief is in Chor Bazaar right now. Just catch her.'

I reached out impulsively to hold her hand, caught her by the waist and kissed her.

We headed south, past a neighbourhood of crumbling houses; past a trio of Hindu temples from which emanated deafening bell-gongs reverberating like a thunderclap; past Dr K Shukla's Surrogacy Clinic (one of the many unregulated clinics springing up all over India); past the office of Gay Rights Now; past an old rundown building which had collapsed a few days previously killing sixty-seven people; past a film studio vandalized by some political thugs, until we finally reached Bhuleshwar at about 8 p.m., just in time for the Navratri Garba and Dandiya-Raas dance programme, which was being held at the New Gujarat Club.

We changed into the special costumes which we'd brought with us. Julie looked stunning in her colourful embroidered choli and ghagra, her bandhani dupatta glittering with mirror work.

She also wore her favourite blue shoes.

'I love your blue shoes,' I told Julie.

'Why?'

'They bring you to me.'

'They also take me away from you.'

'I know. At that time, I feel jealous.'

We danced to the beat of dandiya until 2 a.m., and got lost in the crowd a few times. But I always found her again.

'You are a good dancer, Julie.'

'And you are a good liar!'

Finally, September came, and the monsoon season drew to an end. The intensity of the rainfall had decreased, but there were still some heavy thunderstorms about.

'September reminds me of the Bandra fair. Can we visit the fair tomorrow?'

At the fair on the next day, a young man shouted across at us: 'Hello, Julie!'

'Who is he?'

'Oh, ignore him.'

He followed us for a while and I could see he had a tattoo on his arm, but he stayed far away so I couldn't make out what it was. Julie seemed to be scared of him and I was going to approach him to tell him to stop following us, but he disappeared into the crowd.

'Who is that guy?'

'I don't know.'

'You must know…he knows your name.'

'Look. Forget about him. He's not important.'

So I forgot about him—or tried to—and we continued walking in the cool September afternoon towards the old Roman Catholic Mount Mary Church, where PP Auntie used to go sometimes when she was alive. There we lit candles and prayed. It was another day to remember, one of many, during that unforgettable season.

Alienation of Affection

It was the day of Eid al-Adha, the Muslim festival of sacrifice. David and I met Irfan in Dongri, in order to wish him Eid felicitations. 'It is a tradition amongst us Muslims to slaughter a lamb or a goat as a sacrifice on the day of Eid, and distribute the meat to the poor. I have also sacrificed a goat today.' Irfan showed us packets of meat he was carrying in two large plastic carrier bags, 'I will be distributing this meat amongst the poor at Haji Ali Dargah.'

He had invited David and me to go with him to the Dargah, which had a mosque and the tomb of a Muslim saint, Sayed Peer Haji Ali Shah Bukhari.

We walked along the lengthy, narrow causeway that bridged the shrine, built on an islet off the coast at Worli, with the mainland.

'During high tide, this path is totally engulfed by sea water,' Irfan said. 'Today we are lucky, the tide is low. At night, you get the impression the mosque is floating on the water.'

'It looks like an anchored ship with its lights on,' added David.

It being Eid, there were hundreds of people in the Dargah. The place was crowded with tourists and pilgrims, not just Muslims, but also Hindus and other non-Muslims, saying prayers and paying homage. The fakir was also there. He smiled at me and again said, 'Hello, my son!'

'I hope my confidential prayer paper is still safe with you,' he enquired with a smile.

I nodded.

He spoke as if he had known me for many years. I smiled back.

After distributing the meat packets to the poor, Irfan, David and I said prayers at the tomb of the saint. It was an inter-faith experience that I knew I would always cherish.

Later that afternoon, I went to see Nalini Rampal, a new client who lived in Cuffe Parade, not far from Mumbai's Chinatown, in a neat and tastefully decorated flat. Rekha had told me that some woman had stolen Nalini's husband and she was very upset. It was my job to calm her down and make her happy.

When I arrived, I saw Nalini was about forty and was quite pleasant-looking, if a little plumper than I preferred. But that wouldn't be a problem for me. It was still my job, after all.

'Rekha told me you are good company. I would like you to come with me to the Elephanta Caves.'

'Lovely. Aren't the caves a UNESCO World Heritage Site?'

'Yes. I have arranged for a private boat to take us there.'

It was a pleasant one-hour journey from the Gateway to Elephanta Island. As it was a private boat, we were able to sit and talk in a relaxed atmosphere over a light lunch that she'd brought with her. Her husband's name was Jas Rampal, but she preferred to call him by his last name. They'd lived together before they got married. Nalini, like most of the others, was eager to tell me the story of her life.

'Both our respective parents and relatives disapproved of

it…We are living in a paperless world. Why should a marriage certificate matter?'

Rampal and she had been accused by friends and family of corrupting young minds by promoting premarital sex.

'My mother wanted me to preserve my virginity till the night of my marriage, like most other girls of India.'

At this, I laughed. She went on:

'But I said virginity is not dignity, it is just a lack of opportunity.'

I nodded in agreement, or rather Radium did.

'After that, they never bothered me…until a few years after our marriage, when Rampal left me for another woman.' Nalini showed her anger in the tone of her voice.

'That bitch stole my husband!'

Once in Elephanta, we spent a good two hours touring through the caves, walking around the island and having some food at one of the local restaurants. It was easy money for me. No effort involved.

On our return journey, Nalini told me how Rampal was lured away from her.

'She is a bitch. Her name is Preity Singhal, and she calls herself Pretty Single—single and ready to mingle. The name "Singhal" means leonine, like a lion. She is a lion and Rampal is a lamb.'

I listened sympathetically.

'She is a controlling, calculating, shrewd and strong-willed woman, used to getting her own way.'

Nalini launched into a tirade, stamping her feet like a spoilt child who'd just had a toy taken away.

'I didn't invite her into my life, she invited herself. She got involved with my Rampal, knowing he was my husband.

The bitch knew he had a wife and two children!'

'Is the bitch rich?' I asked this in a sincere way, but my tongue was firmly in my cheek.

'Very. She has millions in the bank and owns shares and stocks and at least ten large mortgage-free properties in Mumbai.'

'Why don't you sue her?'

'Sue her? On what grounds? What would I achieve?'

'Sue her for breaking up your marriage. Sue her for compensatory damages...for punitive damages. Her offence is called "alienation of affection".'

Nalini's eyes lit up. She was interested and, for the first time since I met her, she smiled.

'Alienation of affection is the estrangement by a third person of one spouse from the other.'

She listened intently.

'Here a woman can sue her husband's new partner for taking love and affection away from her.'

'Tell me more.'

'Can you prove that you and Rampal were living together as man and wife in the same house?'

'Yes.'

'In the same bedroom?'

'Yes.'

'And in the same bed?'

'Yes.'

'Can you prove there was still love in your marriage?'

'Yes.'

'Did the bitch cause Rampal to withhold his love from you?'

'Yes.'

'Did the bitch know that Rampal was married?'
'Yes.'
'Did the bitch know or should she have known that her actions would cause Rampal to lose affection for you?'
'Yes.'
'Do you believe the actions of the bitch were malicious?
'Yes.'
'And intentional?
'Yes'
'And do you believe her actions impacted your marriage with Rampal?'
'Yes.'
'Then you have a case against this woman. If you win, you could be awarded compensatory damages.'
'Meaning……?'
'Compensatory damages is money the bitch will have to pay you for your actual loss of Rampal's affection, companionship and support.'
'That would teach her a lesson.'
'You might also get punitive damages.'
'Meaning?'
'Damages to punish the bitch for acting willfully and maliciously, and for actively and deliberately setting out to seduce Rampal, knowing he was married.'
'That will pile more misery on her! More the merrier.'
'With a good and clever lawyer and a sympathetic judge, you might even win.'

She was encouraged by my words and by my smile.

'You talk like a lawyer, Radium. I am impressed.'
'You should slaughter the bitch! Go ahead, you'll make history.'

'I will, Radium!'

Later, when our boat reached the shore at the Gateway of India, she slipped me my envelope of cash and whispered that she'd let me know the outcome of the lawsuit. Her eyes were mercenary, and I contemplated charging her a legal consultation fee. But I had had an amusing time, and the fee was adequate for the performance I gave. There was no need to go too far. She might want to see me again.

Midnight's Children

After some three months, Nalini Rampal got in touch with me. She'd commenced legal proceedings against Preity Singhal for alienation of affection. The case was heard under a fast-track system by a High Court judge who awarded her damages equal to five million US dollars. It was a landmark judgement. The first of its kind in India.

'Have you actually received the money?'

'Yes, thank you.'

I couldn't believe it. I was pleased.

That same evening the news was all over the TV channels in India and in all the papers the next morning.

I had another satisfied client, but after my time with Julie, I didn't know if I could face another.

That same weekend, I had a phone call from Josephine, this time on a Sunday afternoon, when I was having one of my rare afternoon naps, a 'three-five'.

'I have become a mother! Please come home tomorrow evening.'

The next day, I went to Dadar with a gift for the newborn.

'This is my son,' said Josephine as she handed her lovely son to me.

'What have you named the boy?'

'Moses!'

'And this is my gift for your son.'
'A Moses basket!'
'For your Moses.'
'You should have brought two.'

At that very moment, I heard the sound of a baby crying in the next room. The next minute a man entered the lounge carrying another baby in his arms.

'And this is my husband Mark the proud father of my twin sons,' said Josephine, pointing to the man.

'Twin boys! How did you manage that?'

'You told me to eat a high-fat diet. I doubled it,' joked Josephine with a smile, firmly holding both her boys in her arms in a glorious show of maternal tenderness.

'Our children were born at the stroke of midnight,' interrupted an excited Mark.

'When the two hands of the clock meet and kiss,' added Josephine, wetting her lips in a suggestive manner.

'What is the name of Moses's brother?'

'Garfield—named after Gary Sobers.'

'How fantastic! I hope he will also be a great cricketer.'

'Thanks for the Moses basket,' said Josephine.

'And for your "Ten Commandments",' added Mark.

'Look after yourselves,' I said.

'We will.'

'And the twins.'

As I walked the streets home, I decided to give up the life of an escort. Nalini Rampal's victory and Josephine's happy ending seemed to close this chapter of my life. I would look for another, inevitably poorer paid, job. I told myself I had been lucky to get away with it for so long. Julie need never know a thing. I smiled to myself as I hailed a rickshaw, in preparation for my imminent cut in wages.

Paradise Lost

≈

THE NEXT time I saw Julie, I'd never seen her so angry in my life. She seemed possessed by an incomprehensible fury. She handed me a letter she'd received that morning. As I read it, my knuckles whitening on the paper, I realized that as with much in life, I had made my decision too late.

> *Dear Julie Madam,*
> *Did you know that your boyfriend, Rahul, is a gigolo who fucks Mumbai's rich women for money?*
> *A shameless sexual bumblebee, he calls himself Radium.*
> *If you do not believe this, just ask him.*
> *Yours,*
> *A well-wisher*

The letter was unsigned and undated. A photograph of me as Radium with one of my clients was enclosed.

'Is this true?'

'Well...' I stammered, my hands trembling.

'Is it true, Rahul?'

Her face was full of anguish and disappointment.

'Let me explain....'

I tried to explain, but she was in no mood to listen. She was shaking her head bitterly.

'But...that's you in the picture, isn't it?'

'Yes and no...'

There was a brief silence. Then she screamed at me. I'd never heard anyone's voice so loud. 'Get out of here and never come back!'

At 3 a.m., I was still lying on my bed, unable to sleep. It was worse than the night I spent in jail after the VAT raid in Dhiraj Desai's office. It was inevitable, really, that this should happen, but I never expected my cover to be blown like this. A *well-wisher*, whoever it was, I vowed to kill him, if ever we came face-to-face.

With a terrible sigh, I got up and sat at the table in front of the laptop I'd bought with the money I'd earned. I kept a list of my clients in it—their names and addresses, their likes and dislikes. Everything. Everything that had destroyed my life. I picked the machine up and smashed it on the floor.

Ratan had gone to Bilimora on some Parsee community business, and the only other resident in the house was Asif Khan. I heard a gentle knock on my door. Asif smiled at me when I opened it.

'Sorry...I heard a noise.' He looked past me into the room. 'Are you okay, brother?'

I saw he was staring at the broken laptop.

'It slipped. An accident.'

'Ahh...an accident. May I come in?'

I opened the door wide and stepped back to make way for him. Asif had a bottle of whisky in his hand, something he would not have had were PP Auntie still alive. He went to my cupboard and picked up two glasses. He poured the whisky.

'I don't drink.'

'I know you don't. But do have some. It looks like you

need to feel better. Yo-ho-ho!'

Asif sat and sipped whisky from one of the glasses. I sat opposite him and looked at the other glass. I was tempted to drink, but I did not. He smiled at me again and said nothing.

Finally, he spoke sadly. 'I have failed to break into Bollywood.'

'I'm sorry.'

'I am not educated. My biggest disadvantage is that I do not speak English. In Bollywood, you need to speak good English. I will have to try for a role in a Tamil or Telugu film.'

'I hope you succeed, Asif,' I said, unable to concentrate on what he was saying. All I could see was Julie's tearful face, ordering that I leave.

We didn't say much after that. Suddenly, I started feeling unwell. The room began spinning around and I was in tears. I felt as if I was going out of my mind. Asif tried to comfort me, but to no avail. He put me to bed and, thankfully, left the room.

The next morning, my head hurt and the laptop still lay smashed on the floor. The malicious letter was lying on the table. Julie had thrown it in my face as I'd left. I don't know if Asif read it or not. I didn't care. I felt wretched. I wished I'd killed Radium off earlier, and told Julie about him myself. Then she might have understood and forgiven me. My parents always told me honesty was the best policy, and I could see now they were right. I drank some water and read the letter again a few times. Then I went back to my bed and tried to sleep. I woke later in the day and drank more water and sat at my table and read the letter again.

I had a text message.

Hello, Lady Chatterjee's Lover! Having a fantastic time in

Bangkok. Wish you were here. Regards, Alice C.

For a moment, I had to think who it was from. With grim irony, I recalled it was from one of my rare English clients who had married an Asian man from Uganda named Lord (Roy) Chatterjee. For a while, she had taken to calling me Lady Chatterjee's lover. I let the phone drop, and then put my head in my hands and wept.

⌢

The following Monday, I was sitting drinking tea at the Imperial Irani restaurant, waiting for Irfan and David to arrive.

Once they confronted me, Irfan said, 'You look terrible, Rahul!'

I smiled weakly and nodded. 'Thanks.'

They joined me at the table and called the waiter. I showed them the letter.

'Some bastard has exposed you. Do you know who it is?'

Irfan was angry. David read the note. 'Whoever he is, he's a coward!'

Irfan placed his hand on one of my shoulders and David placed his hand on the other, just as they had when I first told them about the C3 Club.

'Did you not explain? Did you not apologize?'

I rolled my eyes.

'It was impossible to talk to her. She went on and on with her piercing protests, hurling scornful knives at me with her tongue and her eyes in rage!'

Julie should have shown me the yellow card. Instead it was the red.

'Have you tried to call her since?' asked David.

I nodded, hoping I wasn't going to break down again.

'Yes, but she doesn't answer. Only a week ago, we were very much in love. But now it's all over.'

'A week is a long time in politics. In love, it can be an eternity,' said Irfan just before we parted.

⸙

The next seven days were the longest and saddest of my life. Time just wouldn't pass. I was insanely depressed and completely heartbroken. Julie's screams still rang in my ears—just like the day Robin was attacked. The echoes followed me wherever I went. The distress etched into her face haunted me, and her tearful eyes stared back at me in my fitful dreams.

It was the most painful time, even more than when Tasmin had thrown me out, because then, at least, I had my parents to support me. In contrast, here in Mumbai, I was all alone.

Ratan noticed something wasn't right when he returned from Gujarat. However, as a polite Parsee, he asked no questions and treated me the same as he always did, as if nothing was wrong. I just sat on my bed in a morbid, catatonic mood, remembering Julie and the wonderful times we had together—how I met her, how I fell in love with her, and how I betrayed her!

I was sitting in the lounge one morning, watching television, but not really registering anything, thinking about what I could say in a letter to Julie, and wondering if she'd even reply. Lying on the coffee table were some old magazines which Ratan had meant to donate to the Parsee Library. There were issues of *Life* dating back to the early fifties, *Reader's Digest* and some film magazines. They were PP Auntie's collections of vintage magazines. I picked up a copy of the *Reader's*

Digest and casually flicked through it, not really interested. There was an article headed 'Laughter, The Best Medicine', about Mumbai's Laughter Clubs. I needed something to smile about, something to lift me out of my stupor, and the thing just lodged itself in my subconscious like some subliminal suggestion.

A couple of days later, I found myself at Chowpatty, where the local Laughter Club members gathered for their daily session. There were about forty of them, men and women. The youngest was around twenty and the oldest, about eighty.

'Would you like to join us?' one of them asked.

I was only looking, browsing really. But they dragged me in. The group leader was called Johnny Walker and he laughed at everything. I didn't find anything funny. He explained the rules of the club and the benefits of laughter, and I just went along with it. It was difficult at first, given the mood I was in, yet after a while, I started to lighten up. There was laughter all round, loud roaring laughter, and it was contagious. It was a kind of yoga, but involving self-triggered laughter. It brought in more oxygen to the body and the brain and had many benefits.

'So...laugh and you will start to forget all your problems!' smiled Johnny.

Johnny Walker wasn't his real name, of course, but here I was at Mumbai's Chowpatty beach, laughing and crying at the same time. There must have been something to it, because I felt better after it. It temporarily lifted the worst, if not all, of the heaviness from my soul.

When you reach for a star, you have a long way to fall. I had climbed a ladder and now a snake had brought me down. Some serpent had exposed me, and Julie had expelled me from the garden of her life. Banished me to hell. I had been thrown into the wilderness, where I was now wandering, not knowing for how long, or what would happen to me next.

My splendid world had been destroyed, and now I was lost.

⁓

Julie rejected all my efforts at reconciliation. My e-mails, text messages, telephone calls, flowers and chocolates all went unanswered, unopened, unappreciated. I went personally to her flat one Wednesday afternoon, which I knew was her half-day. When I rang the bell, she would not even open the door, having already seen me through the spy-hole. After a few more rings, she did open the door but only a few inches and stubbornly kept me out. I stood there like an errant ten-year old, squeezing my hands in anguish, begging for a chance to explain my transgression. She was just not interested. Her expressionless eyes, red-rimmed and inflamed from weeping, her swollen face, her greasy hair, spoke volumes.

'Just go away. Leave me alone,' she said as she firmly shut the door and disappeared into her flat with its curtained windows and trellised screens. Her voice betrayed her many sleepless nights.

She had emotionally distanced herself from me, her love for me having clearly melted away.

I left empty-handed. I had clearly disgraced myself forever in her eyes. I was shattered, like a mirror broken into a million pieces—so small that no image could be seen in them. Mirror dust! Julie's absence left a deep hole in my life. I was totally demoralized, and, over the next few days, I started to become somewhat suicidal. I started to eat like a glutton, six times a day. I even considered drinking. One thing was for certain—if

I didn't pull back, I would soon be as dead as her husband, Robin.

It was now two weeks since Julie had thrown me out. I missed Julie very badly—her fabulous smile, her soft body, her laughter, her smart clothes—and was torn between the magic of her memories and the torment of remembering her.

After a month of inner torture, I decided to write her a letter. I sat in front of my new laptop, trying to come up with words that would explain everything. But nothing sounded right. My bad luck persisted. My laptop screen just froze suddenly. Thwarted by an unresponsive laptop, I gave it a three-fingered salute by pressing 'control-alt-delete' keys on my keyboard, and started all over again.

It was my first letter to anyone in a long time. Sitting down to write felt strange in this age of texting and e-mails. But I had been good at composition in school, and I told myself I could do it. I just needed to concentrate and find the right words and keep it simple. I wrote to Julie, tracing my journey from Rahul to Radium, offering her my obsequious apologies in a repentant tone, imploring her to understand and forgive me.

'Yes, I was making love to the rich women of Mumbai. I won't attempt to deny it. "Radium gate" is now closed. Radium is dead. I killed him,' I wrote in my long letter. *'I killed him in my heart before you found out. The truth was, when I became Radium, I was desperate for money. I had hit rock-bottom. I had been working as a rat killer...'*

I posted it and waited for her reply. But it didn't come. I was devastated. Life became even more hellish. Radium was dead, but Rahul was still alive. Money wasn't a problem, I had plenty of that. But it was worthless without Julie. I prayed for divine intervention.

Then, one day, about a month later, a letter arrived, typed on blood-red notepaper. It was from Julie.

Rahul, or should I address you as Radium?

Thank you for your letter. I know all about the hardships you suffered when you first came to Mumbai. You told me and I was so sorry for you, just as you were sorry for me after Robin died. I was never going to have a relationship with another man. I thought I would never be able to find another man like Robin—as good as Robin. Then I met you and changed my mind. Now I wish I had not.

You asked me to "open my eyes". Well, Rahul or Radium, they have been now opened. Really opened. I allowed myself to be touched by someone who was making love to other women for money. I feel so dirty. So violated. So betrayed. How could you betray me like that—for your thirty pieces of silver? YOU JUDAS!

Love is earned. Not yearned. You did earn my love. Now you have lost it. Forever.

Right now, I would not let you touch me even to save me from drowning. No, sir.

I wish I could completely erase you from my memory, as if you were a bad dream. As far as this nonsense about you not being Radium is concerned—what fiction! More of your lies and deceit.

You say Radium is dead, that you killed him. I WISH YOU HAD KILLED YOURSELF INSTEAD. I WISH RAHUL WAS DEAD.

Goodbye, my paid philanderer.
Yours—never!
Julie Robin Singh

I read the scarlet letter with its shouty capitals several times. I went from gloom to more gloom, wrenching my hands. After a few days, I stood at the very spot where we had first kissed and burnt it. The pieces of carbonized paper were taken quickly by the sea breeze, and I watched them disappear into the empty sky.

The Guru

Now that Radium was dead and Julie gone, I had nothing to do all day but mope around PP Auntie's house and laugh idiotically with Johnny Walker and his friends. I did all the eye-contact stuff, and behaved like a little kid with the fake laughter, but it was the only thing I had, apart from the moping. Even Irfan and David couldn't help me. I just didn't want to talk to anyone except the Laughter Club people. And they weren't real. I went to Chowpatty in the mornings, where the sessions started with warm-up exercises, such as stretching and chanting and clapping and body movement. These helped break down inhibitions, and breathing exercises were used to prepare the lungs for laughter. Then came the laughter exercises, like acting and visualization and group interaction. We finished with twenty minutes of hysterical guffawing and then some smiling meditation—a short session of unstructured laughter; like an athlete cooling down after a work-out. For the others, it was always a powerful experience that led to an emotional catharsis and a feeling of release and joyfulness. I just pretended I was happy, not for Johnny Walker's benefit, but for my own. And I did feel some lightness afterwards, some relief. But it soon wore off and I was back to crying in the afternoons, and sleeping in the evenings, and watching TV all night.

My life, with its immersive events, had become quite

complex with several elements nuzzled inside each other like a Russian doll. I was thoroughly bored and was reminded of a client of Radium who had said, 'I have been bored for the last thirty years.'

Then my father e-mailed me a letter received at my London address from NR Bank, my one-time employer in London before they made me and twenty others redundant due to their mortgage losses. Now, two years later, NR Bank was getting back on its feet and recruiting again. They were offering me my job back. My parents called to see if I was interested.

'Why don't you come back to London and go back to your old job?' my mother asked tearfully. 'A bird in hand is worth two in the bush.'

My father was also on the open line.

'Let him make up his own mind, Patricia.'

'I'll think about it,' I said in a flat voice.

I noticed the call-waiting indicator on my mobile. It bleeped a few times then stopped. Then it sounded again. 'I've got to go, Mum...Dad...I'll let you know what I decide to do.'

As soon as I finished the call to London, the other call came through. It was from an unidentified number.

'Hi Rahul! Guess who!'

The caller was a lady. I recognized her voice immediately. With a strange serendipity, it was my ex-girlfriend.

'Tasmin? Are you in Mumbai?'

'Yes. Can we meet?'

After a moment of hesitation, we agreed to meet at the Gateway of India the following day.

When we met, she said: 'I'm sorry for the way I treated

you back in London. I was wrong and stupid. After we broke off, I began to realize what you really meant to me.'

I said nothing.

'I still love you, and I've come all the way to Mumbai to tell you that.'

'It's too late, Tasmin. I've moved on in life.'

'At least think about it.'

I wanted to tell her about Julie. That I'd found and fallen in love with someone else. But Julie was gone. Forever.

'I am staying at the New Moon Hotel at Khar. Let's have dinner tonight.'

'I'll call you.'

'Promise?'

'I promise.'

The next morning, as I was leaving the Chowpatty Laughter Club, I got a text message from Rekha Jones, asking me to call her. I'd already told her Radium was dead and she should stop calling me. But she didn't. She kept phoning with offers.

'I have a new client. She is really lovely. She will pay handsomely.'

'Radium's dead! How many times have I got to tell you?' I wanted to add that I felt the same way. 'Don't call this number again!'

'She only wants an escort for a party at the Taj.'

'Not interested!'

And I hung up. For the first time, I didn't know what to do. The pain of losing Julie was crushing me. I loved her and missed her very badly. Rekha wanted Radium. NR Bank wanted me. I still wanted to study filmmaking and become a film producer. My mother wanted me back in London. Tasmin wanted to kiss and make up. I wanted Julie back in my life.

I felt as if a thick sisal cord were being tied around my hands and legs, pulling me in all directions, left, right, up, down, the grip clasping more and more and shouting: *Decide! Decide! Decide!*

But, like Hamlet, I couldn't decide.

⌇

Back in London, I had been popular and had had dozens of friends. I thought they'd be happy to see me again and we could party and have a good time. Mumbai had become a prison, and the solitude was suffocating me. Everything began to irritate me and I couldn't think of one good reason to stay, except for a tiny spark of hope, deep down inside me, that Julie would come back. But I knew she wouldn't. I was like an animal in a cage, confused about who I was.

The clock in my room was ticking away faithfully. Tick, tock! Tick, tock! Tick, tock!

Time was flying as it has always done since Adam was a small boy. However, the sand in my life's hourglass had suddenly become mortar and was flowing lethargically down its neck.

I knew I had to shake myself out of this depression and this dangerous inertia. I had to do something. I thought about going down to the municipal corporation and trying to get back my job as a Night Rat Killer, out of desperation. It might take my mind off Julie for one solitary second.

I felt as if I had fallen off from a fast train in the middle of nowhere. I thought I must be having a nervous breakdown. Once a warrior, I had now become a worrier. The demon of loneliness overwhelmed me. I was wandering about in an emotional and logical wilderness. I was also letting personal routines go. Not shaving or showering, I was turning into a tramp. Dirty towels, smelly socks and underwear were strewn across the floor. Rubbish overflowed from the bins. Drawers were left open. Crockery and cutlery lay unwashed in the sink, newspapers and magazines cluttered the chairs and tables in my room, which was now in a state of violent disorder. I remembered a university friend who had committed suicide by drinking himself to death because he no longer had the will to live. He had stopped believing in life and decided to let go.

I started to wish I had a brother, a twin brother perhaps. Maybe he'd be here with me now and I wouldn't be so lonely. We could have come to Mumbai together to join Film International—me studying to be a producer and my twin brother to be a film director. We would've been a great team. After finishing our studies, we could have set up a partnership in filmmaking. Have our own studio; make great films just like Warner Brothers. We could have been 'Saxena Brothers', I thought. But I was the only child of my parents.

One morning, I realized it was too late to go to Chowpatty and the laughing people. The day was gloomy and overcast. It was a Tuesday, a day I never liked. Too many people died on Tuesdays—like the three thousand at the Trade Centre in New York in the 9/11 massacre. The Greeks and the Spanish considered Tuesday to be unlucky, so did I. There was always some bad news on Tuesday—especially Tuesday the 13th. Today was Tuesday the 13th. I knew it as soon as I woke up. But what could happen to me that hadn't already? I didn't care. Bring it on! Then my mother called me.

'Hello, Rahul.'

'What's the matter?'

'Nothing.'

I knew why she rang. I knew my father was standing next to her.

'Please, Mum...don't cry.'

'We miss you...'

'I know. Me too.'

'Are you coming home?'

'I don't know. I need more time.'

After putting the phone down, I realized I had suddenly developed a fear of death. I felt shadows of death coming towards me, clustering to snatch me from this world like some giant King Kong. My life had become like an onion—you peel more, you cry more.

With tears in my eyes, I went to Asif Khan's room. He wasn't there, but his bottle of whisky was. I poured a glassful. I sat on the bed looking at the whisky. Its golden colour spoke to me. A million thoughts went through my mind and it seemed as if I was being hypnotized by the spirit, by the light shining through it, distorting and dissembling and whispering to me like a lover. I didn't realize I was gripping the glass so hard until it shattered in my fist. I watched my blood drip. All the whisky spilt on the floor. I was saved from drinking it. I washed my hands and decided to get out of the house. Where could I go? Whom could I go and meet? Tasmin at her hotel? Yes, I had promised her, after all. I took a taxi there to avoid the Super-Dense Crush Load and it felt familiar, going to a hotel room to meet a woman.

When we finally met, Tasmin was glad to see me and we kissed. It was like she'd never been away. She asked me what happened to my bandaged hand and I told her it was nothing, an accident, a minor cut compared to the wound in my heart.

'Have you had time to consider...?'

'Yes.'

'And...?'

'I'm sorry.'

She turned away from me.

'I need more time to sort myself out.'

This cheered her up, but I also didn't want to give her false hope.

'I think you should go back to London. If I go back to London, then we might get together again. How long are you in Mumbai for?'

'Till tomorrow.'

'That soon?'

'Rahul...it's been ten days since we spoke.'

'Has it? That long?'

'I'd given up hope of you contacting me.'

'I'm sorry.'

We chatted for a while about London and the old days, and my mind was occupied for a while with other things, other thoughts. She asked me to stay the night and I thought about it. If Radium had still been alive, I would have. But in the end, we kissed goodbye and she closed the door softly after me.

It was getting dark and I forgot to ask the hotel to call me a taxi. I wandered about, not ready to go back to PP Auntie's house and begin another sleepless night. The streets looked familiar as I walked along and, by some coincidence, I realized I was suddenly in the backstreet by the hawala office.

The office was closed, and I remembered vividly the knife to my throat, and a blue handkerchief with small white circles.

Then I saw a man was entering the alley at the other end. He walked towards me. His face was in shadow. We approached each other in the centre of the backstreet and, as he passed me, he spoke.

'Hey, you bastard!'

I turned, but he did not. 'What did you say?'

He kept walking. I began to follow him. 'Hey! What did you say?'

The man turned the corner out of the alley and was lost from sight. I followed him and, as I turned the corner, I was struck a blow from a fist that was attached to a powerful arm. Before I lapsed into unconsciousness, I noticed the arm had a tattoo on it. It read: JULIE.

Sometime later, I regained consciousness in the darkness of the alley.

The money I was carrying had gone, and stray dogs were sniffing around me, to see if I was edible. At least they kept the rats away. Very slowly, I made my way back to Tasmin's hotel in Khar West and she let me in.

'Rahul! What happened?'

'Somebody hit me.'

'Oh no, let me call the police.'

'No! No police!'

Tasmin wanted me to stay the night with her, but even in the state I was, I felt I couldn't do that. So she got me a taxi and I went back to PP Auntie's house. The following day, she went back to London. She wasn't the kind of girl to ask twice.

My depression returned and my wandering in the wilderness continued. I went for long walks with only my thoughts for company. All kinds of thoughts—the good, the bad and the ugly. I'd had everything, and I'd lost everything. What should I do? I needed to find some enthusiasm for life again—some impetus to get up and go on. But the lethargy just wouldn't leave me and I was losing weight again, just like in the early days, when I lost my money and was starving. I still had money, plenty of it, but I was still starving. For love.

I tried to sleep but could not. Sleep was not a matter of joy anymore, but a time of worry and apprehension. I would wake up tired, fearful of the day ahead of me.

One day, at 4 p.m., I found myself all alone at home. Ratan was at work and Asif Khan had gone away to South India to try his luck in Tamil and Telugu films. Mahendra Jiwa, the NRI hater, had left a long time ago, after a stay of just a few days, and Ratan hadn't taken on any new lodgers since PP Auntie died. I was sitting in the lounge in front of the TV, changing channels, not really wanting to watch anything in particular, changing channel after channel out of sheer boredom. Every time I switched on the TV, the same thing came up, just like in a toaster. I found myself pausing at Channel 40. It was a religious channel called *Jai Ho*, and the programme showed a guru preaching. I normally didn't watch religious programmes on TV, but, on this occasion, I stopped switching the channels and kept on watching.

Within a few seconds, I found myself impressed by the guru. And within a few minutes, I was completely hypnotized by what I saw and heard. The guru spoke eloquently about joy, inner peace and humility.

...Humility will endow us with the awareness that we own nothing except the consequences of our own actions...

There was a footnote on the screen, saying that it was a live telecast from Goregaon, which I knew was a suburb in

Mumbai. The guru's name was Krishna but, out of respect, he was called Krishna Bhaiji. The footnote also said the live telecast from Goregaon would be shown every day for twelve days, which meant the guru could be heard in person at Goregaon Sports Complex during those twelve days.

I immediately googled Krishna Bhaiji.

I learnt that Krishna Bhaiji was forty-five years old, and had been born in Surat, in Gujarat. When he was a young boy, his parents migrated to Kenya and from there to London. At the age of fourteen, Krishna was blessed with divine revelation. He studied scriptures from all the major religions of the world and learnt devotional songs and music. To my surprise, he was fluent in English, Gujarati and Hindi. He loved literature and had read Shakespeare, Dickens and Milton. Apart from being familiar with the teachings and contents of the Hindu holy books like Gita and Ramayana and Mahabharata, he was also well versed in the Quran and the Bible and the scriptures of the Sikh, Buddhist and Jewish faiths.

What I saw and heard on the TV and what I read on the web so impressed me that I immediately decided that I would go to Goregaon the next day to listen to the guru in person.

∽

The afternoon developed into a very hot and humid evening. I took a cold shower, and then for a few good hours lay on my bed with the ceiling fan on to cool down. I don't remember when I dozed off to a sleep too deep even for nightmares.

I woke early the next day from my deep dreamless sleep, disturbed by Ratan's heavy footsteps on his way to the kitchen. He was an early riser. I cleaned up my room, which had been in a mess for months. I changed my bedsheet to a clean fresh white sheet free of wrinkles. I shaved, took a hot shower and put on a new white shirt and white trousers. My room was clean. I was clean. I remembered my mother who always insisted on cleanliness. Suddenly, I was feeling better.

I left home at noon to go to the Goregaon Sports Complex. The preaching wasn't due to begin till 3 p.m., but I wanted to make sure I got a good seat, right in the front. The event was free and seating was on the ground under a large marquee, with some chairs for senior citizens. Soon the place was full, with up to five thousand people—men, women, young and old, the disabled—all waiting for Guruji to arrive, with millions more watching on TV. The guru was referred to as Guruji. It denoted respect.

On the north side of the ground was a large stage which was decorated with flowers. Behind the Guruji's seat was a larger-than-life painting of Goddess Lakshmi, depicted as a beautiful woman of golden complexion with four hands, standing on a full-bloomed lotus and holding a lotus bud. On the Guruji's left were seated seven singers and musicians.

The Guruji arrived at 2:50 p.m. and the live telecast began exactly at 3 p.m. He started by singing a devotional song in praise of Goddess Lakshmi, and then went on to preach about the benefits of prayer and the need to do good deeds in life. He spoke in Hindi and, from time to time, also in English and Gujarati. This type of religious preaching is known as 'katha' or story-telling. Throughout his katha, which lasted for four hours without a break, he frequently sang devotional songs, with the seven singers and musicians seated near him on the stage joining in. The audience also joined in clapping hands in rhythm over their heads. Many stood up and danced.

The entire katha on that day was in praise of the Goddess

Lakshmi, who he referred to as 'Maa', meaning mother. The Guruji, through his devotional songs and his katha, explained that Lakshmi was not only the Goddess of wealth and prosperity but also of wisdom, courage, generosity, fortune and fertility, and one who would protect her devotees from all kinds of harm and misfortune.

'Just as your mother will listen to you, so will Lakshmi Maa, if you only ask for her help.'

Guruji said this again and again, in a variety of ways. He pointed to the huge painting of Lakshmi standing behind him.

'Maa is always standing by to help you. I am the one who is sitting, but Maa is not.'

At this point, everybody in the ground stood up and clapped for a good five minutes. The atmosphere was absolutely electrifying.

As I sat there on the ground and listened, my heart grew lighter and I felt some worth come back into my world. I couldn't explain it…it was like I was floating back up to the surface after being submerged under black water for so long. I could see the light approaching as I came up. Then, as I broke the surface, the warmth of the sun fell on my face and I knew I was still alive, not dead and buried in the darkness. I'd lost a personal love, a subjective and selfish love that I believed was mine by right. I now found a more all-encompassing love—strength of heart and mind.

'…Prayer is the exit button on your life's keyboard,' said the Guruji as he concluded his katha.

Clearly, the Guruji was hugely loved and revered by the audience. He came across as a spiritual giant, one who could transform lives of people by bringing the Lord's strength through his preaching into the hearts and minds of his listeners.

Great Expectations

That evening, I left the Goregaon Sports Complex enlightened and enlivened. I felt myself again; Rahul Saxena, not some sewer-rat who didn't deserve to live. Alright, I hadn't been honest with Julie, but I hadn't been totally dishonest either. Radium was born out of necessity and now he was dead. Life had to move on and I'd found the will to do so at last.

I reached home at around 10 p.m. and went straight to my room, where I sat on my bed for a few minutes, just thinking. A million thoughts went through my mind. The Guruji's impact on me had been profound indeed. He made me realize that maybe through prayer I might be able to solve my problems and regain Julie's love.

. . . Just as your mother will listen to you, so will Lakshmi Maa, if you only ask for her help.

These words of the Guru had a profound and compelling impact on me.

On the table in my room was that anonymous letter written to Julie, the one that had destroyed my life. In the last drawer was the prayer paper which the fakir at Haji Ali had given me. I swapped them over. I put the bastard's letter in the last drawer and the fakir's prayer paper on top of the table.

I read the one-line prayer. Then I read it again, and again, until I'd memorized it.

Then, I remembered what the fakir had said to me.

You can pray to any god or goddess using this recitation. The Lord will listen. Your prayers will be answered and your problems solved.

I decided to pray at four in the morning to Maa Lakshmi for help, using the fakir's prayer.

That night, I drank a glass of milk and went to sleep at midnight. I woke up at 4 a.m., wide-eyed and enthused with renewed energy, and sat cross-legged on my bed, with the lights in my room switched off and my eyes closed. I started to recite the fakir's prayer in my mind, praying to Goddess Lakshmi.

Concentration was difficult at first, almost impossible. I couldn't hold my mind steady. I tried to empty my head of all thoughts but my mind was running free and undisciplined, rebelling against the effort to get rid of its overcrowded itinerary. I persevered, trying to banish worldly images and regrets and hopes and fears. I tried to relax and to concentrate on my recitations, to withdraw my mind from everything external by using an energy that was internal—an energy I didn't know I had until I began to use it. Slowly, I made progress and increased my concentration. The room was in total darkness and there was complete silence. It was almost magical.

I recited the prayer in my mind. Every recitation brought me strength, more and more strength as I went along. My heart began to feel light. I began to sense the light of the Almighty. I decided to get up every day at four in the morning and recite the fakir's prayer ninety-nine times; then repeating the supplication several times over, making it a one-hour bandagi daily. It was a tranquil hour which brought me peace.

After praying every morning at 4 a.m. for twenty-one

days, I had a dream. I often have dreams. Our dreams are ours, personal, like our passports. There are no shared dreams. I mostly dream of crowded city centres with their hustle and bustle, bazaars, shopping malls, cinemas, skyscrapers, crazy traffic. Dreams are like movies to me. But this was different. Once again this was a city dream. In the dream, I was sitting cross-legged at a street corner in a busy bazaar in downtown Mumbai, cleaning and polishing people's shoes.

'Shoeshine, sir?'

I was calling to the passers-by and people were queuing up for my services. There were many boot-polish boys in Mumbai, working from railway stations, beaches, bazaars—and I was one of them in my dream. It was a Friday. I could see many Muslims walking towards a nearby mosque for prayer. Mumbai's sea of unmoving traffic was as chaotic as ever in the bazaar where I was sitting. A passing policeman saw me polishing people's shoes and just ignored me. He didn't push me away or ask me to pay him a bribe. My mind was focused on the pair of ladies blue shoes I was polishing. Suddenly, I heard a voice. It was a man's voice, a voice that was strange in a familiar way, and familiar in a strange way.

Go to Amritsar and polish shoes there. Your problems will be solved.

I looked up to see who the man was and saw the fakir of Haji Ali, who'd given me the prayer that I'd been reciting every morning.

My dream had been interrupted by a bleep on my mobile phone. It was a text message from my mum: *What have you decided?*

I went back to sleep after reading the text, and woke up again at 7 a.m. I remembered the dream and the fakir telling me to go to Amritsar to polish people's shoes. I didn't know what the dream meant. Where in Amritsar? Polish shoes? How would that solve my problems? I decided to go to Haji Ali and try and meet the fakir in person. He was there most days, but not on that day. I was told he'd gone to Ajmer. No one knew how to contact him or when he would be coming back.

The next day, I met up with Irfan and David at Imperial Irani Restaurant and told them about my dream.

'This fakir has told me to go to Amritsar and polish shoes! I'm confused. I don't know what he meant,' I said nervously as my tea cup clattered on its saucer.

Irfan, who was looking at David, suddenly smiled as if he had just received a text message in his brain.

'He is telling you to go to the Golden Temple of Amritsar and polish the shoes of the devotees and worshippers who come to pray there.'

Irfan was confident he knew the meaning of the dream. David wasn't normally as susceptible to dreams as Irfan, but he could see something in it as well.

'Yes, that's it! He's telling you to do seva at the Golden Temple.'

'Seva is a selfless and voluntary service performed without any thought of reward or personal benefit,' explained Irfan.

'There is a tradition amongst Sikhs of performing seva at the Golden Temple in Amritsar, but non-Sikhs could also take part if they wanted to. The person performing such a service was called a sevadar,' continued David.

'What kind of seva do people do?' I asked eagerly.

'Scrubbing the temple floor, cooking food, helping in the kitchen, washing dishes, polishing shoes, looking after the sick and the aged...'

'For no reward…' interrupted David.

I mulled over this for a moment. Then Irfan spoke.

'Seva at the Golden Temple will give you spiritual fulfilment and bring you tranquility and serenity. It is also considered a form of worship. Although you do seva without any expectation of reward, the Almighty does reward the sevadars in many ways.'

In a matter of minutes, he and David convinced me to go to Amritsar for a while as a sevadar.

I decided that my seva at the Golden Temple would be completely selfless, without expectation of any reward. I genuinely began to believe that my problems would be solved if I polished pilgrims' shoes. I told no one else about going to Amritsar, not even my parents or Ratan. I wanted to do my seva discreetly so that its selfless nature wouldn't be compromised. I suddenly started to feel better. I no longer felt confused. I had a kind of answer within me at last—an answer to something, even if I didn't know what that something was. I also decided against going back to London to take up my old job with NR Bank. I'd keep to my plan of studying filmmaking at Film International. I was still in love with Julie, so Tasmin wasn't an option. I had enough money to achieve my original objectives, and that's all I needed at the moment. Later that day, I called London and told my parents what I'd decided.

'I'll be joining Film International when their new term starts.'

My mother was disappointed. She was missing me and hoping I'd come back. But they both supported my decision to stay on in Mumbai.

The next day, I applied for a new mobile number. This took about a week. I gave my new number only to my parents, Irfan, David and Ratan—nobody else. Before my old number was cancelled, I spoke to Rekha and told her for the last time that Radium was definitely dead. She was disappointed, but finally accepted it. I also spoke to Tasmin in London and told her that I was in love with another girl and she shouldn't wait for me.

With my telephone number changed, there was now no chance of Rekha or Tasmin or any of Radium's clients being able to contact me, and I'd given up on ever hearing from Julie again as well. I prepaid six months' rent to Ratan instead of the normal one month and asked him to keep my room available for me until I came back. He never once asked me where I was going or why or for how long.

I left Mumbai by train for Amritsar, ten days after my fateful dream. Irfan and David came to see me off at Mumbai Central Station. My train, the Golden Temple Mail, left exactly at 9:25 p.m. It was a thirty-two-hour journey, with the train making thirty-one stops.

So, there I was, the son of a Hindu father and an English Christian mother, inspired by a Muslim fakir and a Hindu guru, now a devotee of Maa Lakshmi, travelling to Amritsar to do seva in a Sikh temple. I was quite at ease with the ecumenical nature of my life. I'd prayed in a Hindu temple, a Christian church, the Muslim Dargah of Haji Ali, and lately at 4 a.m. sitting on my bed in my room. I'd never visited or prayed at a Sikh temple, even though Julie was a Sikh, and I was now looking forward to that experience.

My spiritual compass was taking me to Amritsar. The past few months in Mumbai were a monumental torture. I was finally leaving my ground zero with great expectations and heading to the Golden Temple to do seva.

⌢

The Golden Temple Mail was one of the oldest running train routes in India. The fares, by European standards, were quite cheap. But I decided not to travel first class even though I could easily afford it. I wanted a proper Indian travel experience by ordinary class for it to be memorable—to be part of the hustle and bustle of the Indian railway stations, with the tea sellers crying *chai, chai garam, chai*, and the sights and sounds and smells all around me. At the back of my mind was, however, the patchy safety record of the Indian railways. My life had been derailed and I hoped that my train too should not derail. Only two days previously a train had derailed on its way to Indore due to derelict, decaying tracks, killing 139 people and injuring over 200. 'Don't worry. Leave it to the Lord!' I said bravely to myself as I boarded my train with mixed emotions.

I did get a seat in a reserved compartment, and, on the way to it, I passed by some unreserved carriages. I was disturbed by what I saw. The unreserved compartments had wooden seats and were hugely overcrowded. Many people were sitting or sleeping on the ground, some close to, or even inside, the toilets. People and luggage were scattered everywhere, with no place to walk or even stand. There was a foul smell of perspiration, urine and alcohol everywhere. The passengers had to wait in a queue for four hours just to get in, and some would now have to stand all the way.

My reserved compartment was a six-berth, and I got a seat next to the window which had no glazing, just iron bars.

The other five people in my compartment became so familiar they acted like they were my family in no time. They wanted to know everything about me—where was I from, my age, my income and whether I was married and all about my life in London. I tried to sleep as much as I could, but with the train stopping every hour or so, it was impossible. I was also disturbed regularly by an elderly Gujarati couple who farted, snored and burped almost non-stop as the train rattled its way through the night.

I awoke from a broken slumber when the train stopped. It was 4:10 a.m. and the station was Godhra Junction. Everyone in my compartment started to talk about the Godhra train burning incident of 2002. One of the passengers in my compartment, Raziya Begum, a Muslim lady in her sixties travelling to New Delhi, said her husband and three adult sons had been slaughtered by a revenge-seeking mob in the riots that followed.

'Many got away with murder,' said Raziya Begum, sobbing inconsolably.

My first night of travel ended when we reached Ratlam Junction at 7:05 a.m. The overnight journey had been quite an experience for me. There was going to be one more night to go, with the train scheduled to reach Amritsar the next day at 5:40 a.m.

Throughout the day, I sat looking out at the passing countryside, with my thoughts wandering in and out through the iron bars of the open window. It was great to have nothing to do. My mind was completely at rest. Not for me now the tension, torment and constant mad traffic of Mumbai—just the flat landscape passing on the right and the sunlit hills on the left.

My thoughts kept returning to past events in my life—London, my parents, friends at school and university, my life in Mumbai…I thought about Julie, whom I knew I still loved. Every time I switched on my mobile phone, her photograph was there—the one where she was standing against the background of Haji Ali, taken by me on the day I first met the fakir.

Whenever the train stopped, the vendors ran up and down the platform selling tea, fruit, bread snacks, household goods. There were people everywhere—men, women, children, passengers with tickets and some without. And the public-address system crackled out announcements of train arrivals and departures. Every station was like a bazaar, even in the early hours of the morning.

In my compartment there was also a Rajasthani man in his fifties who wore a turban, an angarkha and a dhoti. He kept staring at me continuously, and, if I'd only just arrived in India, I'd have been annoyed. But I knew by now that many people in India loved to stare. Almost everyone did it—in the bazaars, on the trains and in the shops. They did it because they were curious to know whether you were a Gujarati, a Parsee, a Maharashtrian or a Punjabi. They wondered where they might know you from. They could even come up to you and tell you how you resembled someone they knew. Often, they would start a conversation with: 'I am sure I know you, but cannot remember exactly where we have met before.'

They wanted to know everything about you—your name and marital status and how many children you had, your occupation, which car you drove. They would often ask for your phone number and you'd no doubt get a call from them within a couple of days.

The flatulent couple with their expulsive noises and the Rajasthani man got off at Kota Junction. I was very glad. Three new passengers joined us there, one was an American tourist and the other two were university students, Arun and Badal, returning to Delhi after a research assignment.

They both immediately became members of the compartment's 'family'.

But as they talked, I just gazed out through the bars, thinking about what awaited me in Amritsar.

Four eunuchs wearing cheap make-up and lipstick and dressed in ill-fitting ladies' clothes entered our compartment at Mathura Junction, where the train stopped for five minutes. They were clapping and singing a Bollywood film song and begging. One of them was dancing. They appeared jovial on the outside, but I could see the sadness behind their laughs and smiles. We all gave them some money and they quickly left to go to the next compartment.

'They are called "hijras" and we have about a million of them in India.'

Raziya Begum decided to comment on the eunuchs after they left.

'Apart from begging, the hijras, known as India's "third sex", earn their living by showing up uninvited at weddings, birth celebrations and housewarmings to bless the event by singing and dancing.'

I nodded politely.

Raziya Begum continued, 'Some NGOs are working to improve the life of the hijras who are now standing in elections and winning.'

The day-time journey ended when the train reached New Delhi. All the other members of my compartment 'family' got off there and, for a short while, I was left alone. But new passengers soon joined me. They were all NRI Sikh tourists from Canada travelling to Amritsar on a pilgrimage to the Golden Temple. They formed the new compartment 'family' in no time.

They were all called Singh, namely, Arjun Singh, Balbir Singh, Charan Singh, Diler Singh and Ekam Singh. I wondered vainly if any of them were related to Robin Singh or knew Julie Singh.

The second night of my journey was quite peaceful. I slept well. But since it was dark, I missed the views of the lush countryside of Punjab, of which I'd heard so much.

The Golden Temple Mail finally reached its destination on time at 5:40 a.m., after two days and two nights. When I came out of the station, I was delighted to see a murmuration of starlings in the sky and felt as if they had come to welcome me to Amritsar.

Heaven on Earth

~

The city of Amritsar had already woken up. Roadside food stalls and shops were getting ready for the day's business. People were coming out onto the streets. Traffic was building up fast.

I took a rickshaw from the station. The traffic was almost as chaotic as Mumbai. We made our way through shoals of rickshaws, cars, trucks, carts, pedestrians and animals, and finally reached the Golden Temple only after my driver skilfully avoided at least a dozen potential collisions.

The Canadian NRI Sikhs on the train had told me about a free dormitory that had beds set up next to each other as well as shared bathrooms. I headed straight there. I had already had breakfast on the train so, after showering at the dormitory, I went to the Golden Temple where hundreds of people had already gathered.

What I saw was, indeed, out of this world. It was a beautiful temple, with decorated gilt domes and towers, seeming to float calmly in the middle of a vast, shining, sparkling square lake, with a magnificent marble walkway at its perimeter.

A Sikh man in his twenties asked me as I approached the temple complex.

'Are you from America?'

'From England.'

'I have been to London, where I have an uncle living in Southall.'

His name was Dilip Singh and I wondered if every Sikh was called Singh.

He offered to take me around the Golden Temple complex.

'Cover your head, take off your shoes, wash your feet and step into heaven on earth.'

The beautiful white marble floor glowed white-hot in the sun on a scorching day. Hundreds of bare-foot pilgrims walked around on a makeshift path of wet sackcloth. I saw pilgrims circling the courtyard around the lake in a clockwise direction, whilst some sat in cross-legged reverence by the lake, with others just wandering around, clearly awestruck. Some dipped hands and faces, and even whole bodies, in the lake.

'Sikhs from all over the world come here,' said Dilip Singh as we walked around.

He took me on a guided tour of the magnificent interiors, decorated with fresco work and gemstones.

I was awestruck. 'What I like most is the calm and serene atmosphere of the temple,' I told Dilip Singh. In my mind, I was comparing the scene with the noisy madness of Mumbai.

'Can you hear Sikh music and prayers everywhere?' asked Dilip Singh as two of his friends joined us.

One of the boys, Harry Singh, wanted to go to England, and knew what he thought was a lot about London. The other one was called Vikram Singh, a big, rotund boy who laughed a lot and showed off his gleaming white teeth.

'We come here several times a week to help out.'

Inside the temple complex, Dilip Singh and his friends showed me various shrines and memorial plaques.

'There are four entrances to the temple and three holy trees outside.'

We walked towards the main temple, accessed by a sixty-metre marble causeway flanked by nine gilded lamps on either side.

'This is *Adi Granth*,' whispered Dilip Singh, pointing to the holy scripture of Sikhism installed in the main temple under a jewelled canopy.

'I love the music,' I whispered back as I watched the musicians playing and a choir singing reverently in front of it.

Apart from the music and singing, silence prevailed. A sacred, sublime silence that was almost transcendental in its spirituality. I felt totally and utterly at peace for the first time since those golden days when I was in love with Julie Singh and she with me.

It was almost lunchtime, and I suddenly realized how hungry I was. Dilip Singh and his friends took me to the communal canteen, the Guru ka Langar. I was pleasantly amazed at the scene I saw there with orders being shouted around, steel dinner plates and bowls clanging around, water splashing, and people from all over India and abroad happily engaged in a raucous cacophony of talk in a kaleidoscope of Indian and foreign languages.

'These vast kitchens churn out free dal and thousands of chapattis every day for more than twenty thousand pilgrims,' said Dilip Singh as we joined the long queue for a free meal.

On the way in, we were each handed a steel plate and bowl and directed to take a cross-legged place on the floor in a long row of fellow eaters. Meals were served by the volunteers. It was all so amazingly fast and frantic it easily put even the concept of 'fast food' to shame.

Dilip Singh was impressed when he heard I'd come to Amritsar to do seva at the Golden Temple.

'There is a lot you can do. Scrub the floors, work in the kitchens, cook, serve food, wash dishes, clean toilets.'

'I would like to polish shoes!' I announced, suddenly remembering my dream.

'We will help you.'

I looked forward to coming back the next day to start my seva.

⌒

My first night in the free dormitory was quite unexpectedly comfortable. I went to bed early. I was exhausted after the previous two nights on the train, so I fell asleep almost immediately.

I automatically woke up at 4 a.m., and, sitting cross-legged on my bunk, closed my eyes and meditated for one hour. I prayed to Goddess Lakshmi, reciting the fakir's prayer in my mind. Then I went back to sleep. Just before dawn, I dreamt I was walking at midnight towards the main gate of the Golden Temple, along with hundreds of other pilgrims. Someone tapped me on the shoulder. I stopped and looked back. It was the fakir from Haji Ali standing with a lighted candle in his right hand, held in a silver-chamber candlestick. He smiled at me, came close and whispered in my left ear.

'Be brave, my son! Clean and polish pilgrims' shoes at the Golden Temple for forty days and do other acts of seva as well. Your problems will surely be solved.'

I woke up again at 7 a.m., when the alarm clock of the man in the bunk on my left went off. It was an old-fashioned, wind-up, spring-driven clock with two bells. The noise was loud enough to wake the whole dormitory. But not him! It took him one full minute to hear it and switch it off.

Later that morning, I went to the local bazaar and bought shoe-cleaning and polishing materials, including black, brown, and neutral polish, four pieces of cloth, several wooden handled brushes, three dusters, a sponge and a rucksack to carry it all.

Dilip Singh was waiting for me when I got to the Golden Temple. After saying a short prayer inside the temple, we both went down to the northern gateway at the outer perimeter of the temple complex where he arranged for me to be given some space to sit and do my seva. Very soon, the pilgrims were queuing up to leave their shoes with me to be polished. My seva had started! I was really excited. I first cleaned and dried the shoes with a cloth and then applied the polish, using a brush to spread it evenly, and then rubbed in the polish vigorously. I then buffed the shoes with a dry cloth to get a good shine. The results were fantastic. I had never done this before, but I soon became an expert shoeshine boy and my speed increased with practice. I catered for all kinds of shoes—black, brown, and white shoes, men's shoes and women's, children's shoes, new shoes and old, worn shoes and even some torn shoes!

I started to keep a count of the days. For the first two days, I only polished shoes. But on the third day I started doing other stuff as well. Dilip Singh organized a standing sign with a top-loading poster frame and a square piece of white cardboard, on which was written an announcement in English, Punjabi and Hindi.

'You may leave your shoes here to be cleaned and polished.'

This was most helpful, as from time to time I was going to be away from the northern gateway doing other acts of seva.

On the third day, I moved out of the free dormitory to a small bedsit-type room, which I rented from Dilip Singh's aunt. It was on top of a grocery store in the middle of a bazaar, not far from the Golden Temple. When she heard I was doing full-time seva at the Golden Temple, she refused to accept any rent from me.

'Giving free accommodation to a sevadar like you will be counted as my seva in the kingdom of God.'

But I insisted she take the money, as I didn't want anything to interfere with the selflessness of my seva or have anything or anyone else contribute. The fakir had told me this would solve my problems and I wasn't taking any chances. I gave her two months' rent upfront, which she finally accepted.

'I will buy some sugar with this money and donate it to the Golden Temple as my seva.'

In the end, we were both happy.

I liked my room. It was spacious, with two large windows that allowed plenty of sunshine in. Not that it mattered much as I was going to be away from early morning to late evening. A small sofa, a bed, a table, two chairs and a small wardrobe comprised the room's basic furniture.

There were no rats in the room. I did, however, see a lizard on the wall on the first night, staring at me in a steadfast manner, which I didn't mind as I had now got used to being stared at after coming to India.

My other sevadar colleagues were very impressed with me, especially when they realized I was a non-Sikh, and that too from England. In India, NRIs from the West were often regarded as snobbish and aloof. But not me!

I started to grow a beard and stopped trimming my hair.

Dilip Singh laughed at my appearance when he caught

up with me. 'Hello, Noah! You look like Ryan Gosling in the film *The Notebook*.'

I found his comment quite flattering.

When I wasn't doing seva, I sometimes sat cross-legged on the floor of the temple to meditate and pray. I had no problem with praying in a Sikh Temple—after all, I'd prayed in temples and at Haji Ali and at a church in London with my mother. For me, there was only one God and it was to that one universal Lord I was praying.

I took my seva very seriously, working energetically from 9 a.m. to 5 p.m., seven days a week. The days rolled by. There was never a dull moment. And all the while, memories of Julie were receding into the distance. For this, I was both grateful and a little sad.

✧

As part of my seva at the Golden Temple, I tried my hand at washing-up one day. I got to work in elbow-deep soapy water in rectangular tubs the length of 16-seater dining tables, scrubbing dishes along with other men and women all eagerly performing their selfless service. Stacks of metal plates, bowls, cups, spoons and tumblers were continuously being thrown in the water, drenching our faces. No one complained. Everyone was busy grabbing items from underwater in a friendly competition to outperform each other and take away maximum sacrament. We scrubbed, rinsed and laughed whilst cleaning the dishes and our souls. It was hot, noisy and crowded, and I was drenched with sweat and spattered with dal and rice, but when I finished a couple of hours later, I felt out of this world.

Even after twenty-one days of seva—more than half the

time period given to me by the fakir in my second dream—I still looked forward, every morning, to going to the Golden Temple. I was always there at 9 a.m. sharp, going first to the main prayer hall of the temple to say a short prayer, and then coming straight back to the northern gateway. Some shoes would already be there, waiting for me to clean and polish them. I had no qualms about handling other people's shoes. After all, my ancestors were cobblers so shoes were part of my heritage.

One day, I saw an old man with a wooden leg, tall and broad-shouldered, sitting peacefully on the floor on the marble walkway with his crutch next to him. I spoke to him, in case he was feeling unwell.

'Are you ok?'

'Yes. Thank you.'

His name was Dara Singh, and he wore a loosely tied blue turban and came to the temple every single day. He told me he was in his eighties and had himself done many years of seva.

I found the old man quite inspirational and very active for his age. He laughed when I told him that.

'When I was eighty-one, I told everyone I was eighteen. When I was eighty-two, I told everyone I was twenty-eight. When I was eighty-three, I told everyone I was thirty-eight. When I was eighty-four...

'How old are you now?' I interrupted.

'Eighty-eight.'

'So, next year you'll be ninety-eight.'

'There will be no next year.'

As the days went by, Dara Singh grew increasingly frail. 'Age gives us wisdom, but the same age debilitates our faculties and prepares us for our death,' said a sad Dara Singh. 'I hope I die at the Golden Temple in the presence of the Lord.'

Two days later, his wish was granted. He died inside the main prayer hall of the Golden Temple in peaceful prayer and meditation. All the sevadars were very sad. We missed him greatly. But he would have told us not to mourn, not to cry. He would have said that death is universal. Everyone has to die. There are no exceptions.

One day, a pilgrim wasn't happy with the shine on his shoes, and criticized me for it. I wasn't hurt. I simply polished his shoes again. He was humbled by my response.

'I thought you would remind me that you were not getting paid for cleaning people's shoes and that you didn't have to listen to my nonsense.'

I only smiled, thinking of Dara Singh.

The man apologized for his outburst and walked away.

Dilip Singh and his two friends had become very good friends of mine. We had a lot of fun together in between doing our seva. They had the habit of all talking at once, none hearing the other. Harry Singh always wanted to talk about London, and Vikram Singh was always laughing about something or other. When he wasn't laughing, he was eating.

'I would like to lose weight, but I just can't stop eating burgers.'

Burger King? or Burger Singh? What shall I call him? I wondered.

'I'll tell you how to lose weight.'

'How?'

'Eat breakfast like a king, lunch like a prince and dinner like a pauper.'

He didn't know I was quoting Adelle Davis, the American nutrition expert.

'What about the other way round? I get hungrier as the day goes on!'

Dilip Singh complained that Viki could not keep anything confidential.

'We always call him VikiLeaks.'

'I am really Vikipedia,' replied Vikram Singh with a laugh.

Our conversations were like that—haphazard, funny, flitting, like a butterfly, between subjects, never all that serious and very polite.

Harry Singh thought he knew everything about London.

'I know all about Oxford Street, Regent Street, Trafalgar Square, Selfridges, Harrods, Lord's, Wembley Football Stadium, Victoria and Albert Museum, the Ismaili Centre, Wimbledon, Westminster Abbey, Buckingham Palace, Serpentine Lake, Holborn…'

He pronounced 'Holborn' as 'Hol Born'.

'The 'l' is silent in Holborn,' I corrected him.

'How can an 'l' be silent?'

'It just is.'

Viki Singh, who was slow to anger and quick to laugh, started to laugh uncontrollably as usual. How he laughed! He guffawed until his eyes were wet and red.

Harry Singh also knew how to plan a journey on the London Underground. He practised this constantly.

'When I go to London I will stay at the Indian YMCA. I will take Piccadilly Line from Heathrow Terminal three and then Northern Line from Leicester Square to Warren Street and then walk to Fitzroy Square.'

He also knew the queen and her ancestors. 'I love the

abdication speech of King Edward VIII.'

And he could quote from it: '...*you must believe me when I tell you that I have found it impossible to carry the heavy burden of responsibility and to discharge my duties as King as I would wish to do without the help and support of the woman I love...*'

After this he smiled, waiting to be congratulated on his excellent memory. He even had opinions on matters of state.

'I think the queen should abdicate and make way for Prince William to become the next King of England.'

'But what about Prince Charles?' I asked.

'I think Charles should give the throne a miss when the queen abdicates and let his son William become king. I think Will fits the bill more.'

Harry's father, who like many Indians never said anything without first raising his voice, also knew a lot about Britain. I loved talking to him but dreaded his bone-crushing handshake.

It was the twenty-fifth day of my seva. Fifteen more to go. I wondered what the significance of the number forty was. There must have been some significance. I mean, the fakir wouldn't have mentioned it otherwise.

So, I went to the local library in Amritsar to do some research. It was a well-stocked place, much better than anything I'd visited in Mumbai. There were several books relevant to my research, three of which were particularly useful. *Romance of Forty*, *Forty Facts* and *Faith and Forty*. There were other books which weren't so relevant, like *Alibaba and Forty Thieves* and *Forty Alibabas and One Thief* and *Naughty at Forty* and *Forty Carrots* and so on. I spent a good two hours in the library and discovered a few very interesting facts.

Apparently, the number forty was significant in Jewish, Christian, Islamic and Hindu traditions. In Hinduism,

Hanuman Chalisa, a devotional song based on Hanuman, an ardent devotee of Lord Rama, had forty couplets; rain fell for forty days and forty nights during the Flood; Moses was with God on Mount Sinai for forty days and forty nights; Jesus fasted for forty days and nights in the desert; Jesus was tempted by the devil for forty days; Jesus remained on Earth for forty days after resurrection; Mohammed was forty years old when he first received the revelation delivered by the archangel Jibrail; the Quran set the age of responsibility at forty, that being the age when humans reached full maturity; the Israelites spent forty years in the wilderness.

There were also some references which were non-theological. Forty years represented the time it took for a new generation to rise; it was believed by many that ghosts of the dead linger at the site of their death for forty days; forty days of mourning after a bereavement was common in some communities; offenders were whipped forty times in some civilizations; women were pregnant for forty weeks; in science, 'minus forty' was the temperature at which the Fahrenheit and Celsius scales corresponded; forty was often used in medieval literature—forty winks; a fool at forty was a fool forever.

Oh yes, forty was a very significant number indeed. And I remembered that it was on Channel 40, the *Jai Ho* Channel, where I first saw and heard Guru Krishna Bhaiji, whose katha inspired me to pray to Goddess Lakshmi. So, there was obviously some really good reason for me to do seva for forty days.

Dilip Singh was a science graduate and loved technology. One day, he suggested he should write about me and put my picture on Facebook—and maybe a short video on YouTube, showing me polishing shoes at the Golden Temple. I didn't like this idea very much, as my seva was supposed to be selfless and not for publicity purposes. It was alright for Bollywood stars to come here, do some seva and seek publicity. I wanted to do my seva discreetly.

'There is no harm in a little bit of publicity if it can encourage others to do seva.'

Dilip had great persuasive skills, and, after a day or two of his constant nagging, I capitulated. The next day, he brought a camera and a camcorder and took photographs and shot a short video film, showing me cleaning and polishing the shoes. Later that afternoon, he showed me a small write-up which he wanted to post on Facebook. This is how it read:

Hi friends,
This is Dilip Singh from Amritsar!
I would like to share with you the story of Rahul Saxena. Rahul is an NRI boy from England who has recently become a great friend of mine. Rahul is a non-Sikh, the son of a Hindu father and an English Christian mother. He is currently doing forty days of seva at the Golden Temple, cleaning and polishing pilgrims' shoes and also doing other acts of seva.
Rahul says he was inspired by a Muslim fakir whom he met some months back at Mumbai's Haji Ali. The fakir then came twice in Rahul's dreams and told him to go to Amritsar and do forty days of seva at the Golden Temple. Here are some great photos of Rahul in action. You can also see him on YouTube.
Watch this space for daily updates on Rahul's renaissance!

I asked Dilip to remove the bit about the fakir.

'Rahul, it will be good for interfaith dialogue and understanding. The idea of a Hindu boy with an English Christian mother being inspired by a Muslim fakir to do seva in a Sikh temple is very romantic. It will inspire many others to come and do seva as well.'

When he put it like that, how could I object? He went ahead and put me up on Facebook and YouTube. He also set up a Twitter account and started tweeting about my seva. All tweets in 140 character messages of course. That number 40 again, in one form or the other! Five days later he told me his friends had forwarded my details and photos to their friends who in turn had forwarded them to others via different social media platforms. The YouTube video had more than four hundred thousand hits.

'You are already a celebrity! Many young people will follow your example and come to the Golden Temple to do seva. Their seva will be counted as part of your seva and you will surely benefit also.'

Although I'd originally come to the Golden Temple in the hope that my problems might be solved, I'd since forgotten about any reward. The subject had disappeared in the object. From time to time Dilip and his friends would refer pilgrims who needed information or guidance on various matters. I was only too pleased to help with whatever little knowledge I had. Sometimes pilgrims consulted me on their personal problems.

I was once approached by a young pilgrim, a beardless Sikh with a haircut, who had problems with his wife.

'We always quarrel. I have left my wife. I want a divorce.'

'I would strongly suggest you go back to your wife with flowers and apologize to her. Try and reconcile with her. Try and see her point of view.'

A week later he came back to the Golden Temple sporting a beard and wearing a green turban. His wife was with him.

'I had deviated from my Sikh traditions and my wife. Now we are back together. Thank you.'

'Yours is a seva with time and knowledge,' said Dilip Singh.

'It's a *nazrana*,' said Harry Singh.

'*Nazrana*?' I asked.

'An offering.'

'Yes. TKN,' said Dilip Singh.

'TKN?' I asked. I was confused.

'A time and knowledge *nazrana* to the Lord and his children,' added Viki Singh who, for once, was talking seriously without laughing.

As I progressed through my forty days of TKN at the Golden Temple, I felt the presence of the Almighty Lord in me and around me, in this glorious place of pilgrimage—a true heaven on earth.

The Last Day

On my last day, I got up at four in the morning as usual, and sat cross-legged on my bunk with my eyes closed and the lights switched off. I meditated and prayed, reciting my bandagi in my mind. Maa Lakshmi was really looking after me. This 4 a.m. bandagi had become an integral part of my life and I intended to continue with it for as long as I lived. I was at the Golden Temple at 9 a.m. sharp. Dilip and his friends were waiting for me. He had posted a final update on Facebook.

> *Hi friends,*
> *This is Dilip Singh from Amritsar!*
> *Today is the 40th and last day of my friend Rahul Saxena's seva at the Golden Temple.*
> *Here are some great photos of Rahul in action, taken yesterday.*
> *Rahul has become extremely popular with many regular sevadars at the Golden Temple and will be badly missed after today.*
> *We wish him all the best.*

When I arrived, Dilip greeted me warmly. 'We will all miss you from tomorrow, Rahul.'

'I'll miss you all too. I'll miss the Golden Temple. I'll

miss the peace and tranquility that I attained here. I'll miss the seva!'

My three friends were all emotionally charged. We were both happy and sad. They were gossiping non-stop, all talking at the same time and laughing and roaring with jollity. I had to tell them to stop their ceaseless chatter and get back to work immediately.

'Work No Words,' I told them quoting an interesting phrase I had come across on the internet when doing research about seva and voluntary services the day before I travelled to Amritsar.

I spent most of the morning helping in the temple's kitchen, chopping onions, cutting potatoes, peeling garlic and washing dishes. At 1 p.m., I returned to the northern gateway to clean and polish the pilgrims' shoes. There were at least thirty pairs of shoes waiting for me. I sat down cross-legged on the floor and started to work. Then I noticed something that looked very familiar. A pair of ladies' shoes. The cobbler in me began to assess them—blue shoes, with a slingback and peep-toe design, lower wedge heel and suede upper and leather lining. They had a cork base with a heel height of around seven centimetres...I'd seen those shoes before. They were Julie's shoes! Her favourite shoes, the ones she'd worn so many times before, the ones which brought her to me, making me happy, and also took her away from me, making me insane with jealousy.

I looked quickly around to see if she was nearby, but she wasn't. Perhaps they belonged to someone else...No, they had to be hers! I decided to proceed as if they were, so I cleaned and polished her shoes with extra care, using the neutral polish I'd bought at the beginning of my seva.

I carried on cleaning and polishing, and waited and waited and waited. But Julie didn't appear. I felt a strange tightness in my stomach. My heartbeat began to surge and my breathing was heavier than usual. Time passed slowly.

I was waiting, and I realized I was still in love. Time was slow. Time was eternity. An hour, two hours, three hours passed. It was 4 p.m.—close to the time I was due to finish my seva at the Golden Temple—forever.

Then I saw her. My heartbeat surged as she slowly walked towards the northern gateway. She was coming closer and closer. She looked at me but didn't recognize me. My beard had grown and my hair was longer and hung around my face. She came closer still. As she did so, I tried to think of all the reasons she could be here—of course, being a Sikh, it wouldn't be unusual. She had told me she returned almost every year. But what were the chances of us finding each other here?

Thirty metres…What if she just took the shoes and said nothing?

Twenty metres. Should I tell her who I was, or just let her go?

Fifteen metres. I wasn't here for reward or to find Julie again. I was here for the good of my soul.

Ten metres. Her pace slowed. She was looking at the ground, searching for her blue shoes. The space between us seemed enormous. She was dressed in a simple white salwar kameez with blue embroidery, and no make-up except for a little smudge of lipstick.

As she walked towards me, hope and happiness pulsed through my veins.

Five metres. Now, suddenly, I was nervous and tense. I wanted to turn my face away from her. I wanted to get up and run. But I didn't.

Two metres.

She looked as beautiful as ever, but sad. Sadder than I remembered her—apart from on that final day when she threw me out. She smiled as she bent down to pick up her shoes, obviously pleased with the cleaning job this sevadar had done.

But her smile disappeared when she looked at me. Her face was close to mine, the face I loved—just inches away. She looked into my eyes and recognition appeared in hers. She looked at my beard and my hair and my face and back into my eyes again. A myriad of emotions flashed in hers—surprise, confusion, pain, happiness, pain again. I stood up. She did the same, holding onto her shoes as if some thief was going to try to take them from her.

'Rahul?'

'Julie…'

I could see the tears brimming in her eyes, ready to spill over any moment.

'Your shoes…I cleaned them.'

'Thank you.'

She began to cry, some of her tears falling on my hand.

'I still love you…Julie.'

'I love you too, Rahul.'

At these words, I almost fell over. Could it be true?

She stood there searching through her salwar kameez and then she pressed a letter into my hand. I was so stunned I took it without question. I looked down at it and, when I looked up again, she was gone. Disappeared into the crowd of pilgrims milling around. She had just vanished. And I wondered if she had been there at all, or was she just a mirage, a vision brought on by the intense spirituality and transcendental nature of the temple.

I sat down on the ground and tore open the letter. At least *that* was real.

My dear Rahul,

I was hurt and wounded when I learnt about Radium.

At the time, my love for you drained like blood from a wound. A few weeks after I broke off with you, I began to realize how much you meant to me. How much I missed you. How much I loved you. My wounds began to heal. I tried to call you, but your mobile phone was disconnected.

I thought you must have gone back to England.

Then, two days ago, I heard about an NRI non-Sikh boy from England doing forty days of seva at the Golden Temple, polishing pilgrims' shoes. I saw photos of that boy on Facebook and his video on YouTube. I knew it was you, Rahul.

From the daily updates on Facebook I realized it was already the 38th day of your seva, so I decided straightaway to fly to Amritsar to see you.

I don't know how I will react when I see you, Rahul— or how you'll react when you see me. So, I'm writing this letter just in case we do not get to talk. You hurt me deeply, or rather Radium hurt me. You said you weren't Radium, that he was dead. Is he, Rahul? Is he really?

I am sorry for shouting at you, for the way I threw you out, for my anger, for calling you Judas.

You taught me to 'smile, open your eyes, love and go on'. And I did—for you. Then you hurt me and I wished I hadn't. Now I want to try again. Now I want to 'forgive, love and go on'.

You made me laugh and you made me cry, you made me love and you made me hate. I miss the laughter and the love.

The question is, Rahul, do you miss the laughter and the love too? If you do, then I will believe that Radium is dead. If you do, then meet me tomorrow at 1 p.m. at the Golden Restaurant not far from the Golden Temple.

If you do not turn up, I will know that Radium is still in your heart.

Yours,
Julie Singh

I continued to sit on the ground, reading the letter over and over with trembling fingers, not believing it was true, expecting the paper to dissolve in my hands at any moment. I replaced it in the envelope and held it tightly, in case it caught on fire or blew away or was grabbed from my hand by some passing pilgrim.

It was miraculous! Julie had forgiven me. Then I remembered the words of the fakir.

Bo bravo, my son! Clean and polish pilgrims' shoes at the Golden Temple for forty days...your problems will surely be solved.

And they had been! It was the fortieth day of my seva at the Golden Temple, and my soul was cleansed from the stain of Radium, and Julie was back in my life! I could go back to Mumbai and love the only woman in the world for me, and also join Film International. My life was back on track.

I'd faced my demons and they had been defeated. The fakir's covenant had been fulfilled.

It was 5 p.m.

My forty days of seva were over. I left the northern gateway and went to the main prayer hall of the Golden Temple, the sanctum sanctorum. I was completely overwhelmed. I just stood there in the majestic spiritual presence of the Almighty whose hands I could feel on my shoulders. I said a prayer of thanks and asked for the Lord's forgiveness for all my errors and omissions, my shortcomings and sins. I prayed for my parents, and for the soul of PP Auntie. I prayed for Julie. I prayed for Irfan and David. I prayed for the fakir. I prayed for Guru Krishna Bhaiji. I prayed for my three Singh friends.

On my way out, I met Dilip, Harry and Vikram, who were all waiting patiently at the northern gateway to say goodbye to me.

'We will miss you so much.'

Dilip gave me a gift. It was a box of forty scented candles.

'Blow them out on your 40th birthday.'

We laughed, especially Viki, who thought it was the funniest thing.

'We have another surprise for you. We have organized a blood donation campaign in honour of your seva. Our aim is to achieve forty pints of blood. We are now short by some 400 millilitres.'

'I'll make up the shortfall.'

We walked towards the transfusion camp set up by the three Singhs, just outside the Golden Temple, where I made up the target of forty pints. Was it a coincidence that the amount of blood I was required to donate to make up the target of forty pints was 400 millilitres? A multiple of forty, that number again! But it was time for me to take leave of my Golden Temple friends, who had become my golden friends.

'Goodbye,' I smiled.
'Au revoir.'
'Dasvidaniya.'
'Kwaheri.'

I guessed those were the only foreign phrases the boys knew.

'We'll meet again, I'm sure of it.'

My mission accomplished, I could leave now. I felt a deep sense of satisfaction. I'd served at the Golden Temple for forty days with sweat, tears and toil, and now blood as well.

The next day was Sunday. My first free Sunday in forty days. I reached the Golden Restaurant at exactly 1 p.m., just as proposed by Julie. At first, I couldn't see Julie and started to panic. Then I saw she was already there, looking fabulous in a blue and red salwar kameez. I'd planned to rush to her and hug her, cover her face with kisses. But I just stood in the doorway looking at her. She looked back, not smiling, but not frowning either. She stood up as I walked slowly across to her. We were almost touching.

'I'm so sorry…'
'So am I. I read your letter a hundred times.'
'I love you.'
'I love you too.'

Julie sat down and I sat with her. She smiled at me and I smiled back.

The Punjabi thali which we ordered was all a vegetarian fare—jal jeera to drink and papad, salad and paneer fingers for starters, and then naan, kadai vegetables, methi dal, chole, peas pulao and cucumber raita for main course, and rabdi for dessert. It was the loveliest meal I'd ever eaten, even though I hardly tasted it. Finally, we spoke again.

'It's my first restaurant meal in a while.'

'Same here,' she said in that familiar voice. It was like we'd never been apart.

'As a young boy, I went to Ngorongoro Safari Park in Tanzania and had wildebeest curry in the restaurant.'

Julie looked at me and I looked at her and we both burst out laughing simultaneously. The sound of her laughter thrilled my whole body. I missed it so much.

'What made you come to the Golden Temple?'

'Where do I start?'

'At the beginning.'

I told her everything that had happened. It took over half an hour. At the end, there were tears in her eyes. She said, 'It is a fascinating story.' Then she laughed. 'Do you know, I almost missed you after I was let down by Budget Air?'

'Why, what happened?'

'I was booked to travel from Mumbai to Amritsar, with a change of flight at Delhi, to reach Amritsar on the 39th day of your seva. When I reached Delhi, I was told that my onward flight to Amritsar had been cancelled due to weather conditions. This was a lie.'

'How did you find out?'

'Everyone was saying so. The cancellation of the Delhi–Amritsar flight is a regular feature with Budget Air. Passengers are lured into flying with the airline by being offered cheaper fares and then made to travel by coach to Amritsar. I was furious. The airline was doing this to grab business and then making extra profit by putting passengers on a coach at the last moment. It had almost derailed us ever meeting again.'

She paused to drink water.

I looked at her, waiting eagerly to hear what happened next.

'I had no other choice. The night-time coach journey from Delhi Airport to Amritsar was a nightmare.'

'It must have been bitterly cold.'

'It was, and the coach had no heating. The journey took thirteen hours instead of the six hours advised by the airline staff at Delhi airport.'

'Another lie,' I interrupted.

'I finally reached Amritsar at 5 a.m., after thirteen hours, when the local temperature was about minus five. I was dropped off in freezing temperature at some isolated place in Amritsar with not much light, and where I could have been easily mugged and robbed.'

'Thank God you were alright!'

'I could easily not have reached the Golden Temple in time, and would have missed you.'

There was again a pause, during which I reached over and took her hand. It was the first time we'd touched since meeting again.

And so, we kept talking to make up for lost time.

'I'm sure the Lord wanted us to meet again and brought you to me in good time on the fortieth day of my seva.'

'And the torturous coach journey was my redemption.'

'Our love actually was always with us,' I told Julie as we left the restaurant, hand in hand by now.

*

We spent the next three days in Amritsar. Julie knew Amritsar like the back of her hand, having spent a few years of her childhood in the city, and also from visiting the city almost every year since.

'Have you seen much of Amritsar?' she asked.

'No. I've only been at the Golden Temple since coming here.'

'I'll take you around and show you the zigzagging narrow streets of the city with its shops and bazaars.'

After spending a full day seeing Amritsar, we visited Jallianwala Bagh, the scene of the Amritsar Massacre in 1919. We stood there in silence, holding hands, thinking solemnly of the many dead.

The next day we visited the Wagah Border crossing with Pakistan, twenty kilometres from Amritsar. We got out of the auto-rickshaw and walked the last kilometre to the Indo-Pak border. The crowd of tourists and sightseers had to be organized into a single-file line. This was done in true Indian fashion, with complete chaos, people pushing and pulling in all directions. There were two stadium-like seating areas, one on each side of the border. We took our seats in the India stadium. Like many in the crowd, Julie and I waved the flag of India. People on both sides sang patriotic songs and yelled insults at each other. Every three minutes or so, a young woman sitting next to me stood up and blew a trumpet. The crowd responded with a standing ovation and patriotic slogans. There was dancing and shouting and clapping everywhere.

Just before sunset, guards from each country performed a ceremony to mark the end of the day and the closing of the frontier. With the beating of drums and the blowing of whistles, Indian guards marched towards the Pakistan border. The crowd in the Indian stadium jumped up and cheered and yelled and waved, carrying on as if their last batsman had just hit a six to win a one-day cricket match against Pakistan off the very last ball of the match. From the Pakistan side of the border came loud jeers and mocking laughter, and boos and shouts of ridicule. The Indians responded in similar fashion minutes later when the Pakistani guards appeared.

I overheard a couple of old men talking on the way out. 'I hope one day India, Pakistan and Bangladesh will be reunited into one single country, like before 1947.'

'That can never happen, my friend. But let us hope that one day we may have some kind of a loose political confederation of the three countries.'

The Punjab was famous for dhabas, which were small, open-air local restaurants, open 24×7 and selling heavily spiced and fried Punjabi food which you ate sitting on cots. Later, Julie took me to one and I loved the experience. I was learning more about where she came from, who she was—she was showing me her soul.

Afterwards, we walked hand-in-hand along the streets of Amritsar at three in the morning. Her eyes beamed with radiance, brighter than the stars above us in the clear sky. We stopped in the middle of the road. There wasn't much street light, any traffic or pedestrians, only a stray dog and a bird cawing once or twice.

I looked into Julie's eyes and moved closer to her and touched her face lightly. Then I bent my head and moved my lips towards hers, which parted slightly and I could feel the tip of her tongue as we kissed. It was our first kiss since our reunion. I'd been waiting patiently for it to happen, for the time to be right, not wanting to rush things. Her arms reached around my neck and she clung to me. The past and all its mistakes and sorrows seemed to dissolve.

My arms tightened around her body and I deepened my kiss, moving one hand from her back and sliding it to her breasts. My mouth left hers to probe her ear and then across her cheek and then gently back to her lips again. We were locked together like one person. Our faces pressed together and Julie's arms locked around my back. I imagined hearing the folks singing, somewhere in the Rajasthan desert, the fakirs chanting and the gurus praying, and we kissed each other until blood exploded in my ears. It was our longest kiss!

Once we pulled apart, Julie said breathlessly: 'I feel like I'm sixteen years old again!'

'So do I!'

Our months of separation had dissolved like sugar in hot milk. Life was sweet once again. The winter of solitude was over. Spring was at our doorsteps. No more tears. We walked on. It was 5 a.m., a new dawn approaching.

The past few months had been a nightmare. But I knew I would eventually forget what I'd been through. Experience had picked me up like a small boy and taught me some of life's bitter truths. I felt lucky to have come out of it victorious and would now be able to use that experience to build a bright and happy future for myself and Julie. I felt more mature, wiser, older. It seemed to me as if my life had always been influenced in one way or another by a series of women—my mother, Tasmin, PP Auntie, Rekha, Radium's clients, and now Julie, turning me this way and that, steering me to port and then to starboard. I hoped that Julie would keep me on an even keel from now on.

After wandering in the wilderness for days on end, and overcoming all challenges and temptations, and after forty days of seva at the Golden Temple, I'd regained Julie's love and trust. We both realized now that love was the greatest force in the universe and it could hurt as well as heal. There would always be good times and bad times. Right now, we were going through a good time. The cold winter was over at last. We quickly forgot all the difficulties we'd been through in the recent past. Our memories of those events were already becoming vague, like the sub-plots of a bad movie, long-forgotten, a film which we would never see a second time. I thanked the Lord.

The Good Die Young

~~

I DECIDED TO shave off my ragged Ryan Gosling beard and get a haircut. I was back to being Rahul, the way I was when I first arrived in India from London. Julie and I had some things to catch up with when we finally got back to Mumbai. She went home, and then to her shop. I went straight to PP Auntie's house. It was Ratan's day off and he was sitting in the JFK rocking chair in the lounge reading a newspaper. He was excited to see me but then suddenly looked unhappy.

'Ruby and I have split up,' he said.

I could see the sadness in his eyes and it reminded me of my own sadness the last time I was here in this house. I didn't ask him for any details, only whether he still loved her.

'Yes, I do…'

In those few seconds, while talking to Ratan about winning back Ruby, my own experiences from the moment Julie threw me out to the time my paradise was regained flashed across my mind like a video in fast-forward. It had been a marathon journey. Now, at last, I was back in Mumbai and ready to restart the rest of my life.

The next day I met Irfan and David, who were both excited to learn that Julie and myself were together once again.

'Thanks to the fakir,' I said as my two friends cheered me.

It was a cold Sunday morning, three weeks since Julie and I returned from Amritsar. We hadn't met since that day, but we'd been in touch with each other by phone, e-mail and text.

Now it was time to meet again. The dust of our lives had settled long enough.

I phoned her at nine in the morning. 'Can we meet today?'
'Twelve noon at Haji Ali?'
'Fantastic!'

Julie arrived exactly at noon. I was there before her, waiting at the Juice Centre on the main road near Haji Ali. She wore no make-up, but still looked wonderful with her film-star sunglasses and her hair in pigtails, shining in the sunlight. She was wearing a cream-coloured angora cardigan, blue scarf and leather boots, and she looked as if she had just stepped out of a fashion magazine. I was so happy to see her. My spirits soared.

'I love you.'
'I love you too.'

I was always relieved when she whispered this sentence back to me. I knew I would always be afraid of losing her again.

We hugged. My arms encircled her, and my eyes looked deeply into hers. But I didn't kiss her. There were too many people and police around. And this was Haji Ali, a sacred place.

The tide was low. Fast-moving, radiantly white clouds skimmed across the sky overhead as we walked unhurriedly along the causeway to the main shrine, along with dozens of other pilgrims.

As we approached the mosque, we saw a crowd of about

ten people gathered near the front of the shrine. There was a commotion going on, a rush to see what had occurred. We quickened our pace. We pushed our way through to the front to have a better look and saw that a man had collapsed and was lying on the ground in obvious pain. I was shocked to see it was the fakir. He was wearing his green knee-length one-piece robe. His hair and beard had grown longer than I remembered, but it was him alright—there was no mistaking him. I went forward and took his head in my arms. His breathing was short and he was perspiring. Julie stood next to me. He'd lost a lot of weight, and looked quite ill with his sunken cheeks and diminished eyes. He was clearly in the last stages of physical and mental debilitation.

He recognized me at once. 'I am dying, my son.'

He looked into my eyes and his arm went around me. 'No...you'll live for many more years.'

'It's my 50th birthday today.'

'Happy birthday, Baba!' I said, in an attempt to lift his spirits.

Someone in the crowd had called for an ambulance. It was on its way. I shouted at the people to move back and give him some air to breathe. His voice was low but audible.

With what little energy he still had, he asked, 'When did you come back from Am...?'

But he was unconscious before he could complete his sentence. I'm sure he meant to say Amritsar. Did he recognize me? He had given me the prayer paper. Did he remember that? Was I the only one to whom he gave that prayer paper? He had then featured in my dreams twice. Did he know that? Was it just a coincidence that I was at Haji Ali at the very moment he collapsed? What was our connection? Was

I a son of his from a previous life? Plenty of questions but no answers.

Julie, her eyes full of compassion, gripped my hand, sensing my emotion, as I quickly composed myself.

'Three weeks ago. My problems were solved, thanks to your guidance and prayers.' I said sadly, talking in the hope that he could hear me. But his eyes remained closed. I felt for a pulse in his upper arm and wrist. It was very faint. Then his pulse faded completely and his face turned blue. He stopped breathing at exactly 12:40 pm, with his arms still holding onto me.

I was overwhelmed with a sense of sadness and grief. I felt very alone and somehow abandoned, even though Julie was at my side. I felt a part of me had died. One old man in the crowd said, '*Inna lillahi wa inna ilaihi raji'un,*' the phrase Muslims recite on hearing the news of someone's death which meant: Surely, we belong to Allah and to Him shall we return.

The ambulance arrived after about ten minutes. The paramedics ran up the causeway with a stretcher and a medical kit.

'He's dead,' I announced.

The male nurse I spoke to looked quite distraught.

'I knew Noor Baba very well. The fakir suffered from prostate cancer.'

That was the first time I'd heard him being called Noor, which meant 'light'. I remembered the words: *And God said, 'Let there be light, and there was light',* and I felt that, through Noor Baba, God made his light shine in my heart.

Julie and I went with the ambulance to the nearby Worli Hospital. One of the onlookers in the crowd said he'd like to attend the fakir's funeral. I took his mobile number and promised to call him later with the details. It struck me that the last time we'd been in a hospital was when Julie's husband had been admitted. The ambulance weaved in and out of traffic, driving over Mumbai's notorious potholes, at times grinding to a halt. I phoned Irfan and David, who met us at the hospital a few minutes after the ambulance arrived.

David quickly dealt with all the formalities at the hospital and arranged for the death certificate to be issued. Irfan made half a dozen phone calls to various people to arrange Noor Baba's funeral at Eternal Gardens, a Muslim cemetery in south Mumbai, an idyllic setting often used to bury Bollywood Muslim luminaries.

In Islam, bodies are buried within a few hours of death, so the funeral was held at 5 p.m. that same afternoon. I phoned the man whose mobile number I'd taken earlier in the day at Haji Ali and informed him of the funeral arrangements.

'I will pass the word around.'

Julie then went home from the hospital. She said simply: 'I will pray for Noor Baba at home.'

Irfan, David and I went to the funeral, which was also attended by fifteen or so other people.

'Noor Baba had no relatives. His wife had died many years ago,' a mourner at the funeral told me.

'Did he have any children?'

'One son, who died a few days after he was born.'

'Since then, he'd been all alone in this world,' another mourner joined in.

'The dead body is first washed to cleanse the corpse, then wrapped in a simple plain white cloth called the kafan.'

Irfan explained the rites and rituals of an Islamic funeral to me as it happened.

'Collective prayers are offered for the forgiveness of the dead.'

Noor Baba's body was then placed in the grave, without a casket. Those present at the funeral symbolically poured three handfuls of soil into the grave. The corpse was then buried by the gravediggers. Prayers were recited throughout the burial process.

'Flowers and perfumed rose water will now be scattered on the grave.'

Incense sticks were lit and placed on the grave, followed by collective prayers.

Noor Baba was now laid to rest with his eyes shut, sleeping peacefully in the bosom of mother earth, his body committed to the ground—earth to earth, dust to dust, in the midst of silence and soothing greenery.

I heard one of the mourners tell another: 'In this same grave was previously buried Sultan Khan, a Bollywood superstar of the 1960s.'

'Old graves are dug up to bury new bodies due to lack of space,' another mourner explained, when he saw the amazement on my face.

'But Sultan Khan was a superstar,' I said. 'Surely his grave should have been preserved.'

'Every Muslim is equal before God; no concession can be made for artistes and celebrities,' the cemetery manager explained. 'We regularly turn over the graves due to shortage of space.'

'In England, this would not be allowed.'

'This is India, my friend!'

Yes, this was India. Noor Baba's death certificate and other formalities were all completed very quickly and he was buried in just a few hours. This surprised me, as it was such a contrast to the length of time it took for someone to get buried in England.

'We don't have grave diggers' strike in India,' Irfan told me as we walked away after the burial.

'Nor are our Christmas-time funerals postponed until after 5th January in the New Year,' added David.

'Our VIP memorial services are held within a week or so. Not some six or eight months after the person has died,' asserted Irfan. How different to England, I thought.

I turned back and had one last look at Noor Baba's grave. It was a simple grave for a simple person. I remembered an Urdu couplet which I'd heard a long time ago about the grave of a proud and arrogant man:

O you proud man!
You! Who always walks straight in arrogance with your head high!
Just bend once only and look how small your grave will be!

'You come naked and you go enshrouded,' I heard a mourner tell Irfan.

'Noor Baba was born poor and died poor,' one of the mourners told me.

'Kafan has no pockets,' I replied.

Some years ago, I'd attended the funeral of the two-year-old daughter of one of our neighbours in London. I recalled a passage read from the Ecclesiastes at the church service:

A time to give birth and a time to die.
A time to weep and a time to laugh
A time to mourn and a time to dance...

We cry when we are born and when we die others cry. Today was Noor Baba's time to die and my time to weep and mourn.

The sky started to darken and clouds thickened overhead as we prepared to leave. Soon it started to drizzle. Tears came down from heaven. After Noor Baba's death, I became more philosophical about life and death. We remembered the dead. Then we were remembered ourselves. And so, life went on. Death loved life and wouldn't rest till it captured it.

Noor Baba was only fifty when he died. The good die young. So they say.

Guess Who's Coming to Dinner

~

A WEEK AFTER Noor Baba's death, Julie invited me to a cricket match. It was a One Day International match between India and Pakistan. I remembered how worked up my father used to get in London about cricket. Now I witnessed first-hand the cricket mania in India. The pitch was a substitute for a battlefield. There was hype and hoopla and frenzy before the match, and sound and fury raging everywhere during it. A carnival-like atmosphere ran riot in the stadium, with trumpets and hooting and frequent fireworks. From the first to the last ball, the tension in the ground rippled right across Mumbai, and beyond, across all of India. The contest went to a nail-biting finish, which India won on the very last ball, batting second. I already knew from my father that cricket was a religion in India, and that people get very emotional about it. But this was something else. In India, ace cricketers and Bollywood superstars were worshipped like God. Streets, offices, schools, shops, cinemas and even mosques and temples were empty on a day when there was an important cricket fixture, especially when India played Pakistan. Incidents of heart attacks during a tense last over, or even suicide at a loss by the Indian side, weren't uncommon.

That evening, kids all over the country would have been playing cricket in small back streets to celebrate India's win.

A few days after the India-Pakistan match, Julie invited me round for dinner. She looked grave when she opened the door.

'I have received another letter from that guy.'

'Which guy? What letter?'

'I received this in yesterday's mail.'

She handed me the letter. It was typed on a plain A4 paper and was undated.

'Dear Julie Madam,

After my previous letter, you broke off with Rahul, but now it seems the two of you have got back together again. I am absolutely horrified to see an intelligent girl like you falling for a guy who is a complete fake. I have seen him on YouTube and have also read about him on Facebook. I can tell you that Rahul or Radium or whatever name he calls himself is a first-class liar.

Can you not see? He just put on an act to win you back. He created this fantasy of a Muslim fakir. He then devised a scheme to go to the Golden Temple knowing very well that you, as a Sikh, would be impressed and go there so he could then win you over.

It's all adding up nicely. Is it not?

Of course, he would deny all this. He would, wouldn't he?

The guy is sick. Just leave him. If you do not, you'll regret for the rest of your life.
Your
Well-wisher

I was shaken when I read the letter. I went to sit on the sofa, stone silent, with the letter next to me. I felt very angry. This evil-minded person was out to destroy me.

'This guy is sick!' said Julie, and came to sit next to me.

I gave her a tight hug and whispered in her ear, 'I love you. No one can separate us again.'

'I love you too…but I'm scared.'

'Don't be…come on…cheer up! Let's have dinner.'

I tried to change the subject as we walked across to the dinner table.

Julie was obviously very concerned. After dinner, I took her hand and led her back to the sofa. There was fear in her eyes and it wouldn't be long before the tears followed. She forced a smile. I tried to console her. She snuggled up against me, resting her head on my shoulders, not speaking.

The next morning, I sent Julie a bouquet of thirty-six red roses to cheer her up with a love message on a card with a foot note: *P.S. I Love you.* But I knew the malicious letter from her 'Well-wisher' would be on her mind all day.

∽

With my filmmaking course still way off, I had time on my hands—time to think and time to worry. Julie had hired a full-time manager in the shop and could run her place without having to spend much time there.

We visited the tree in Julie's neighbourhood on which I'd once carved 'Rahul loves Julie'. I now added the word 'always'. We spent time walking under the shade of trees in the Friendship Forest not far from Mumbai. I love trees. They represent birth, growth, death and rebirth and provide us food, fuel, shelter and, ironically, wood for our cremation or coffins when we die. I also love the sea. We spent a lot of time in the sea. We swam in the morning and afternoon and sometimes at late evenings in the phosphorescent glow of the full moon.

Most days were sunny, which made swimming popular, but we also liked to swim in the rain, with nobody else in the water but ourselves. Kissing in the sea was magic and there were plenty of kisses. Time had brought us together as never before. We weren't married, but we felt as if we were on one long honeymoon. Togetherness brought us great happiness, but it wasn't all smooth sailing. We sometimes argued and frequently disagreed, like all couples, but Julie was not a sulking type, like Tasmin, and we always made up quickly—laughing and hugging and kissing and making love.

Born on 11 July, Julie was a Cancer, which made her emotional and intuitive, determined and forceful, exciting and magnetic, powerful and passionate with a romantic impulse. I wasn't worried about the other side of Cancer—jealous and resentful, obsessive and obstinate. Nobody was perfect, especially me. In real life, choices determined our character. Our real character was forged in the choices we made when we were under pressure. The more intense the pressure, the louder the proclamation of who we really were, and what our true character is. To me, Julie was the girl next door. I loved everything about her—her beauty, her courage, her confidence, her smile, her laughter, the compassion in her eyes, her ambition and her idealism.

The most important three words in life are *please, sorry* and *thank you*. But there are also three more. *I love you.* Then there are four more. *I love you too.* And then there are still four more—important and magical. *Will you marry me?* And, finally, there is that all-important one-word reply: *Yes*.

Weddings in India are majestic occasions and celebrated like festivals. Extravagant and colourful, they are glamorous affairs, celebrated in the grandest fashion. A month after we returned from Amritsar, Julie and I attended one such wedding. It was held at a sports' venue, with a grand pandal decorated with exotic flowers and bright lights. The two-mile drive from the main road to the marriage grounds was adorned with illuminated columns in blinding white colour and statutes in erotic poses. The groom was dressed like a prince and made a grand entrance on an elephant. The bride wore a heavily embroidered red sari and her hands and legs were decorated with henna. She wore exotic jewellery and walked down the aisle accompanied by six drummers. There was live music and a sumptuous buffet extravaganza after the main ceremony. The boy and girl were both from very rich families, but in India, even a poor man's wedding was a small festival in its own right. Some poor people even borrowed large sums of money from local moneylenders to host weddings beyond their financial capacity. I thought it ironic that every time I go to the airport to see someone off, I feel like travelling. Every time I attend a wedding, I feel like getting married.

Julie and I talked about marriage and married life, but not about getting married ourselves. I knew Julie missed married life, and that she had also lost her baby. She wanted to be a mother. She imagined her life like a great Bollywood love film from the 1960s. Boy meets Girl. Boy tries to woo Girl. Girl says 'no'. Boy keeps trying. Girl then agrees to meet Boy. They meet. They meet again a few times. No kisses at first. Then comes the first kiss. Girl is shy. Boy is not. They fall in love. Girl brings Boy home to meet her parents. There's also a third person in the story, maybe another boy who also likes the Girl or another girl who likes the Boy. Who will marry whom? In the end, true love always triumphs. The Boy and the Girl get married and settle down. From then on life is like a TV commercial. A young, lovely couple with two children and a dog entering a car showroom and happily driving off into their new, idyllic sunset. Of course, the reality of life was quite different, as I knew well, having heard from all the women during my time as Radium.

But Julie didn't think about the stresses and strains which would inevitably arise from time to time between husband and wife. There would be financial worries, issues with budgets, bringing up kids, sex, snoring, getting older and familiarity. There would always be screams. There would always be shouts. A few plates might get broken, maybe many plates, as Connie Corleone did in *The Godfather*. I knew this from my mum and dad. They argued from time to time, but had an understanding which worked quite well. They had two golden rules. One, all bust-ups had to be finished before 7 p.m., that way, the evenings were always peaceful in our house. Two, no bust-ups between 4 p.m. on Fridays and 9 a.m. on Mondays, making the weekends peaceful too. During evenings and weekends my parents displayed the divine gift of silence and, overall, we were quite a happy little family.

I wasn't worried about future fights between Julie and me, rather it was always the threat of the past returning—of her changing her mind, or even her husband's murderer tracking us down. She had told me several times that the police had failed to catch him, and this worried us both.

I was convinced our emotional investment in each other was secure and was bound to grow and yield dividends every day. Our emotional assets would also appreciate year after year. I was quite sure of that. We both knew love was a plant that needed to be watered 24×7.

'Marriage is like a corporation,' my father once told me.

'To be successful, it has to be well managed.'

Sometimes Julie would fall silent, but only for a few minutes.

'We don't have to talk if you don't want to.'

I'd say stuff like that and within seconds she'd be fine and back to her usual bubbly self. She was like a diamond, full of sparkle and life, a joy to be with.

For some weeks after our return from Amritsar, I'd been thinking about proposing. I imagined presenting an engagement ring to her. I imagined going down on one knee and asking her to marry me. I was pretty sure she'd say 'yes'. I wanted to make it a surprise. I had to find a moment when she wouldn't suspect anything. I went down to Zaveri Bazaar in downtown Mumbai and bought a 14-carat white gold classic solitaire engagement ring. I devised different scenarios and possibilities in my head. I practised the moves and the words I'd say. I decided the best place would be Julie's own flat. That was where we'd first consummated our love.

It was a Thursday, my favourite day. My lucky day. The date was 13th December. Julie had invited me to dinner and I went nice and early with a bouquet of seventy-two red roses. Double the normal! The dinner was romantic and candlelit and she'd cooked mutton biryani and samosas and two vegetable curries and parathas.

This was the first time Julie set up a candlelit table, and it made things just right for what I was about to do. By 7 p.m., the only sound in the room was that of the ticking clock. She started to tell me something, but I put my fingers to her lips to keep her from speaking and for a long time we just looked at each other. Then I got down on one knee and took out the ring.

'Julie…my life has never been the same since I met you. You've inspired me and made my life happy and joyful. I can't imagine being without you. Will you marry me? I want the answer in one word.'

Julie was suddenly silent, which disconcerted me a little. She replied after what seemed like an eternity and a day.

'No.'

I was dumbfounded. It took me a while to get over the shock, but I finally got my voice back.

'You were supposed to say yes.'

'You wanted the reply in one word. That word is "No". I have met your conditions.'

She stood up and walked away from me. The silence returned. It was a long silence. I kissed her, held her, told her over and over that I loved her and, just when I thought I'd won the argument…

'Have you spoken to your parents?'

'No.'

I wondered why she needed to ask me that.

'I am not from your community. Will they accept me as a daughter-in-law?'

'My father's a Gujarati Hindu. My mother's a white English Christian. There won't be a problem.'

'I am also a widow. Will your parents still accept me?'

'Why not?'

I knew Julie mentioned her widowhood because widows were generally looked down upon in India, where they have often been marginalized and mistreated.

'Your widowhood would mean nothing to my parents.'

'Are you sure?'

'Positive.'

For the first time that evening, she smiled shyly. 'I will marry you if your parents agree.'

'But what about this ring?'

'I will take it and I will wear it, but only after you have your parents' permission to marry me. In the meantime, I'll keep it safe as a sign of my conditional acceptance of your marriage proposal.'

It all sounded rather formal to me, but it was the best I was going to get—for now at least.

'So, do I take it that we're engaged now?'

'Definitely, maybe.'

⁓

At my university, back in London, two students in my group, a boy and a girl, were once asked by the lecturer to write on a piece of paper the things they wanted most in life. The boy wrote down three items. Love, Wealth and Health. The girl wrote down just one item. Everything.

Women, it seems, want everything in life. Julie was no different. But she was practical and down to earth and knew where to draw the line. Right now, she wanted my parents' agreement to our marriage. I was overjoyed when Julie accepted my engagement ring. But it was a conditional engagement. Julie would marry me only if my parents approved.

I decided to send an e-mail to my parents seeking their approval. The next day at six in the morning, when the birds were just beginning to chirrup, I sat in front of my laptop with a cup of tea and some hard round toasts, which I'd bought from the nearby New Parsee Bakery. After a dozen amendments, the e-mail to my parents was finally ready.

My dearest Dad and Mum,

I decided to send you this e-mail rather than talk to you over the telephone.

You remember how shattered I was when Tasmin broke off with me? You were both really wonderful at the time and supported me day and night and helped me pull through my worst emotional crisis. Thank you.

You encouraged me to take things easy and assured me that, given time, a new girl would come into my life and that I'd fall in love once again.

Well, you were right. Yes! I'm in love again!

The feeling is out of this world.

Her name is Julie. Julie's parents died when she was a little girl. She's immensely beautiful, kind and loving. I attach a recent photograph of her.

However, there are two issues which she feels might stand in our way. The first is that she's a Sikh, not a Hindu. Her full name is Julie Singh. The second is that she's a widow.

I first met her more than a year ago when I witnessed her husband being gunned down in the middle of a Mumbai street. Her husband died a few days after being shot. He died in Amritsar, as he wanted to be near the Golden Temple.

I met her again some months later in a Mumbai film bookstore, which happened to be owned by her. Since then we've met regularly. I was the first to tell her those three magic words.

We've had our ups and downs, and once even broke off for a good few months.

Why we broke off and how we got back together is a long story which I'll tell you some other time. But we're now back together and love each other like never before.

She's everything to me. My heart. My soul.

Julie is prepared to settle down with me, but only if both my parents accept her without any reservations and approve of her.

I need your understanding, agreement and your blessings, without which Julie won't say yes. I told Julie you'll welcome her with open arms but she wants to hear from you that you have no objection to us getting married.

Julie has accepted the ring I gave her a few days back, but will only wear it if you approve of her.

Dad and Mum, will you accept Julie Singh as your daughter-in-law?

Will you love her and cherish her as your own daughter until death do us part?

Love,
Rahul

For the rest of the day, I checked my incoming e-mails to the point of obsession. The only e-mails I received on that day were junk spams, selling Viagra and scented condoms, or offering me huge returns on some fake and obscure investments, like tiger breeding, or telling me I'd won a massive lottery and asking me to send them money to claim my prize.

Five hours later, I found the e-mail I was waiting for.

Our dearest son Rahul,

Thank you for your e-mail, which we read with great interest. In fact, we read it twice. Father Brown happened to be at home when your e-mail came. He also read it with much interest. We are all very excited to learn that our son is once again in love with a girl who also loves him.

We have seen Julie's photograph and are very impressed with her. She looks really lovely and graceful. We are also touched by her requirement that we as your parents should approve of her. There is no question of us having any objections. We approve of Julie Singh wholeheartedly. We do not believe in these outdated notions and restrictions relating to inter-caste marriages and the position of widows in society.

There is one and only one reason why a boy and girl should get married, if they want to, and that is love. That is why your mother and I got married. And that is why you and Julie should get married.

Yes, Rahul dear, we will accept Julie Singh as our daughter-in-law. We will love her and cherish her as our own daughter till our last breath. We want to meet Julie and we will be flying to Mumbai within the next few days.

Love always,
Dad and Mum

I wanted to tell Julie immediately that my parents had approved her, and that they were coming to Mumbai to meet her. But how should I do this? By phone? By e-mail? Personally?

Instead, I sent her a text message:
Guess who's coming to dinner.

Psycho

~~

As soon as I could, I told Julie about my e-mail to my parents and their reply. She was delighted to hear they'd consented to our marriage and that they were planning to come to Mumbai to meet her. We decided to meet that evening at 6 p.m. under the soothing green branches of the tree in her neighbourhood where I'd carved 'Rahul loves Julie. Always.' It was the only tree in a small park which Julie called the Love Park. I'd named it the Love Tree. It was a quiet neighbourhood with not many people around at that time of the evening. The park was off a small road which was sometimes used by motorists and taxi drivers as a shortcut to miss the traffic on Hill Road. That evening was particularly mild and quiet.

I got there first, and Julie arrived a few minutes later, at exactly 6 p.m. She looked ravishing, as usual, wearing a red and white, thigh-skimming evening dress, with red peep-toe shoes and carrying a matching red clutch bag—all brand-new.

'You look out of this world.' I whispered in her ear as I kissed her lightly on the cheek. She smiled.

'You don't look too bad yourself.'

We sat on a bench near the Love Tree for a while. It was cool and peaceful. It felt as if we were far away from crazy Mumbai, somewhere in a remote hill station. Eventually, she said:

'I am so happy. Your parents have accepted me.'

'There was never any question they wouldn't,' I replied, giving her an affectionate squeeze.

'Still, it is good to get their approval.'

'So…is our engagement still "conditional"?'

'Of course not!' she said as she squeezed back.

She took the ring from her bag and placed it on the palm of her right hand. I took her left hand and slipped the engagement ring onto what the Romans called the ring finger. They believed the vein in that finger led straight to the heart. I drew her close to me and kissed her. Now we were 'unconditionally' engaged.

'We will get married with bells and banjos,' said Julie.

'You mean with band baaja barat?'

'Yes! There will be pomp, pageantry and party at our wedding.'

'And our wedding car will have a special number plate J…U…5…T…W…E…D—JU5T WED!' I added.

'Be original, Rahul, for God's sake! Don't just copy like the Indian film producers do.'

'OK. So how about J…U…L…1E.,..JUL1E?' I asked.

Nodding with exuberance, she went on to say 'I now officially name this bench as Love Bench.'

I then put my fingers to her lips to keep her from saying anything further and for a few minutes we just sat basking in each other's adoring eyes.

'Take me to some place on the other side of the moon,' she whispered in a seductive tone.

I wanted to carry her in my arms to paradise. However, I'd booked a table for two at the Love Restaurant near Carter Road for a romantic dinner, to celebrate our engagement.

Better and better!

Just as we were about to leave the Love Bench, I saw a man in the distance approaching us. He was conspicuous because there was nobody else in the park at the time, also because he was very dark, with an oddly-shaped head, and thick bushy hair. At first, he walked slowly towards us, and I didn't pay much attention to him, but then he started to pace with long strides. I knew at once that something was wrong. I had a sense of imminent danger. He stopped about ten feet away from us. To my horror, I saw it wasn't his head that was strangely shaped. He was wearing a helmet with the visor down.

'Rahul…' Julie was trembling and pointing towards the man's headgear. 'I recognize that helmet.'

It was the red helmet with black spots on it. The same as the one worn by Robin's killer.

Julie suddenly screamed as she lunged towards him and hit his face with her red clutch bag.

The man pushed her away effortlessly, then took off the helmet and threw it to the ground. I could only see his eyes. His face was covered with a handkerchief mask. I recognized the handkerchief. It was blue with small white circles on it. I knew straightaway that this was the man who had mugged and robbed me when I first came to Mumbai!

The man kept coming closer to us, removing the handkerchief as he walked, and rolling up his right sleeve. He had a tattoo on his arm. It said—JULIE. I could now see his face for the first time.

Suddenly Julie screamed out: 'This man is Akash Sandeep Chinoy! I know him! He's been stalking me! You saw him at the Bandra Fair the other day!'

Chinoy was only a couple of feet away now. He shouted

at Julie.

'You rejected me! That is why I killed your husband. Then you fell for this bastard...' and he gestured to me with contempt, '...who calls himself Radium. I tried to break the two of you apart by writing those anonymous letters, but you are back together,' he screamed venomously.

So, he was the phantom letter-writer too! We stood frozen, facing each other down, like a Mexican standoff.

To our horror, Chinoy then removed a length of rolled-up cloth from around his waist and, quick-as-a-flash, swung it around my neck before I knew what was happening. Hissing at me, he tried to manoeuvre himself round behind me. Some voice told me I couldn't let him do that. If I did, I'd be dead in seconds. I shouted in a strangled voice for Julie to run, but she stood stock still in terror. Then she screamed at the top of her voice.

'Help! Help!'

I vaguely heard a dog barking from some distance away as my vision began to blur. But I knew there was no one around to help us. I managed to get my fingers between the noose and my neck, but Chinoy was working his way round behind me and twisting the noose tighter and tighter.

Finally, he released his grip on the cloth and pulled a knife from his pocket. It was a folding knife, a one-handed opening and closing type with a sharp eight-inch blade.

'I am now going to kill you,' he said hissing psychotically.

The man spoke in a calm voice. But his face betrayed a flaming internal furnace.

My limbs were trembling. I felt giddy and started to crumple. Sweating profusely, he grabbed me by the chin and looked deep into my eyes. Forcing me to the ground, he knelt on top of me, shoving the knife against my head. He placed the point of the knife against my temple, squeezed his eyes shut for a few seconds, and then, opening them, he pointed the knife first at my left eye and then at my right eye and back again.

At that moment, Julie grabbed his hair and yanked his head back.

'Don't kill him, please,' pleaded Julie, tears rolling down her cheeks.

But he was too strong and pushed her off.

To my horror, Chinoy wetted his lips and then grabbed me by the neck. Sucking in a deep breath, he then lifted the knife in the air. It was a new knife, its chaste, taciturn edge designed as if just for me. He slammed it down. He heaved it up again. This time the knife was stained in blood. My blood. The blood of my father and mother. The psycho stabbed me repeatedly, in my stomach, in my inner left leg, and then again in my chest, and back in my stomach. It was a frenzied attack. He had turned into a crazed butcher, possessed by the devil.

I was vaguely aware he smelt of alcohol, and that he was grinning viciously as he stabbed me with murderous frenzy... And then I heard the sound of an approaching car.

And then all was darkness.

∽

When I opened my eyes, I felt intense pain all over my body. My mouth was parched and my head was throbbing. I didn't know what was happening to me. I began to slip back into unconsciousness. When I regained consciousness, everything was foggy but my vision gradually improved over the next few minutes. I glanced above my head. I realized I was connected to tubes, drips and monitors. I was in a hospital. I slowly remembered what had happened to me. I felt my neck and it was extremely sore and tender. Then I noticed that my chest and stomach and left leg were heavily bandaged. At first I was fearful, then terrified. The pain in my body was excruciating. But at least I was alive. I looked around. I could slowly make out the features of the people around me—my father, mother, Julie, Irfan and David, who were all standing near my bed.

I heard my mother's voice first, taking me back to childhood: 'Everything will be all right…'

Julie sat close to me on the hospital bed. I asked her what had happened, and she told me quietly, gently.

'Do you remember a car approaching Love Park?'

'Yes…I think so.'

'Well, that car belonged to David, who was on his way to downtown Mumbai with Irfan.'

'They must have been on the way back from the airport.'

'Yes. David stopped the car. They were all shocked to see me shouting for help.'

'Then what happened?'

'They saw you lying unconscious on the ground in a pool of blood and quickly brought you to this hospital.'

It was Bandstand General Hospital, where I'd first come more than a year ago with Julie and Robin, after he'd been shot by the same bastard. Julie pointed as Dr Mittal and Ratan entered the ward.

'You are under the care of Dr Mittal. He saved your life.'

'No, I did not,' said Dr Mittal solemnly. 'It was the Almighty who heard our prayers.'

'Irfan telephoned me in London and told me what had happened,' continued my mother.

'We immediately flew down to Mumbai and David brought us straight from the airport to here,' said my father.

'You are in the intensive care unit,' Dr Mittal said. 'You had lost a lot of blood. Your surgery lasted for five hours and, afterwards, you didn't regain consciousness for a long time.'

Then my mother spoke, almost in tears. 'You were not responding to treatment. Your life hung in the balance…'

'We were all so worried about you,' said Julie.

'Your mother and I spoke to you and held your hand and pinched your fingers and told you we loved you and begged you to wake up.'

'We gave you so many kisses, but you would still not respond.'

'I told them to pray for your recovery,' said Dr Mittal.

'We all prayed for you,' said my mother. 'And now, after many days of prayers, you have finally opened your eyes.'

∽

I was in the ICU for several days. I was fully conscious but still in pain. My father and mother and Julie stayed by my bedside, taking turns to be with me so I was never alone. The nurses and the ICU staff were fantastic and wonderful, and I couldn't ever praise them enough. They kept watch on me night and day, and were always smiling and cheerful and full of support.

I was then moved to a general ward where there were already four other patients. The nurse in charge was called Jane Iyer, a South Indian Christian lady of great warmth and energy.

'You are as compassionate as Jane Eyre,' I told her.

Two police officers came to interview me on my second day in the general ward. They'd already interviewed Julie, Irfan, and David.

'We have been down to the park where you were attacked and have recovered your assailant's knife, helmet and handkerchief,' said one of the police officers.

'He was traced and arrested the next day and charged with attempted murder, along with a number of other serious offences. Akash Sandeep Chinoy is now being held in a jail somewhere in Mumbai, pending a full trial,' said the second officer.

I noticed that the psycho who attacked me had three names.

'How come all these assailants and assassins have three names?' I asked Julie after the police officers left.

'You are right, Rahul. We had Nathuram Vinayak Godse, and Lee Harvey Oswald, and Mark David Chapman.'

'Not to forget John Wilkes Booth,' I added quickly, not to be outdone.

'Sorry, I didn't tell you I was being stalked...'

She was silent for a while, and then she took my hand. 'I didn't want you to worry.'

Apart from my parents and Julie, who were always at the hospital, I had regular visits from Irfan and David, and Dr Mittal came to see me whenever he could. He was a man of great confidence and authority and tried to reassure me that everything would be alright, given time. I knew I was in good hands. Ratan came at the start of his shift, and again just before leaving at the end of each day. He'd insisted that my parents stay in his house while they were in Mumbai, in the room next to mine.

Yet, despite everyone's reassurance, the pain in my body did not subside. My head pounded as if I'd been hit by a cricket bat. Shooting pain would travel down my spinal cord into my arms and legs and my chest. The healing process was slow. From time to time I felt really low, as though any solid ground I'd gained had vanished again and was replaced by quicksand. My spirits would slip every now and then. The days were bad, but the nights were worse. Whilst I was in the ICU, I was mostly unconscious and protected from the pain and fear, but here in the general ward I was wide awake. All my senses were active. All kinds of thoughts and fears started to grip me and made me panic. The pain and the panic kept rising. I was scared and scarred. I was given painkillers and sedated, but they didn't help much. I was full of all kinds of demons—fear of the scars the knife attack would leave, not just on my body, but on my mind as well. I could imagine and hear, with growing horror, noises such as I had never heard before in my life—the growl of bears, the grunt of camels, the scream of eagles, the howls of the three witches from *Macbeth*, the wailing of people jumping from the sinking Titanic and, finally, would you believe, the marching of the soldiers of the Terracotta Army. Now, how could clay soldiers march? I asked myself in a state of utter confusion, suffering tormented imagination like never before.

Many nights I drew my knees into my stomach and tried to sleep. I closed my eyes to calm my nerves, but pangs of fear kept assaulting me, and dark thoughts bombarded my head mercilessly.

I remembered the fakir. The image of him dying in my arms came flashing back to me. I'd experienced his death at first-hand and now it was my turn to die in the arms of my father and mother and Julie. I started to cry like a small boy. Within a few seconds, I was a weeping wreck, and my face was puffy and swollen with tears. I tried to scream, but no words came out of my mouth. My teeth started to chatter and my limbs started to shake.

One day, I started to sink. My eyes closed. My hands and feet went cold. I began to shiver. Julie gave one long scream. Everyone made such a commotion that Jane Iyer rushed into the ward, followed by Dr Mittal. The noise they made brought me out of my state of semi-unconsciousness. I was now awake but gasping and very sleepy. Suddenly, I felt the light in the room diminishing, as if filters were blocking the brightness, creating a late afternoon type of darkness, that of a cold and miserable winter's day.

'I'm going to die,' I managed to murmur.

My dead body was on a funeral pyre at Varanasi on the banks of the Ganges River—whistling, blazing and expectorating red and yellow embers into the pitch-black night. This frightful image flashed across my eyes, making me shudder. Thankfully, I was still live.

'No! No!' Julie's voice sounded clearly distraught. 'Open your eyes! Look at me! Look at me! Please do not leave me, Rahul!'

My father and mother were also pleading. Dr Mittal was issuing orders. After a few minutes, my eyes opened slowly. I felt blood pounding in my head. Dr Mittal was examining me. He looked concerned.

Suddenly, I heard the azaan, the Muslim prayer call from the nearby Muslim neighbourhood, just north of the hospital. It was being broadcast over the loudspeaker from the local mosque in a beautiful, soothing and melodious voice of the muezzin. I then remembered the fakir again. Not his death this time, but the prayer he had given me.

The next moment, my eyes fell on the gold chain my mother was wearing. It had a cross pendant. I had five wounds in my body from the knife attack—two in my chest, two in my stomach and one in my inner left leg. The cross reminded me of the five wounds of Jesus Christ when he was crucified—two on his hands, two on his legs and one on the side of his chest. I suddenly realized my suffering was nothing compared to His!

This calmed me somehow, and, after a while, I started to feel better. The calmer I became, the more determined I became—determined to fight my fear, just as I'd fought against the strangling noose in the park. I realized fear was my real enemy now. Fear is an enemy of life. It comes to you step by step and grows inside you molecule by molecule, suffocating you. It first comes to you as doubt and makes a small home in your mind. It then refuses to leave and stays on like a squatter. It starts to challenge you. You try to fight back but fear is evil and merciless. Having created doubt in you, the squatter then creates anxiety in you. Now there are two squatters—doubt and anxiety. The two of them do everything to terrorize you. To suffocate you. Fear attacks not only your mind but also your body. It is now in full action. You try to fight back. Fear is winning. But fight back… you must. Otherwise fear will destroy you. But you have no weapons. You need to seek help from a friendly king, asking him to send in his best troops. But how do you ask? You are a prisoner. Luckily, the friendly king is within you. You have to just remember him and ask him for help in your mind. He will listen to you. He has powerful ears. He responds by sending his most powerful fighter. Hope. Hope will destroy fear, that oppressive dictator.

My friendly king was not a king. She was a Queen. She was an Empress. She was a Goddess. Goddess Lakshmi! She had previously come to my aid. I used to remember her every morning at 4 a.m. but lately I had forgotten her. But she, I was sure, had not forgotten me. She was just waiting for me to call her. Her line was always busy, but she had many extensions and could deal with multiple calls all at once. She would definitely help me this side of the grave and the other.

I tried to concentrate and asked for her help, reciting the fakir's one-line prayer over and over again.

I asked Goddess Lakshmi for her help silently and repeatedly. And she came to me and stayed with me, near me, in me. She held me and banished my fear. I was no longer afraid. The fakir and Guru Krishna Bhaiji had showed me the path to my Queen. To my Empress. To my Goddess. I thanked them both.

A week later, my pain started to ease. My recovery accelerated. My confidence returned. I started walking exercises in the ward, helped by my mother and Julie. Everybody cheered me, helped me, looked after me. My father assisted me in shaving and washing and walking. My mother applied scented, cooling oil on my head, rubbing it soothingly and combing my hair. Julie made sure I ate properly. They were all wonderful. I was now possessed by a mighty urge to live. I knew I wouldn't die. Having conquered my fear of death, I was now no longer afraid of dying. That didn't mean I wanted to die; no, I wanted to live. Live a long time. There was a lot I wanted to achieve in life. To help others to achieve in their lives. It just meant I wasn't afraid of death anymore.

One day, I heard Jane Iyer speaking to Ratan as he entered the ward.
'He is feeling much better now.'
'Who?'
'The English patient.'

Yes! The English patient was feeling much better. My recovery was on track. I was out of danger and would soon be out of the hospital. I was really looking forward to it.

My family, which now included Julie, only came during normal visiting hours. Irfan and David came to see me once a day for five minutes or so, and, one evening, Mr Dharsi the beggar also turned up with a basket of oranges to see how I was getting on. I was touched by his kind gesture, so characteristic of India's poor people. He was carrying a cloth bag with him, which I assumed contained his day's takings. The bag looked heavy! His mortgage deposit for his house purchase was no doubt building up nicely.

I was in hospital through no choice of my own. I was brought here, unconscious and almost dead. But the patient in the bed next to mine had admitted himself. He looked perfectly all right, except for his unsightly Adam's apple and an even more unsightly trickle of saliva from the left corner of his mouth. There appeared to be nothing wrong with him. I wondered why he was in hospital at all. As I watched and wondered about him, the police entered the ward with Dr Mittal. I thought they'd come to interview me again. But, instead, they went straight to the next bed and asked to see the man's medical report. They took Dr Mittal to one side and spoke quietly to him, and then they took the patient away. After he was escorted out, Jane Iyer told me he was a notorious builder called Cobra Das, who was allegedly involved in financial fraud on a massive scale. Das had checked himself into the hospital complaining of chest pains. But his real aim was to evade arrest on medical grounds and dodge jail for as long as he could while his lawyers tried to get him bail. Medical papers filed on his behalf at the court showed that Das's condition was stable and normal.

As his condition remained stable and unchanged, the police acting under the orders of the court arrested him. Jane Iyer told me that this kind of delaying tactic by entering hospital to avoid jail was quite common in India.

Das's bed number was 420, and this was quite appropriate. In India, a fraudster, a cheater or a confidence trickster would be called a 420. The term derived its origin from Section 420 of the Indian Penal Code, which dealt with cases of cheating. When I first came to Mumbai, Mr Dharsi had said to me, 'Mumbai is a callous city, where buildings are made of cement, and people's hearts are made of stone.' He was quoting another beggar from a very famous and popular 1955 Bollywood Hindi film, *Shree 420*. It was a film about confidence tricksters which my father watched every time it came on Indian TV in England. My mother often chided him about it.

'How many times will you see this film?'

'Four hundred and twenty times,' my father would reply in a teasing tone.

I read in the papers the next day that Cobra Das insisted he was innocent and that he would be fighting for justice with the 'simple sword of truth and the trusty shield of fair play'. Now, where had I heard that phrase before? Ha! Ha! Ha!

Life and death…so close together. Two sides of the same coin. It made me think about the fragility of life and how vulnerable we all were, us mortals, us human beings, who thought we were immortal.

By the third week, my wounds had all healed. At last I felt as if my mind, body, soul and spirit were all coming together like never before, releasing me from a muddled maze. The clock in my ward had stopped working. Time, however, had not stopped. Time kept flying. Hours became days. Days became weeks. In all, I was in the hospital for forty days. The forty days of my seva at the Golden Temple of Amritsar brought me close to the Lord. Now forty days in hospital brought me even nearer to Him.

I was discharged from the hospital on a bright Thursday morning, my favourite day of the week. I thanked the Almighty with my own interpretation of Psalm 23. The Lord was my shepherd, as I was lying on the ground in Love Park dying, and then on the operating theatre, and later on the hospital bed. The Lord saved me and made me lie down on green pastures. I walked through the shadow of the valley of death without any fear for He was with me, always. His rod and His staff comforted me. Using my mother's hands, He anointed my head with oil, making me feel serene. Drawing strength from Psalm 23, I prayed that goodness and love would follow me all the days of my life, and that I would dwell in the house of the Lord forever.

One Enduring Lesson

~

It was now two weeks since I had been discharged from hospital. The worst was over. My recovery was continuing. My strength and confidence were returning. Soon there would be no pain, I told myself. The scars on my body would remain, however. There was nothing I could do about them. I decided to soldier on. Exuberant optimism now engulfed me. I had come to Mumbai to do a two-year course in filmmaking. What I had seen and experienced from the moment I arrived in Mumbai was in itself a film. A real-life film with an original script—written, directed, produced and edited by the greatest producer in the galaxy, who also provided the music and made me dance and sing to His tunes and act as per His direction with His constant cue 'Lights, camera, action!'

My days of travelling wearily through rough and stormy seas and a barren featureless desert, devoid of shade and full of reptiles, vipers, scorpions, had come to an end. I had now reached a hilltop and could see the Promised Land below. Life was no longer breathless but breathtaking. It had been a long and interesting journey through Mumbai, through India and through life. It had been a journey of discovery. India was the museum of the world. India was a myth. It was fiction. It was fact. It was fable. It was fantasy. India was everything—a country of innovative ideas, where things fell into place at the last minute. India was a bazaar. It was bizarre. India was chaos, a fully functional chaos. India was incredible. And India was life. Real life. India was shining and not shining at the same time. There were two Indias. Three Indias. Multiple Indias. India was beautiful—a riot of colour and sounds and sights and smells and tastes and everything the senses could imagine. It was something I only dreamt about before I came here, but now it was my India. Mother India.

I am proud to be British, but I am also proud to be Indian, an Overseas Citizen of India. I have the best of both worlds.

I was no longer myself. India had changed me. I could have done my two-year filmmaking course back home in England, but now I was glad I had chosen India. I loved India as never before, despite everything.

And I loved Mumbai more than anywhere now. It was a fascinating city. A city that couldn't be intimidated, upstaged, suppressed or ignored. Mumbai never slept, never stopped, never conceded, never complained. It could neither be crippled nor killed. It could not be controlled. Mumbai was Mumbai. It would never die. The world is a small place, but Mumbai is a large space. It is truly a Maximum City, a city of many chronicles. A city of my dreams, joys and sorrows.

As my health returned, my eyes sparkled. Every day started with a golden morning which tingled me with ebullient positivism and I felt like crying out:

Indiaaaaah! Indiaaaaah! Indiaaaaah!

My *annus mirabilis* had at last started. I hoped.

'*Achhe din aane wale hain,*' I told my father excitedly.

'Yes, Rahul. Good days are coming,' replied my father, with my mother looking on and sharing our excitement.

One day, to my surprise, David turned up in a new seven-seater silver Vauxhall Zafira air-conditioned car.

'The loan company kept on offering me cheap finance. I finally caved in.'

He was with Irfan, as always. 'India is changing. Some years back, borrowing would be frowned upon. Now young middle-class India is building up a debt mountain.'

'Buy now. Pay later,' added Ratan, who had just joined us in the lounge.

David and Irfan took my parents, Julie and me around for a week in the new car to see Mumbai. They were seven glorious days in glorious company in a glorious city. I'd completely recovered and was ready to start my filmmaking course at last. To my great delight, Julie also decided to join Film International to do a course in directing. Like mine, hers would also be a two-year degree, of which the first year would be a foundation course common to both of us, when we would be together.

'The two of you can then jointly make films,' my father laughed.

'And babies!' My mother who had grown golden and graceful over the years was always looking forward to becoming a grandmother.

I was brought up by my parents to tell the truth in life. Honesty was the best policy. And so, I felt compelled to tell the truth to my parents about my life in Mumbai. I told them how and why Rahul became Radium. How I met Julie, lost her and won her back. About the fakir. About the Guru. About my forty-day seva at the Golden Temple in Amritsar. About all that had happened after I returned from Amritsar, leading up to the knife attack. They seemed to forgive me, and for that I was both surprised and grateful.

My mother had tears in her eyes. 'All is well that ends well!'

One Sunday afternoon, we had a small informal ceremony to celebrate my engagement to Julie, attended by fifteen people including Ratan, Irfan, David, Dr Mittal and my parents, of course.

'Marriages are made in heaven, but divorces are made on earth,' said my father.

'So be careful,' said David, showing off his newly grown pencil-thin moustache.

Irfan became philosophical: 'Throughout the centuries, there have been lovers in history and in literature. There were Salim and Anarkali, Shah Jahan and Mumtaz Mahal, Jane Eyre and Edward Rochester. And now we have Rahul and Julie with the same initials as Romeo and Juliet.'

Then he informed me that his mother had agreed just the day before that he need not now marry his first cousin after all.

'I hope you also find a nice girl, Irfan,' I offered, smiling warmly.

My parents then prepared to return to England, but delayed their trip by four days as there was some sad news.

Dr Mittal had died suddenly of a massive heart attack. He was only thirty-eight. It was a shock for everyone. We all attended his funeral. I thought about the people I'd lost—first PP Auntie, then Noor Baba, and now Dr Mittal. Three important people in my life who'd died one after the other in Mumbai. It made me feel sad for a time, until I reflected on my earlier thoughts about the fragility of life. We'd all die one day. 'Live till the last day,' Dr Mittal would often say. But, until then, life was for the living. It went on, and we should honour the dead by making the most of it.

There was some good news too. Ratan Pestonji and Ruby Daruwalla were now back together and were due to get married in two months' time.

Finally, Julie, Irfan, David, Ratan, Ruby and me, all of us went to Mumbai Airport to see my parents off. It was an emotional farewell. As usual, my mother's eyes were brimming with tears. So were my father's, this time. It was bitter-sweet for me. They were the best parents in the world, and I told them so. But I had my own life to lead now.

While waiting in the airport departure area that day, I found myself sitting next to an egg-bald passenger reading the final page of a dog-eared book, with scraps of paper tucked in-between pages as bookmarks. He was an Englishman, also flying to London on the same flights as my parents.

'It's a fascinating book, an autobiography of a great person,' said the man as he handed me the book and suggested that I read the last paragraph.

I did and then quickly voice recorded it on my iPhone.

Life in the ultimate analysis has taught me one enduring lesson. The subject should always disappear in the object. In our ordinary affections one for another, in our daily work with hand or brain, we most of us discover soon enough that any lasting satisfaction, any contentment that we can achieve, is the result of forgetting self, of merging subject with object, in a harmony that is of body, mind and spirit...

I looked at the cover. The book was titled *The Memoirs of Aga Khan*.

I put the book down and sat silently for a while. Guru Krishna Bhaiji showed me the path of righteousness. This path, my daily prayers to Goddess Lakshmi at 4 a.m. prescribed to me by the Muslim fakir, and my forty days of seva at the Golden Temple helped me in my days of crisis. Satan was defeated. I realized I was alive because of my sincere prayers and seva and the prayers of my nearest and dearest ones. Again, Satan was defeated. Death was delayed. For as long as God would give me life. I was finally at peace with myself. Satisfied. Contented. Liberated.

But I still had to achieve lasting satisfaction, lasting contentment. I'd tried to forget the self, tried to let the subject disappear in the object, tried to merge the two together. I hadn't always succeeded, and I would have to try even harder. So, Lord, help me, please!

We were in prime tearjerker territory as we waved off my parents, and they said they would return for our wedding the following year.

And so on 21 March, my two-year course at Film International began, and I attended every lecture with my wife-to-be Julie at my side. I hoped, in our professional lives as filmmakers and in our personal lives, that Julie and I would always remember that Bollywood was an illusion, whereas India was not.

I hoped we would always remember that *one enduring lesson* for our lasting satisfaction and contentment: *The subject should always disappear in the object.*